Chapter One
Angela

Before you think I might have killed him, let me tell you that I didn't. I wanted to, many times, but I was never that brave. For God's sake, I wouldn't even answer him back. But I didn't help him, either. I heard his frantic calls from his room and I chose to ignore them. Why would I volunteer to go when I could stay outside in my perfect garden? I let him yell. I left him alone for the rest of the day. I suppose deep down I knew something was wrong but I couldn't bring myself to find out. So no, I didn't kill him, but I didn't save him either. Thank God for heart attacks.

Well, I didn't actually mean that last bit. What I meant was that it was over, finally over, and I was happy. Of course, neither of the boys felt the same. Who could blame them? He was their father, after all. Nobody other than Jeannie had known the truth about my marriage. Mark was my husband's golden boy, made in his own image. Josh was mine, my lifeline.

I'd asked Jeannie to come with me for the will reading. She was my best friend, my only friend but she'd refused; the only thing she ever had, and it hurt. I could understand her decision, of course, but I don't think she realised how scared I was. In the end, Josh came to collect me. Mark insisted on meeting us there. That was typical of him wanting to be first. I guess he had been waiting some time when we arrived; his impatience always showed. Josh ignored him and protectively put his arm around me.

I looked at my two sons and shuddered; if only they knew what had happened, how I had let their father die. They would never forgive me. I knew this was a secret I would take to my grave.

The solicitor was a stranger, apparently a friend of George's but I had noticed he hadn't attended the funeral. Not a close friend then. He seemed to sense Mark's urgency and immediately starting reading the last will and testament of Mr George Theobald Trippett. I struggled to pay attention to the solicitor as he droned on. I watched the boys' reactions. They had always been so different. Mark was perched on the edge of his seat, taking notes verbatim as the will was read. Josh was on his phone. I could see that he was scanning through his photos. I wondered if there was any of George. I thought not.

The solicitor stopped abruptly and I saw Mark's head snap up from his notepad.

'I am afraid that not all the estate has been left to you, Mrs Trippett. There's an extra bequest that I hadn't noticed before. Sorry.'

He asked to be excused.

Josh put his phone down and went to the window. The SS Great Britain was moored across from us. I remembered taking the boys there when they were young. George had refused to come; as always, he had things to do. Mark began to drum his fingers on the table. I knew the warning signs well. 'This is bloody ridiculous,' he said, the drumming got louder.

I went to put my arm round him, but Josh stopped me. 'Leave it, Mum,' he whispered.

Thankfully, the solicitor returned. Mark ceased and picked up his pen once more, now Josh was paying attention. My hands began to shake.

'It appears that a tidy sum has been left to someone else. An amount of fifty thousand pounds has been left to another,

The Other Mrs Trippett

Christine Seddon-Kaye

The Other Mrs Trippett

Olympia Publishers
London

www.olympiapublishers.com
OLYMPIA PAPERBACK EDITION

A CIP catalogue record for this title is
available from the British Library.

ISBN: 978-1-80074-602-2

This is a work of fiction.
Names, characters, places and incidents are either products of the
author's imagination or are used fictitiously. Any resemblance to actual
persons, living or dead, is purely coincidental.

First Published in 2024

Olympia Publishers
Tallis House
2 Tallis Street
London
EC4Y 0AB

Printed in Great Britain

Acknowledgments

Thank you to Jenni, Suzy, Dean and Rob for always believing.

About the Author

Christine grew up near Manchester. Before leaving her job in a bank, she became part of a cabaret duo with her best friend. This led her to Somerset, and she has been there ever since. A mother to three grown-up children, she spent twenty years working in the holiday park industry before leaving to spend more time in her beloved Kenya.

You can find her online at www.christineseddon-kaye.com, on Facebook at Csk author and Instagram at @seddonkaye

Mrs Trippett.'

'But Grandma is dead,' Josh said.

'A Mrs R Trippett, in Kenya.'

'There isn't any Mrs Trippett in Kenya. The Mrs Trippett sat here used to live in Kenya for a while. But she left. We all did except Father – many years ago.' I saw the muscles tighten against Mark's jaw. The solicitor, I think, saw it too. He wiped his face on a tissue, leaving bits of white fluff in the bristles on his chin. 'No mistake, Mr Trippett. He left this money to a Mrs R Trippett and it states here that she is his wife.'

Chapter Two
Angela

I can't remember one single thing that happened for the rest of that day. I don't even recall getting into bed that night. I awoke with one thought only: my husband had another wife and I'd known nothing about it. My head felt it was going to burst. I went downstairs and phoned Jeannie.

'Load of old codswallop, I reckon. There'll be nothing in it, mark my words.'

'But it was written in his will signed, dated and witnessed ten years ago by Daniels and Partners in Nairobi,' I said. 'Proper lawyers!'

The solicitor had given me a copy of the will, and as I made myself a coffee, it sat sneering at me from the kitchen worktop. *To Mrs R Trippett, I leave the sum of fifty thousand pounds for her to do with as she desires without restriction.*

I felt George laughing at me, as he always did when he knew he had bested me. He had done it one final time, his last revenge, and I couldn't do a thing. The solicitor had explained that he believed it to be legal. Even though it had been signed overseas, the process remained binding. We were to meet again once he had looked into it further.

I left the coffee, made a peppermint tea to ease my pounding headache, and went back upstairs to bed. There was no missing George on his side of the bed; I couldn't remember when we had last shared a bed, let alone been intimate. He'd had his room and I'd had mine. He'd had his life and I'd had mine. That was the way it had been for many years now. There was no warmth of affection to miss now that he was gone; I couldn't remember there ever being any. Jeannie had known what had been going on. She'd witnessed the bullying and the put-downs and had held her tongue for my sake.

The key in the door and the sound of the boys shattered my thoughts. It was unusual for them to come together. It was unusual for them to even speak to each other.

'Mother, we need to do something about this,' Mark yelled from downstairs. 'We can't just hand over this money to some bloody woman.'

I heard footsteps bounding up the stairs and braced myself.

'Hey, Mum, how are things?' Josh's blond curls appeared round the door. I let out my breath.

'Mother, get out of bed. We have to sort this.' I could hear Mark clumping his way about. Even his footsteps sounded like George's. I grabbed my dressing gown and met him on the landing.

'I was just coming,' I said in my brightest voice. Josh followed. Mark had removed his jacket and rolled up his sleeves. He meant business.

I didn't. 'Lovely to see you, boys,' I said, 'But can we do this another time? I have something I must do.' I put on my bravest face. I couldn't deal with this now; I needed some time to think. For once I wasn't going to be bullied.

'And what the hell is that, Mother?' Mark had picked up the will and was waving it in my face. 'Something more important than this?'

Out of the corner of my eye I saw Josh take a couple of steps towards his brother. I had to stop this now.

'Yes… I'm going to Jeannie's.'

Jeannie never locked her door in daylight and wasn't at all surprised when I walked in unannounced. She sat in her favourite chair, looking out through the open French doors.

'Come on in, dear. Throw your bag upstairs and come into the garden. It's a beautiful day.'

I bundled my way through her small hallway and up the narrow staircase.

'Don't be long now, or we'll miss the sun.'

Jeannie loved the sun and loved her garden. Her little piece of heaven, she called it. The minute I walked out there, I felt the sense of peace that I always did in this place.

'Right, my love, what are we going to do about this little mess? We need to think good and strong on that one.' Jeannie tried to lift herself up and I rushed to help her, but she waved me away. 'I can do it. I'm not ready for the nursing home yet.' She struggled over to her writing desk and switched on her laptop. 'Now let's have a look here. See what we can find.'

For the next hour we looked up everything we knew. The solicitors in Kenya were small but legitimate, and George's ex-company was no longer in business. We even tried looking up any Mrs Trippetts in Kenya. There was none.

Finally, frustrated and annoyed, Jeannie said, 'You could, of course, go and find her. I mean, you don't even know if this bloody woman exists, do you?'

'Whoa, a little minute, Jeannie, I'm not going to head off to Kenya at the drop of a hat, like that. I couldn't dare think about it.'

'Why not?'

'What do you mean, why not?'

'Exactly that, child. What is stopping you from getting on a plane right now and going to see this Daniels person in Nairobi to find out who the hell this woman is?'

'Oh Jeannie, you know I just couldn't. I wouldn't know where to start… just the thought of it scares the hell out of me. It is best to let the two solicitors deal with it. Maybe they can negotiate with her.'

'Wait a minute, let me get this right. Your git of a husband leaves a pile of money to somebody he supposedly married in Kenya, and you're going to negotiate with her. Negotiate, my arse, girl! Don't you want to know who the hell she is? Aren't you in the least bit angry? If you aren't, you bloody well should be.'

'I'm fucking furious, if you must know.' I only ever dared to use the F word with Jeannie. 'So furious I don't know what to do. I can't think straight. You know, what I can't get out of my mind is just how he treated her. Was he nice to her? Did he love her? Or was he just as cruel to her as he was to me?' It hurt to imagine George really loving someone, being the attentive husband that I always wish he'd been with me. After all I'd put up with, he'd married someone else. George's greed had even stretched to his wives. One was not enough; I was not enough. He needed another.

'Well, sitting around doing nothing isn't going to help. You've done that for almost your whole married life and look where it's got you. We both know the mind games he used to play, but that's over now. George is gone. It's what happens now that's important. You can just sit there and get angrier and moan about your life, or you can do something about this mess. Unless, of course, you're happy to just hand over fifty thousand smackers to a bloody stranger, that is.'

'Well, I don't know what else to do. I came to you because

15

you are my best friend and all you are doing is yelling at me.' The tears came quickly, but Jeannie ignored them.

'Okay, my girl, you go back and sit in your beautiful home and cry, even walk around your beautiful garden, but think of your mother and father while you're doing it. Think of all the hard work it took them to earn all that money they left you. They wanted you to have money of your own, to give you the chance to leave him. But you never did. You stuck it out; I'm not sure whether you were a hero or a fool. You gave all their hard-earned money to George and now you're giving it away again to this bloody woman. What is the matter with you?' Jeannie's face was bright red as she flopped down on the sofa.

I rushed to her and got hold of her hand.

'I am getting too old to be this angry.' She smiled. I could feel her pulse racing.

'Oh, Jeannie, I'm so sorry, you're right. I have all this fury boiling inside me, but I'm scared.'

'Scared of what? He's gone; it's over.'

'Jeannie, I'm scared of everything. It feels as though he's still around. Waiting for me to do something wrong, to put me down, to make me feel stupid. Because let's face it, I am stupid. I must be not to know that my husband had another bloody wife.' I let go of her hand. She took it back.

'Angela, my dear, listen to me good and proper. You are not stupid. You were married to a horrible man. You weren't to know that when you married him; nobody does. He made your life a misery, but now he is dead. However, if you let him get away with this, then he'll continue to give you misery for the rest of your life. Is that what you want?'

Before I had chance to answer, Jeannie headed into the kitchen. 'I need cake,' she said.

'I hope you can understand my anger for you?' Jeannie said as she sliced into the fruit cake. 'It's a frustration that I can't make it all okay for you. But I've said my piece and you know I'll help you in whatever way I can. Although at my age, I'm not sure what use I can be.'

'What do you mean, at your age? You still have plenty of life left in you yet. I don't want any of this old age talk coming from you. What would I do if anything happened to you, Jeannie?'

'But that's my point, Angela. Something will happen to me one day and none of us know when that day will come. I promised your mum that I would look after you and I've done my best. But now you'll have to do something for yourself. You need to decide how important this money is to you and whether to let it go without a fight or not. Surely at least you must find out the truth.'

The cake was wonderful, but I found it hard to swallow. Jeannie had hit a nerve. George's legacy to me was another wife, another life and, who knew, maybe other children and the bastard had left my money to them. I did need to know the truth, regardless of how painful it was going to be.

'Jeannie, will you come with me to the solicitors?'

She turned to me, her mouth full of pastry. 'Hallelujah!' she laughed.

Chapter Three
Angela

'Ah, glad to see you again,' the solicitor said. His eyes said different. He raised himself slightly from his seat indicating the chairs we should sit in. Our last meeting had been in a grand oak-panelled room. Presumably reserved for will readings. Today we sat in his cramped, spartan office wedged in chairs as uncomfortable as we were. I introduced Jeannie.

'We're here to get at the truth,' she said, stabbing her index finger firmly on his desk. 'Time for you to tell us exactly what the hell is going on.'

'As I said to Mrs Trippett here, at the reading of the will, her husband has bequeathed fifty thousand pounds to a Mrs R Trippett in Kenya. Now, I can understand your frustration in this...' He refused to look at either of us as he spoke.

'Frustration? That doesn't even come close to what she's feeling.' Jeannie struggled to her feet and leaned over the desk. I gently placed my hand on her thigh and patted it. She plumped back down. 'We know what's in the damn will, but what I want *you* to tell us is how the hell we stop this happening.'

'The problem, we have, and it's a big problem, is that your husband didn't appear to have any life insurance, unless you know different. Looking at the bank account, there's very little cash in there. I was hoping that you would know of further funds to cover this bequest.'

'What do you mean further funds? I don't understand.'

'Mrs Trippett, it seems your husband wasn't in a good place financially and had significant debts, some of which are still outstanding. I can't locate any other funds, no insurance, no savings account, nothing. If this is the case, then the only real asset left in his estate is Saddle Bank House. I am sorry to say it will have to be sold unless you yourself have the means to pay this money to this other Mrs Trippett.'

'But it can't be sold. It's my home. It's not his to sell. It belongs to both of us.'

'Unfortunately, Mrs Trippett, and once again I've looked into this; your name doesn't appear on the deeds of the property. There's also a mortgage on the house. Normally, contesting all this wouldn't be too much of an issue, because you could challenge the terms of the will, being the spouse and having lived in the home etcetera etcetera…. But in this instance, there are complications making it rather more difficult to do that.'

Jeannie clenched her fists as he spoke.

'Mrs Trippett… I can understand how you're feeling.'

'No, you can't.' Her fists banged on the desk. 'You have no idea. Her home is everything to her, and now you're telling me she'll have to sell it because of some bloody woman her husband probably shagged once, who likely blackmailed him? You call yourself a lawyer, yet you sit on your arse gloating over the downfall of this poor woman. You make me sick. Come on, Angela, I think it's time we left this man to his business.'

He finally looked me in the eye. 'Before you both go and accuse me of being the bad-guy, there's something more that you should know. Since we last met, Mrs Trippett, I've had the chance to delve, so to speak, a little further.

'It appears that there is real substance to this lady's claim.

19

There are documents that support her case of being legally married to your husband.'

Jeannie scrambled to her feet and for a moment I thought she was going to hit him. 'Come on, let's go. No point in sitting here listening to that man's drivel.'

We reached the door just as a young woman appeared with coffee.

'Stuff it,' Jeannie snapped.

I was amazed at her strength and energy but feared this was taking its toll. We took hold of each other's hand as we crossed the busy roads outside. I began to cry.

'Now then, young lady, don't you dare take on so. We'll not have any tears. He isn't worth it. Never you mind what that stupid man has to say, we'll get our heads around this.' Jeannie kept a strong grip on my hand as we push our way into the Royal Oak and the comforting surrounding of dark wood, stale beer, and peace.

'God, I need a drink.' She looked over the wine list and was suitably impressed. 'Time for a nice Fleurie, and two of those lovely roast beef and horseradish baps, me thinks.'

'Oh Jeannie, I couldn't eat a thing…' I struggled to stop the tears. She looked over the top of her glasses and I shut up.

'Right, time to have a think on things and then get a plan together.'

'I'm not sure there's any point. I've lost everything. When this is all finished and I've sold my house, there'll be nothing left. I didn't even know we had a mortgage. I thought my parents' money cleared it.'

'Will you quit with all this talk and pull yourself together? You said you wanted to find out the truth and that's what we're going to do. The bastard must have spent all your money, and has left you in a right pickle, that's for sure, but just because the man in the suit says something doesn't mean it is gospel. Bloody hell, Angela, your mother would be horrified that you're giving up so quickly.'

I looked at Jeannie, she was worn out but she was right; I was giving up. I couldn't see any way forward. George had finally won. This is how he'd planned it all along. He knew I would have nothing when he died. He was having the last laugh and I was letting him.

I took a deep breath. 'Okay, what's the plan?'

Chapter Four
Angela

'Have you been to Kenya before?' My neighbour peeled back the silver foil from the food container and, like me, peered cautiously inside. 'This is our first time and we are so excited. We are going to do the Maasai Mara, then head to the coast. What about you?'

'I used to live in Kenya.' I stabbed at a piece of what I assumed was chicken. I wasn't in the mood for small talk. I dropped it back in the container and covered it with the paper napkin. Bile stung the back of my throat and I fought hard not to vomit. Never in my wildest dreams did I ever imagine I would be heading back to Kenya.

It'd been easy to let Jeannie and Josh make all the decisions. It was what I did. I let others decide what was best and this time was no different. Mark had had his say; of course but I don't remember any of it. All I could think was that I'd let my husband die and my punishment was to lose everything. Maybe after what I'd done, I deserved everything that was heading my way? Josh wanted me to go to see the lawyer in Nairobi first, but Jeannie had insisted on a trip to the coast to "get myself together", some hope!

As we began the descent into Jomo Kenyatta airport I hung tight to the armrests. Somewhere out there was the woman who could take everything from me. I closed my eyes.

'Don't worry, I don't like the landing either. Here, grab

hold of my hand.' My neighbour took my hand in hers. This contact from a stranger felt invasive; I wanted to pull away but it would've been rude.

Rushing from the international terminal to domestic gave me little time to think before I was sat back on a plane heading to Mombasa. I tried to remember how long it was since I'd been at the coast. The boys had loved snorkelling in the clear blue shallows of the Indian Ocean on the few times George had taken us. I felt a twinge of excitement as I caught sight of Kilimanjaro above the clouds. 'Simply breath-taking,' I whispered to myself.

I felt the heat immediately the doors opened on the plane to reveal the terminal at Mombasa and I fumbled to find my sunglasses. As I walked through the tiny arrivals, I was swamped by taxi drivers desperate to help me with my luggage. I heard my name above the bedlam and my knight in shining armour appeared barging his way through the crowd.

'Angela, my dear, lovely to see you, still looking as gorgeous as ever.' Joseph waddled up to me, as rotund as I remembered, and within seconds I was engulfed in a huge bear hug.

'He's still a silly old arse. I think he's getting worse.' His wife, Binty, moved in to hug me too as Joseph grabbed the luggage trolley and headed to the car park. 'But he is right, you are looking gorgeous. Now come on let's find Karisa and get you back to the bungalow so you can freshen up.' She linked her arm through mine and followed her husband as he struggled ahead. It was good to see them again.

Joseph had worked with George for many years in Nairobi and when he'd retired he'd moved permanently to his holiday home in Nyali. Binty had, for the short time I'd lived in

Nairobi, been my constant companion. Being ten years older, she'd shown me the ropes and looked after me when George had been on his business trips out of Nairobi. We'd kept in good contact for many years after, but as tended to happen in life, we drifted to birthday and Christmas cards and the odd phone call for major life events. But since I'd told them about George's death and my plans to visit Kenya, they'd been a real support in helping me to get organised for the trip.

They'd wanted me to stay with them, and I'd seriously thought about it, but in the end I'd said no. I didn't want anybody, even Joseph and Binty, knowing the true reason I was in Kenya. They'd organised a single room for me at a small hotel overlooking the beach. I didn't have the money to stay there long but it gave me time to think what I was going to do. They'd even sorted out a driver for me whenever I felt the need to venture out, and it was to him that we headed.

'*Karibu* Kenya, madam, my name is Karisa,' he said as we approached the vehicle, and very formally shook my hand. I attempted to say thank you in Swahili, and his face broke into a wide, bright smile.

We piled into Joseph's land cruiser and onto the chaos of Mombasa town. As I sat languishing in the cool luxurious leather seat in the back, I finally let out the breath that I felt I'd been holding since the funeral. I was here in Kenya, and I felt the freedom that only a foreign land could bring. Even the traffic jam as we headed through the centre of the city to Nyali brought a smile to my face, as I watched everyone going about their daily business of earning a shilling or two.

I jumped at the boom of Joseph's voice as he greeted the security. The electric gates opened to reveal a long gravel driveway encircling a luscious garden. There was a huge

Jacaranda tree in the middle of a large, pristine circular lawn, which, coupled with the vibrant swathes of bougainvillea, assaulted my every sense.

'Are you sure that you don't want to stay with us? You know you're more than welcome, Angela.' Binty waited for Karisa to open her door and then gingerly swung her legs out. 'Damn legs, can't get them to work as good as they used to.'

He gently offered his arm and helped her to her feet.

'Honestly, Binty, I feel like I need some time on my own to get my head straight, but thanks for the offer. I promise that you'll see a lot of me.'

George had talked about the house that Joseph and Binty had bought at what he thought was a bargain price, overlooking Nyali beach. But nothing could've prepared me for the amazing view from the back garden. The sea was a translucent turquoise against the brilliant white sand. The only evidence that we were anywhere near Mombasa was the distant line of container ships on the horizon, patiently queuing to offload their cargoes in the docks.

After a lunch of chicken salad and the sweetest fruits that I've ever tasted, Karisa reappeared to drive me to my hotel.

'This man is at your disposal for your stay by the way,' Joseph said. 'He's a very good driver and a great friend. So, should you want to have a trip up the coast or into town during your holiday, he'll sort it for you.'

'Just the hotel for now, please,' I said, returning the smile that Karisa was beaming at me. 'Maybe in a day or two when I've rested.'

I was on a strict budget. Although it would've been cheaper to stay with Joseph and Binty, I still didn't feel up to company, and so Joseph had chosen this modest hotel for me. Knowing the price I was paying, I was surprised to find that my room contained a huge four-poster bed and was situated at the very front of the hotel, with panoramic views of the Indian Ocean. I said a silent thank you to him as I flopped on the bed.

I hadn't intended to sleep and woke up with a start. It was dark. I walked to the window to witness a magnificent full moon, illuminating the sky and turning the ocean to a sea of glitters. Looking at my watch, I was surprised to see that it was only eight o'clock. I'd forgotten how quickly night comes here, and rushed to shower before dinner.

'Another first,' I thought, as I sat at my table for one amongst the couples and the families. I ate little; I felt very self-conscious and twiddled with my wedding ring. I felt the urge to remove it but it wouldn't budge. I wanted to be away from the dining room, from any prying eyes, and so stuffing a couple of bread rolls in my pockets, I made my way back to the room. I felt completely lost. What was I doing here? I tried again with my wedding ring. I glimpsed a faint white mark as I tugged to get it over my bulging knuckle. It would go no further. I took a sleeping pill, got back in bed and cried.

Chapter Five
Karisa

Joseph's *rafiki* from England had the look of someone who was feeling great pain. She had that look ever since I met her at the airport. I could see she was very troubled about something big. She tried not to show it but she could not hide it. I liked her.

I felt sad leaving her alone at the hotel, but that was how she wanted it to be. I phoned Joseph and he allowed me the rest of the day without work, so I travelled to visit my brother, Katana, and his family in nearby Mtwapa.

The hustle and bustle of the place gave me comfort, so very different from the tourist areas where the woman stays. Here was where I belonged. I liked this place in the daytime, but at night not so much. I turned off the main road to the houses behind the *dukas* and bars. I always drove carefully here, there were many children playing outside the huts. So many children, families of ten or more living in one room. They smiled and waved at me as I passed by. They would think that I was rich because of the car. They would be very wrong.

My brother and his wife were pleased to see me and welcomed me into the small room that they rented. Their new born was lying on a small piece of foam on the floor that was their bed. She seemed content having just taken the breast and was happy for me to hold her. Her name was Zawadi, a 'gift' in Swahili. This was their third child; the first-born passed at birth, and the second-born, a boy of two years, died from malaria, so this child was all their hope, although deep in his heart I knew my brother wished for another boy child.

It was good to catch up on the news of all my close family and cousins, and the afternoon passed quickly drinking *chai* and sharing their meal of *ugali* and greens. But I wanted to return to my room in town before dark; my safety was not assured once night-time fell.

Leaving the car at Joseph's, I caught a *matatu* home as the light was beginning to fade. I was happy to get home before the darkness came. I flicked the light for my one small bulb but there was nothing; for the third day running, there was no power. To be without light in a place like this was dangerous, so I lit the kerosene lamp. As it spluttered into life, I lay my thin worn mattress on the floor and folded all my clothes neatly. My small charcoal *jiko* was ready for my *chai* in the morning. I had little, but I had everything I needed.

I began to cough; the fumes from the lamp hit my throat and made my eyes sting. I opened my door a little but the sound of shouting and someone screaming made me quickly close it tight again.

A few years ago, I would have gone to investigate the screams and maybe helped but not anymore.

Chapter Six
Angela

The sight of Joseph and Karisa, striding into the dining room at breakfast, was most welcome, and I begged them to sit down and have some coffee. I could see that Karisa felt uncomfortable, and he made an excuse to go and check on the vehicle, leaving Joseph and I alone.

'Now then, my dear, I trust that you slept well and are raring to go today, so how about a trip into Mombasa? Binty tells me there's lots of good shopping to be had there. I expect she would be happy to accompany you.'

'Thanks for the offer, Joseph, but to be honest, the last place I feel like being is in a crowded city. '

'Well, what about a trip up the coast? Karisa knows some lovely places where the bad old tourists don't get to. I'm sure he would love to take you.'

Joseph, I could sense, was itching to help, and so I agreed. It might do me some good.

'Right-oh! Give me a minute for Karisa to get organised, and he'll be back. I just need him to drop me at home first.'

By the time he had returned, my rucksack was packed and I was sat in reception waiting.

As we turned onto the Mombasa-Malindi highway and drove through Mtwapa, the difference with the hotel hit me head-on. Here was life in its rawest, and the noise was deafening. The *matatus* honked their horns constantly to attract

29

passengers, people yelling from three-wheeled *tuk-tuks* weaving in and out of the small stalls, and everyone trying to avoid the *pikipiki* motorbikes pushing their way through the crowds, sometimes with a whole family perched precariously on the one seat. The smell of wood smoke and burning rubbish seeped through the air vents, invading my clothes, reminding me of bonfire night at home. The overwhelming sense as we drove through this town was that of a powder-keg. The people, the noise, the traffic, and the energy, all ready to explode. It made me wonder if the place was ever calm and quiet.

The journey gradually eased into sisal, field after field and row after row of the spiky plant forming a giant matrix on the dusty land. Mud dwellings peeked out between the palm trees by the side of the road, the ground swept clean around them and iridescent colours of washing draped on the bushes to dry.

"Madam, please come to the front seat right away." Karisa slowed the vehicle almost to a stop. "Please do so now."

I heard the urgency in his voice and so, without questioning, I clambered over the back-rest and squeezed myself into the passenger seat. Moments later we were stopped at a roadblock. Two policemen, looking not much older than sixteen, rifles slung over their backs like school bags, approached the car, motioning to Karisa to open the window. They requested some documents which he duly handed over. A heated conversation ensued between them with much hand waving, and then, out of the blue, the policemen broke into laughter, gave back the papers and waved us on our way.

'What was all that about?' I asked.

'They wanted money; they said that as you were a *mzungu* tourist then you could pay them money. I told them that they were wrong that you were not a tourist at all.' He started to smile. 'I told them that you were my wife. That is why I told you to get into the front; if you had been sat in the back, they would have made us pay. I also told them that you could understand everything that they were saying and would not be happy in being treated that way. They told me to have a good day and that I was lucky to have such a beautiful wife!'

We both burst out laughing and I had to admit to feeling a little bit smug that the police could believe that I was Karisa's wife. He must be at least fifteen years younger than me.

'Of course, many Kenyan men are with older white women, mostly for money, I think,' he said.

My bubble was well and truly burst.

Eventually, we turned off the road and headed towards the ocean along a bumpy, dirt track through small villages of tin shack businesses, mud huts, and children playing in the water-filled potholes. Apart from the children, the places were deserted.

'No business now,' said Karisa. 'No tourists, no business.'

This was a shock to me. Where I was, there were plenty of tourists and the hotel was pretty full, but here it was desolate and the businesses boarded up. We pulled up outside a hotel that looked to be closed.

'Come, we will leave the car here. Follow me.' Karisa picked up my rucksack and his bag and headed into the empty hotel. It was open, but there were no guests, not a single one. We walked through unimpeded to the beach.

'Welcome to Kikambala.' He spread his arms wide. 'One of my favourite places.'

I immediately understood why. Here, the Indian Ocean was a thin dark line boiling on the distant reef. Between this and the white-hot sand was an expanse of dusty pink coral dotted with many exposed pools. A few local people were casting their nets in the larger ones, others gingerly walking out to the reef with their snorkels and spears to try their luck. The only sounds were the far-off roar of the waves breaking over the reef and the cries of egrets trying to beat the fishermen to their catch.

We sat down at a sun-bleached wooden table and a waiter appeared from nowhere to take our order. We settled back to look out to sea. We didn't speak. There wasn't any need. I was mesmerised watching a man and two boys, digging in the sand with a large stick. There was a rhythm as they stuck it into the sand, one boy poured water on the sand around the stick while the other pushed hard to make it go deeper, and so it continued until they felt it was deep enough. Then they both pulled on the stick with all their might to lever the sand up.

'They are searching for worms.' Karisa's voice startled me, 'To go fishing.'

'Oh, I remember doing that with my father in North Wales. Such happy times.'

His face turned solemn. 'That time with your father was just to pass the time, yes?'

'Yes, it was. He was trying to teach me to fish, but we never caught anything, and I always got bored and demanded ice cream.'

'For these people, madam, it is a matter of life and death. They do not have time for boredom; it is the difference between eating today or not. It is their survival. Life is very different here; the divide between the rich and the poor widens. Life is very difficult for the people here, but they are proud and work hard for their few shillings a day.' Karisa continued to watch the man and the boys, deep in thought, as he poured out his *chai*.

I turned away from him. I'd felt the sting behind his

comments.

After we'd finished our drinks, we decided to walk. We passed a couple of fishermen with a few thin fish hanging from a piece of string.

'They are lucky, they will eat today. But there is not enough for any spare to be sold.'

They greeted us and carried on their way.

As we rounded a small headland we stumbled on an abandoned hotel, the *makuti* roof destroyed and the windows of the rooms swinging open. Every pane of glass was still intact, milky from the spray of the waves giving the interior a ghostly sheen. We tried to see inside. It felt like the last guests had only just checked out and closed the doors forever. It was eerie.

'As I said, no tourists,' Karisa broke my thoughts. 'No tourists, no need of hotels.'

The buildings looked so forlorn but beautiful in their own way, a relic of better times past. The bright pinks and vivid scarlet of the bougainvillea spilled over the whitewashed walls and the burning orange of the flame trees bent inland from the ocean wind. The birds had claimed this area for themselves, undisturbed and overfed, unlike the local children scrambling over the rocks.

'This is paradise,' I said.

'Only for some, madam, only for some.'

Again the sting!

'Why did you come here?' He asked, as we stood looking out towards the reef.

'Because you brought me here, Karisa,' I laughed.

'No, madam, I mean, why are you here in Kenya?'

His simple and direct question made me stop. It'd all seemed clearer when I was back in Somerset, I'd trusted

Jeannie's judgement but now that I was here, I was confused…and scared.

'I don't know. I thought I did, but it's complicated and I'm not sure that I can do what I came for any more.'

He was no longer listening. He was staring out to sea. His presence disturbed me. I felt I was intruding in a way of life I didn't understand.

I didn't belong here.

Chapter Seven
Karisa

I upset the English lady. She did not make conversation all the way back to the hotel, and it was not my place to do so. I thought that taking her to Kikambala would have pleased her, and I think it did, but then my proud Kenyan mouth had to say too many things to bring her down. Why do I have to do this? What did I want her to say?

I was very rude and it cannot be forgiven. The anger inside came of its own accord and I could not stop it. The past always returns. If only I had not been out that night, I would feel different now, and if only the police had not been attacking that group of young boys and I had not got involved. I went to the aid of those boys but nobody came to mine.

Ten thousand shillings the cost for the hospital. This is a debt I pay to this day.

But I praise God the day, he brought Joseph into my life. The many scars on my body have faded, but those in my mind remain. That day, they took away my dignity as they broke my bones, but worst of all they took my courage and left a coward. My anger cuts deep but yet I do nothing.

Chapter Eight
Angela

I wasn't sure how to take Karisa yesterday. I wondered if I'd upset him; I'd thought we were getting on very well but he hadn't spoken at all on the way back. I needed an excuse to see him again. Although he disturbed me, he also interested me. I'd heard about a wood carving place near the airport and thought it might be worth taking a look. I wasn't really interested in the carving but I hoped to find a little souvenir for Jeannie.

Joseph had given me an old Nokia phone yesterday.

'It has mine and Karisa's number in, for you to contact us. And I'll be bloody miffed if you don't,' he'd said. So I rang him to see if Karisa was free. I wasn't brave enough to phone his number directly.

'Bloody wonderful idea.' He told me that Karisa would be with me inside thirty minutes. Once again, I was all ready and sitting in reception by the time he pulled up in the Land Cruiser.

'Madam, if it is okay with you, I must drop the vehicle back at Mr Joseph's; it is not running good. Then we will travel by *matatu* to the place. I think you will like the journey this way.' He bought two bottles of water from a *duka* by the hotel entrance and handed me one. His smile was strained. 'Sorry it is not *baridi*, madam, no fridge.'

The sun had burnt away the early morning cloud and now scorched overhead as we left Joseph's and walked up the dirt road leading to the main Mombasa highway. There was no shortage of the brightly painted *matatu*s, most of which were crammed to over capacity with people, shopping, children, and even the odd live chicken. There was an overwhelming stench of body odour as we boarded a bright green and yellow vehicle emblazoned with 'God is King' and loud reggae music blasting out. It was difficult to resist putting my handkerchief over my nose. On one of the very few journeys I ever did in a *matatu* with the children when I lived in Nairobi, the vehicle for some reason did an emergency stop, and the seat we were sitting in broke clean away from the floor, throwing me with a wallop into the seat in front, not an experience that I cared to repeat. I can still remember everyone laughing, including the children, as I tried to get my straw hat back from the chicken in front.

I told Karisa of this and he laughed his great belly laugh. The tension released.

'Much safer now, there are laws. We even have seat belts now.' I hunted to find mine. 'Of course, no one ever uses them!'

We sat crammed in with the rest of the passengers, trying to speak over the deafening music. I was aware of his thigh pressing onto mine and I pushed towards the window to put space between us. We got off where the blue and white buildings of Mombasa began. 'They have painted the city for the tourists, not for the people.' His face was serious; I asked if he had a problem with tourists.

'Not at all, they bring employment. But to paint a whole city blue and white for them is crazy, when people have no food and children are going without education. How important is this to you?'

As I looked around, the blue and white definitely made the area look better, cleaner, more in order, but Karisa was right. Was this a priority for the local people, beautiful buildings or food in their bellies?

He grabbed my arm as we dashed through the city traffic,

finally letting go as we arrived outside a large gate with a sign proclaiming "Wood carvings and local crafts". I pretended to be enjoying myself and picked up many articles to look at. Karisa was keen to do the bargaining for me but in the end, I bought nothing. The more I watched him, the more interesting I found him. I thought of the boys back at home waiting for me to sort out everything, and here I was playing tourist and with a young Kenyan man. I felt embarrassed and stupid and asked to leave. We headed back to Nyali for afternoon tea with Joseph and Binty.

Karisa disappeared to check on the vehicle, but reappeared smiling when it was time to go. Joseph volunteered to drive me back to the hotel but Karisa insisted on trying out the repair. So leaving them to their first sun-downer of the evening, we set off back.

The answer to his question from yesterday had been on my mind and I needed to talk. I wasn't sure whether telling him about the mess my personal life was in was a great idea. But the need to share it with someone was overwhelming and maybe someone who didn't know either George or I would be able to give me better advice. It'd got to be worth a try.

'Do you have time for a quick coffee? I've a bit of a problem that I need help with.'

'I would be happy to be of help to you, madam.'

We stopped at a corporate coffee house which could have been anywhere in the world. It brought a sense of the familiar to me.

'So what is this problem?' he asked as he returned with the coffees.

'Where do I begin? But first, I need you to stop calling me madam. It makes me sound ancient and decrepit.'

'I do not understand what decrepit means,' he said, and when I explained, he laughed too. 'Oh, no, you are very much not that. But if I am not to call you madam, am I to call you Mrs Trippett?'

'Oh God no, definitely not that, you must call me Angela.'

'Angela.' He tried it out for size. 'Angela… the angel.' For the first time ever my name sounded sexy.

I told my story and he listened intently, his eyes never leaving my face.

'Angela, you talk about finding out the truth, but what if the truth is not what you want to hear? What if you lose your home?' He touched my hand gently and a shiver ran through me. 'You are cold, Angela?'

I told him I was fine and he carried on. I sat on my hands; I couldn't trust them not to reach out.

'The decision to proceed can be only yours to make. But I will help you if I can.' His words gave me comfort and courage. Crazy though it sounded, I no longer felt alone. But he was right. As good as it had been to tell someone else, only I could decide what to do.

It was coming up to dinner time when we parted. Back at the room I dug out my iPad and brought up my emails. Staring back at me was one from the solicitor, informing me of all the gruesome details and what the consequences could be. And there at the bottom of the email glared that name. Mrs R Trippett. Rose… I hated roses, their cloying perfume, their insipid colours, but most of all their thorns!

I felt the heat flash through my body as I read the name again. Now it was real. All of the anguish hit me that instant, and I knew what I had to do. I needed to find her, I needed to meet her, I needed to know exactly who this other Mrs Trippett was.

Chapter Nine
Angela

I'd decided to come clean with Joseph and Binty. I needed their help, plus, I could hardly keep it secret any more now that Karisa knew why I was in Kenya. I was sure he wouldn't tell anyone, but I felt it was unfair to keep them in the dark when they'd been so kind to me. It appeared that it came as little surprise.

'We had our suspicions, of course, darling,' said Binty.

'But we never saw any evidence that was the problem. There were always rumours about George but then that was the same with many people. Sorry, Angela, but it wasn't unusual for a man working away from home to have his bit on the side, so to speak. But another wife, well now that's a different matter.' Joseph was obviously uncomfortable with the conversation and was pacing round the room. 'It might be an idea to visit the lawyer's office in Nairobi, though.'

I'd been putting it off but I knew that it was the logical place to start. Josh had wanted me to go there straight away and now I couldn't put it off any longer. Joseph was upset, I could sense it.

'How about instead of flying up, you do a bit of a road trip with Karisa and let me book you on a little safari en route? It'd be a shame not to have some sort of a holiday. I know the manager of a great place. It's not exactly five-star but it has a view to die for.' I began to speak. 'Now before you start saying no, I won't accept it. This is my treat. I feel bad enough not knowing what was going on with George and you must believe me, I definitely didn't, so please let me do this for you.'

How could I refuse? The idea of a safari didn't appeal but I couldn't say no, and who knew, it might be fun. I gave them both a hug to hide the tears of relief that these wonderful people didn't think me a fool.

'When are you thinking of setting off?'

By this time, Karisa had joined us in the room.

'To be honest, Binty, I want to get this over and done with, so the sooner the better.'

Karisa looked questioningly at us all and Joseph explained to him what the plan was. Thankfully, he seemed to be very happy to be help. 'It sounds like we must begin soon.'

This was unanimously agreed. In less than forty-eight hours we would be beginning our journey upcountry.

I needn't have worried, as once the decision had been made, both Karisa and Joseph set to in sorting out a vehicle that was going to be suitable for any kind of roads we might encounter. As always, I was happy to leave the organisation to someone else.

Joseph had hired a Land Rover for our use and refused to accept any payment at all. 'This is Kenya, my dear; tarmac is a scarcity in a lot of areas. You have to be prepared for a bit of off-roading.'

I allowed myself to be swept along with it all without really thinking about what I was embarking on. This was it, I was beginning my search, and it felt so unreal. I'd thought of Jeannie a lot and had managed a quick call to her to let her know I was okay and what I was doing. She sounded tired and this worried me. The sooner I got back to Somerset the better.

Although it was a Sunday when we left, the roads were almost as busy as when I'd arrived. We passed the turnoff for Moi International Airport and the unfamiliar set in.

'Bloody hell, girl, I hope you know what you are doing,' I whispered to myself. I closed my eyes, took several deep calming breaths, and sat back in my seat.

I still couldn't begin to understand how my life had come to this, and thinking back to life back in Somerset before George's death, none of this made any sense. I'd truly loved him at the beginning and I'd honestly believed he'd felt the same. But as time went on, I let him take over my life, the finances, the decisions, everything.

Jeannie called it emotional abuse and tried to get me to seek help, but I was too frightened. He never laid a hand on me, but he expected me to be at his beck and call twenty-four hours a day, even when he wasn't in the country. The money had been my hope and, like a fool, I had surrendered it all. He said he'd paid off the mortgage, but now I knew different.

'Are you okay?' The words woke me from my memories. 'Your face looks angry.'

'Sorry, I was just thinking of home.'

Leaving the city behind us, we continued on the main route out towards Mariakani and onto Voi, where we would be spending the night on our safari.

'Today this road is very, very quiet.' Karisa was concentrating on avoiding the huge pot holes ahead. I wasn't sure that I felt the same, as I cowered in the front passenger seat while container lorries headed straight towards us on the wrong side of the road, in their bid to be first to the port.

At regular intervals, we passed a line of trucks parked by

the side of the road at each pit stop to rest, and, according to him, take full advantage of what the prostitutes had to offer in the local bars. In between these places stretched a landscape of scrubland with acacia and the peculiarly majestic baobab trees. The road gradually became less manic but none the less without order.

Chapter Ten
Angela

The gate to Tsavo East Game Park was a short distance from the main road, and Karisa eagerly parked up the Land Rover and jumped into the back of the safari vehicle.

'This is a dream to me, Angela. All these many years I have been on this earth and I have never seen wild animals in my own country. This is an adventure I never dreamed I would have and I have to thank you for it.'

'Don't thank me. This is from Joseph and Binty, not me.'

'Yes, but if I had not met you and you had not decided to do this journey, I would not be here.' His enthusiasm was infectious and, for once, I forgot the purpose of the journey. I forgot the threat to my home, and dare I say it, I even forgot my family, I just sat back and relaxed as we entered the game park.

I could smell the dampness of the burgundy earth, so dark from the recent shower, as it stretched through the greens and browns of the bush. The acacia trees giving shade to unseen animals hiding in the tall grass and, in the far distance, the hazy purple of the hills which were our destination for that evening.

Once past the hanging elephant wires, we were able to stand up and take full advantage of the view as we drove through a land unchanged forever. The driver offered his binoculars, and we snatched them off each other whenever we thought we saw something move. We spent a wonderful couple of hours shouting out the names of any animals we saw as we drove down the many tracks further into the park.

The recent rain had been enough to provide water for the animals in distant watering holes meaning sightings were scarce. But the anticipation was excitement in itself to keep us on our feet.

'I remember when there were many animals here,' our driver said. 'Many, many elephants, zebra, even rhinos were in these parts, but now they are all gone and the others are few.' In the absence of any animals, Karisa told me a tale from his childhood.

'There were donkeys that decided that they did not want to be tamed to do all the hard work that other donkeys were doing, and so they went to visit the hare. He was very wise, and he decided to paint them black and white to disguise them, and therefore they would be able to remain wild and free. But, donkeys being donkeys, they rushed as one and knocked over the paint, leaving some with stripes and some still untouched. And that is why the smart ones are zebras and the others remain as donkeys, destined for a life of hardship and toil.' I was fascinated as he related story after story that'd been told to him by his *Babu* as he was growing up in the village.

'We did not have books, we did not have a school in the village, no television, nothing, and so these stories were a very important part of our learning. They had been taught to every generation before us. This was how we learned our history. Nowadays, the young have so many distractions to pull them away from their heritage, but our culture and our stories must remain.' As I watched him tell these stories, I could see a passion that I hadn't seen before. Here was a man who was totally of his tribe, a man so different from any I'd met before.

We stopped at a small encampment for a simple meal of

salad, rice, and chicken. We sat side by side looking at the view across the bush. This time, I didn't move away from the touch of his thigh. Thankfully, the arrival of a family of elephants by the perimeter fence proved to be more than enough of a distraction. I was enthralled at the antics of the little ones, trying to cause mischief with their older siblings. They reminded me of my own boys when they were young, playing imaginary games in the garden. The guilt stung that I was having such a good time without them.

'Time to go, Angela.' Karisa stood up. 'The driver is waiting.' We headed into the full glare of the early afternoon sun, the oppression of the heat absolute.

'Most of the animals will be lying in the shade asleep,' the driver said. 'You will hear how much quieter it is now; they will wait until the cool of the day before they move again. This is a good time to spot lions.' And as if on cue, he received a message on the radio to say that a pride had been spotted. We set off at speed to find them.

The spurt of power was exhilarating and I couldn't resist standing up and feeling the wind on my face. It felt so good and I couldn't help laughing out loud. Karisa stood up too and we hurtled through the African bush, laughing so much we could barely breathe.

We sat back down with a bump as the vehicle slowed down quickly and the shushing from our driver brought us to our senses. The vehicle crept very slowly alongside those already stopped, and there, in the shade of an enormous baobab tree, were eight lions slumbering. . The male was trying to sleep but was persistently being badgered by three young cubs, which were determined to get him to play. Occasionally, he would lose his patience and let out an earth-shattering roar to scare them away. But they didn't stay away for very long before they were back jumping all over him. We spent almost an hour watching these beautiful creatures doing what they did every day, and finally we had to say goodbye, as the driver reminded us that we had to make our hotel before darkness. Reluctantly, we moved.

We arrived at our safari lodge just in time for dinner. The light was fading fast and the view that had greeted us over the flatlands disappeared in the blackness of the African night, the only light appearing from a floodlit water hole just below us.

Once again, the food choice was simple but exceptionally good and the South African Chardonnay was surprisingly delicious. The bottle didn't last very long, even though Karisa took very little. After dinner, we retired to a small lounge overlooking the view, and we spent some time staring into the darkness, sometimes spotting zebra, buffalo or elephant at the watering hole, before heading off to our rooms to sleep.

We stopped outside our adjacent rooms to say goodnight. I took a step towards Karisa and felt his breath on my forehead.

'Excuse me, may I pass?' The guest pushed between us and the moment was lost. He squeezed my elbows and turned away to his room. His light still shone under the connecting door as I slid under the mosquito net and into the covers.

Before dawn I was awoken by a gentle knock on my door. Having decided not to do the early morning game drive, we wandered down to sit by the swimming pool at the edge of the ridge, to watch the sunrise. It was coming up to five o'clock and Africa was still in darkness. We found two battered wicker chairs and sat down to wait, wrapped in a blanket to keep out the cold. Everywhere was silence.

As the minutes passed, shadows emerged, the glistening of

the last rays of the moon on the watering hole on the plain beneath us, the bare branches of the baobab trees reaching to heaven in supplication, and the distant plains slowly being lit by a faint glow of light as the sun started to show. As if on cue, the world around began to wake: first, the bird song, so very different from the dawn chorus back home, screeches and whistles mystical in their sounds. Down below, I could just make out a small herd of elephants making their way through the trees towards the watering hole. The herd led by a colossus of a matriarch treading a path in search of food and water for her family. The young babies were guided by the other females with a gentleness that defied their bulk.

I gave a sigh of contentment and instinctively slid my hand into Karisa's. He clasped it tightly as we watched two giraffes wandering through the trees breakfasting on the highest sweetest leaves they could find. Presently, a few zebras arrived to drink at the watering hole, obviously very nervous being out in the open, but the need for water greater than the risk of attack. They were joined by gazelles equally as nervous.

As the sun rose totally over the plains, the whole vista came into view, and there in all its splendour stood Kenya. The wonder of the sunrise instilled in me a great sense of peace. To witness the dawning of an African day felt so primitive, so precious, that I had to fight back the tears. This happened in this land every day, but I felt so privileged to be here at this moment in time, and like a fool , I let it show.

Chapter Eleven
Karisa

Yesterday, a dream came true. I saw a lion, the king of animals. I saw many lions. I was a happy man. I heard the sounds of the night. I felt the presence of my ancestors. Sleep would not come.

Angela stirred me in a strange way, a way that no African woman had ever done. I see a child within her; I saw that today as she laughed with the wind. This was dangerous, very, very dangerous. There were feelings within me that must not be allowed to grow. They cannot be.

Yet I knew I saw those feelings in the face of Angela, too. That was why they could not be. I turned to look at her and she quickly turned from me but I knew she watched me. I also watched her when she was not looking. What should I do? I could not leave her, I made a promise but I cannot love her because I made a different promise... to another.

I used to think of Kadzo always and dream of a time when I would fulfil my promise to her.

But if I gave her the freedom she yearned for, she would never be welcomed back to her home. She would have disrespected her parents, my parents, and me. To the village, respect was everything, and so we remain promised without a future.

But my feelings for Angela were getting stronger. I had this attraction to her that I could not explain. I wanted to kiss her as a man should, but it was too dangerous, because it would lead to more feelings and this could not be. She was not mine to have and never could be. So forgive me, Angela. It cannot be.

Chapter Twelve
Angela

Karisa jumped up like he'd been shot.

'I am sorry, I must go.' He ran back up the track at full pelt. I turned to see if anyone had seen my humiliation but, thankfully, I was alone. I felt very, very stupid. What the hell did I think I was doing? For Christ's sake, I was almost twenty years older than him, and here I was acting like a lovesick teenager with a man I had only just met. What on earth was I thinking? I waited until the coast was clear and then I quickly made my way back to the room. I could hear him moving about in his. I didn't understand his reaction, all I had done was lay my head on his shoulder nothing else and yet I felt ashamed.

He didn't show for breakfast and I was both thankful and concerned. What if he couldn't bear to face me? He was waiting at the vehicle though when I emerged from the lodge. We both avoided eye contact but tried to at least smile in each other's direction. Neither of us spoke as we left the park and returned to the Land Rover.

His mobile sprung to life almost immediately. He pulled over to the side of the road, and walked into the bush out of sight to speak. I was worried something awful had happened when he came back into view looking very grave. I was right.

'My uncle has died. I have to return to my village immediately for the burial. They have been trying to contact me since yesterday but there was no signal in the game park. We will stop in the next place and I will phone Joseph to arrange someone to come and collect you and the vehicle. It should take no time at all, maybe only two hours. I must head home to my village. Do not worry. I will wait with you.' Karisa looked broken-hearted. 'This man brought me up after my father died. He paid my school fees, he helped clothe me and he brought us food. I have to pay my respects.'

'How will you get to your village without transport?'

'I will get *matatu*s and then a *boda-boda* or two. I must be there by sunset.'

'Take the Land Rover. It's important to you that you get there quickly. I can wait for Joseph or someone to pick me up. I will square it with him, he will understand.'

'I cannot take the vehicle from you, Angela. It is not mine to take.'

I knew it would be so much easier for him to have the vehicle. I felt his pain and I wanted to make amends for last night. He wouldn't hear of it.

'Well, then, you will have to take me too. That way no one need know that we've made a detour to your village. What do you think?'

Karisa slowly walked back into the bush and I was worried I'd frightened him off again. He returned after a couple of minutes.

'Thank you, madam that will be good. You are very kind. I just phoned my mother, she says she is very happy to welcome the *mzungu* woman into her home. I hope that is okay?'

'That's very kind of her, but surely it would be better if I stayed away from your village. This is about your family. Just find me a small hotel close by.'

'She will not hear of it, madam. You are her honoured

guest, the first white person in our village. You must stay.'

'On one condition, Karisa that you go back to calling me Angela. All this "madam" stuff is just a bit much for me.' And for the first time today, his face broke into that wonderful smile I loved, as we set off back down the road we'd come only yesterday.

After some time, we turned off the tarmac road and travelled down a bumpy dirt track through coconut palms. I scanned through the palm trees looking for houses but I couldn't see any, until at the end of the track we came to a large open space. The sound of the engine brought children running and as we moved slowly through they continued to run alongside the vehicle, until we finally came to a halt outside a solitary mud hut.

Karisa fought his way through the children as they grabbed hold of him and disappeared inside the hut, leaving me marooned in the Land Rover, surrounded by laughing children climbing over the bonnet and the roof. He re-emerged with a frail old lady on his arm.

'Angela, this is my mother. Please come and greet her.'

The door was wrenched open by a couple of older kids and I was half carried, half dragged out of the vehicle by a whole host of eager little ones. The lady let go of her son's arm and walked towards me. She looked very serious, as if she was studying every inch of my face. Then, she took my hand in hers with a strength that belied her frailty and shook it vigorously, all the time with the biggest smile on her face, just like her son's.

'*Karibu! Karibu*!' He explained that she was welcoming me to her home. As she didn't speak English at all, I managed to convey that I was very pleased to meet her, with a lot of flapping hand gestures and a little help from Karisa. Once she understood, she clasped me to her bony chest like she was never

53

going to let me go. 'This is my home and the home of my fathers. You are most welcome.'

He turned over a large metal cooking pot for me to sit on. Both Karisa and his mother crouched low on their haunches, while I gingerly lowered myself onto the pot. I was worried I might dent it. Surprisingly, they looked very comfortable and set about catching up on each other's news I assumed. I watched them and thought of Mark and the distance between us.

He'd grown up so like his father. Once he reached his teens, anger engulfed him and he delighted in being cruel to both his younger brother and me. George seemed almost proud at the disrespect he showed me. He knew it hurt me and he relished in that. He could be so nasty and he had taught my eldest to be the same.

After chatting to his mother, Karisa told me he had to go to the mortuary with his brother to pick up the body. I told him I would be fine and watched him drive away. I had lied; I was far from okay.

The women began to prepare food for the arrival of other family, friends and neighbours later. Feeling useless, I was left to my own devices. I could see all the people around looking at me and I began to feel uncomfortable. The children also still crowded round me and held their hands out to touch my skin and then ran away laughing. This soon became a game for all the children in the village, and the touching became pinching, and pulling my long blonde hair. They meant no harm.

The body duly arrived and the children's attention was diverted. Karisa explained that he would be expected to spend the night with his family and the body in the tent. He glanced back at me as he went inside. I felt my heart quicken; even in grief, the attraction was there. Almost immediately, I felt someone take my hand and lead me to where everyone else was congregating in a circle around the tent. She didn't speak

English but I felt a bond instinctively, and I was happy to stay with her throughout the night.

As darkness fell, the gathered women broke into song, wonderful melodic music whilst the men formed a group of their own.

For the second day running, I was privileged to witness an African dawn which, within less than an hour, had brought the hot blazing sun to warm us all. The men disappeared early to prepare the grave just a short way off on another part of the *shamba*. I could see them working in the distance. A cup of *chai* was brought by women from the neighbouring village who had also joined us to pay their respects. This *chai* would be the only thing allowed to pass my lips until after the burial, and was most welcome to shake away the chill of the night. Hanging from a nearby tree was the goat that had been slaughtered and skinned in preparation for later.

The pastor arrived and, after all the greetings had been made and money had changed hands, the burial could begin. The body in its simple coffin was carried from the tent and the singing began once more. Everyone was keen to be part of it reaching out to touch the coffin as it was shaken and juggled by all to its resting place in the rich red soil. The pastor began the service, punctuated constantly with 'Amens' and 'Hallelujahs'. After it was over, the whole group sang a final hymn to wish Uncle a safe passage to heaven.

Watching all the weeping and outpouring of genuine grief was a stark contrast to George's funeral. I was feeling more emotion at the funeral of someone I'd never even met than at my own husband's. Surely that wasn't right?

I walked away from the crowd and sat behind a baobab tree away from view. I began to cry and, once I started, I couldn't stop. I buried my head in my hands and let the memories flood back. I could never admit to anyone what I had done. I didn't know that a part of me could be so callous to let a man die and not try to help. I felt shame and now I was paying for it. George as always was going to win.

As I turned to go back to the burial, I was conscious of Karisa standing a short way away watching me. I walked over to him, frantically wiping my face on my arm.

'I did not want to disturb you. I saw you leave. You looked so sad. I left you to cry alone, but I was watching closely.'

'Thank you,' I said, finding my stiff upper lip and pasting it firmly back in place. 'I am fine.'

I knew by the look on his face that he didn't believe a word of it, but he remained silent as we walked back to join the others. Proceedings over, it was time to say goodbye to everyone, and there was quite a gathering to wave us off. The awkwardness was back.

'Karisa, I am sorry if I made you feel uncomfortable at the game lodge. I didn't mean to. I just got carried away with the emotion of the sunrise that I forgot myself. I'm very sorry. It won't happen again.'

'Angela, it is fine. Once again, I was very rude to you and I am sorry. Maybe you would be better doing this journey with someone else?'

'But I don't want to do that. I trust you, and I know that you are only doing this because of Joseph, but I would really appreciate it if you carried on the journey with me. Please.' I couldn't let him go now.

I held out my hand for him to shake to secure this new deal, but he continued to stare ahead. Feeling foolish, I lowered my hand. Finally, he turned his head and said, 'I would like to do this journey with you also. But if I am to accompany you then it must be as *rafiki,* as friends. I took you to my home, my mother welcomed you, you are my friend now.' He took my hand and held it. 'Are we *rafiki,* Angela?'

I nodded and thanked God. It was a relief to turn back towards Nairobi. We hadn't gone very far when once again his phone rang.

'It is Joseph,' he said, glancing at the screen. 'Can you please answer it?' I picked up the phone.

'Mark's coming over,' Joseph was shouting. 'He phoned me an hour ago; he says he can't trust you to sort this bloody mess out. His words, not mine, darling. So he's flying from Heathrow tonight and should be in Mombasa tomorrow morning. I tried to dissuade him but he was adamant. He seems to be very like his father, that one. What do you want me to do?'

'Sorry, Joseph, I'll have to phone you back.' I was so shocked at this news and couldn't think straight.

'That's okay, sweetie. I've said that I'll meet him at the airport and bring him home with me. He can even stay with us, if you want. But I think it will be difficult to keep him here in Mombasa. He wants to find this bloody woman.'

I could imagine Mark pacing the floor as he spoke to Joseph, another habit he'd picked up from his father. I was just surprised he had taken so long before getting on a plane.

I phoned Joseph back and told him that we'd be returning to Mombasa to pick up Mark, and that I'd book a twin room at the hotel for a night or so, for both Mark and I. Joseph, bless him, tried to argue but I could hear nothing but relief in his voice as he put the phone down.

Chapter Thirteen
Angela

The dust on the runway kicked up as the flight landed from Nairobi and taxied to the terminal, scattering the egrets as it juddered to a halt. It was the only plane at the airport. People rushed to attach the steps and remove the bags, a flurry of activity that belied the abandoned feeling of Moi International airport.

I spotted Mark immediately as he marched across the tarmac. He was leading the pack, as always, pushing to be at the front, always wanting to be first since he was a child. Nothing had changed. As he emerged from the baggage collection, I was grateful that he was only carrying hand luggage. Maybe he wasn't staying long.

'Mother.' He kissed the top of my head like I was a child. I introduced him to Joseph. He barely shook his hand before complaining loudly of 'The bloody heat' and handing me his case.

Once in the air-conditioned Land Cruiser, Mark became more amenable, and made polite conversation with Joseph. It was only when he realised that he had known his father for many years that the conversation turned frosty.

'So you knew what he was doing?' I noticed that he struggled to say the word 'Dad' or even 'Father' any more. 'You knew about this other woman, I take it?' spat Mark.

'Actually, I'd no idea, my boy. It came as much as a

surprise to me as it did to you.' Joseph was concentrating on weaving through the city traffic.

'I bloody doubt that,' said Mark, continuing to stare at him as he was driving.

I decided that we'd be better going straight to the hotel rather than breakfast at Joseph and Binty's, as had been offered. I pretended to have a migraine, and I sensed that Joseph would be glad to be rid of Mark as soon as he possibly could.

My old room had been available, and the four-poster hastily changed for two singles, leaving Mark bunking down with me until it had been decided what exactly would be happening next. We went to breakfast and of course, Mark had it all worked out.

'We are going to hunt this woman and her people down,' he said, banging his fist on the dining table and making the crockery rattle. 'They're not going to get away with it. We'll find them and destroy them for this.'

All this talk of hunting and destroying made me feel very uneasy, so melodramatic and so typical of Mark. 'And then what? When we find this woman, what the hell are we going to do?'

'We're going to bring her down. That's what we're going to do, Mother.'

'Mark, for God's sake, we aren't going to war. Please keep your voice down.' I could see heads swivelling in our direction as he continued to slap the table.

'Yes, we are, Mother! I won't keep my voice down, and I won't be cheated out of money that is rightfully mine by some woman who was obviously his bit on the side.'

'Ours, actually.'

'What?'

'The money you claim you're being cheated out of is ours actually, not just yours, but the whole family's.'

I could see the flash of anger in his eyes as I spoke out.

'Whatever,' he said; giving the table once last punch he walked out. The pitying looks from the other guests in the dining room said it all.

Leaving him to his own devices for a while, I found a seat overlooking the beach and let the sound of the Indian Ocean wash over me. A group of young boys were performing acrobatics on the sand. They were very, very good.

'They come every day and practise,' said the security guard, who'd wandered up to me. 'Local boys trying to earn a few shillings to take back for their families.'

'Shouldn't they be in school?' I asked.

'Where they come from, they have no choice. You cannot learn without food and they have to provide for their families now. There will be no school for them.'

I stood up to reach over the decking to hand the boys the two hundred shillings I had with me, when I heard the familiar angry voice behind me.

'And what do you think you are doing, Mother? Don't you dare give them any money? They are beggars. Once they know you're such a soft touch, you'll never get rid of them. I forbid you to give them anything!'

A vision of George popped crystal clear into my head. George forbidding me to choose my own car, forbidding the children sweets, forbidding me to go and visit Jeannie, forbidding, forbidding, forbidding anything that would have been fun or brought me happiness. And here was my own son doing exactly the same thing. When did he become such a monster? I waited until Mark reached my side, then, smiling sweetly; I leaned over and handed the money to the eldest child.

'Asante, Mama,' he said, giving me a beaming smile. 'God bless you.' And they were off, running down the beach to the next hotel.

'And don't you bloody come back,' shouted Mark, determined to have the last word. 'We don't like beggars.'

This time it was me who walked away, furious that my first-born should've grown up to be so uncaring, so rude and so like his bloody father.

Chapter Fourteen
Karisa

So we began the journey again, this time with the son. Angela had seemed distracted when she phoned. She said that Mark thought it best that we leave soon. But before I could journey, I was to meet with Kadzo. She was home from university for a few days and had requested to see me. She was staying with her family, but I knew she did not like to be there. She did not see her duty as I saw mine.

We met outside the village in a cafe where nobody knew us, and where we could talk. I ordered *ugali* and goat meat and she ordered hamburger and chips. I drank *chai*, she drank *Coca-Cola*. I felt nervous, she smiled sweetly. She looked so beautiful in her brightly coloured dress, with her hair bound up in a matching scarf. 'So, Karisa, how are you?'

I knew she was not interested in my health, she was just giving the greeting that was expected and so I played the game. 'I am fine. And how are you, Kadzo?'

She muttered that she was fine too, and then we sat waiting for our food.

'My mother says it is time we married. I think she is hoping for the dowry soon or at least an advance.' She found it amusing. I wished I could be as cool about this as her, but I could not.

'Oh, come on, Karisa, you look in pain. Cheer up.'

But I was unable. I knew that when she went back to

Nairobi, I would restart the journey with Angela and I remained stuck. I wondered if Kadzo ever felt stuck. Was she faithful to me or did she have someone who shared her bed? Someone who held her close? Someone she gave her body to? But I was too much of a coward to want to know the answer.

Once upon a time, I was brave. Once upon a time, I stood up to the police, but not anymore. So I sat quietly drinking my *chai* while she told me all about her exciting life in university. The food arrived and she stopped only to fill her mouth with hamburger and carried on. Finally, I got the courage to interrupt. 'Why did you want to meet, Kadzo?'

'Just to talk, Karisa. We never have chance to just chat like the old days. Life in the village is so boring. I just wanted someone to talk to and have a laugh with.'

She continued to speak until the meal was gone, just chat, nothing important, nothing about us, or about any decision to be made. Talk of the wedding and the dowry forgotten, she kissed me on both cheeks and we went our separate ways.

But the promise remained; it could never be broken.

Chapter Fifteen
Angela

'I need to pee,' Mark yelled above the din of the engine. 'We need to stop at the next toilets.'

Karisa raised his head to glance at me in the rear-view mirror before answering, a slight smile on his face.

'I am sorry, sir. There are no *wazungu* toilets for at least one more hour, but I could stop for you to relieve yourself in the bush, if you wish?'

'I'm not pissing up a tree around here. God knows what or who is around.'

'Maybe, sir, I could stand guard for you?'

'No fear. I don't want you watching me. Mother can do it.'

So, five minutes later, I found myself engrossed in a group of young children, giggling as they watched my grown-up son having a pee in the bush. Luckily for them and me, he was completely oblivious to their presence as he concentrated on watching out for 'bloody snakes'. Just before he was finished, I quietly called the children over and handed them a bag of boiled sweets I kept in my pocket for long journeys. They couldn't believe their luck and ran off, squealing and clutching their treasure to share among themselves. Mark thankfully remained ignorant of the entertainment he'd provided.

Back in the vehicle, our journey continued as before. The small groups of huts along the side of the road, festooned with washing hanging from the trees, and the children dressed in nothing but a pair of tattered shorts playing with a coconut shell or rolling a tyre with a stick, oblivious to the heavy traffic just feet away. Hunger took over, and an hour later we stopped for lunch at a roadside café and ordered chapattis, rice and stew. The minute the food was brought to the table, I saw the look of disgust on Mark's face.

'I can't eat this muck,' he said, shoving the bowl across the table. 'I need some proper food.'

I felt my face burn and my temper rise.

'We are in the middle of nowhere in Kenya and you're bleating that you want proper food. Well, this is proper food and you're being a damned idiot. Have you any idea how many people around here would love to sit down to this food?'

He leapt from the table, knocking the plastic chair over, giving me a look of pure hatred and stormed outside.

'I'm so sorry for my son's behaviour,' I said to everyone around, and the tears caught in my throat as I saw their sympathetic looks. Bad behaviour was bad behaviour in any language and culture and they all felt my shame.

Karisa reached across the sticky plastic table and touched my hand gently. 'You have nothing to apologise for, Angela. He is a grown man. His behaviour is his responsibility, not yours.'

We ate our food in companionable silence, but I could sense that this was only the beginning.

'How dare you talk to me like that?' Mark lunged at me the minute we walked out of the café. 'Who the hell do you think you are?'

My fury broke.

'Let me just tell you who the hell I am. I'm your mother, the person who gave you life, who fed you, who looked after you when you were sick. The person who brought you up.

65

That's who the hell I am, and I deserve some respect from you.'

The anger on Mark's face increased. 'Ha! You think you're so wonderful, do you?' I backed away from him, needing to put some space between us. 'You think you deserve my respect, do you? You couldn't even get the respect of your own husband. You couldn't even hold onto him. He obviously didn't respect you, did he? So tell me, why on earth should I?'

The slap was instinctive and immediate, and I saw Mark lift his hand to strike me back. In an instant, Karisa was between us, and he had Mark's hand firmly in his grasp before he could do anything about it. Karisa's face was set like stone, and he remained holding onto Mark's arm until he showed signs of calming down.

'You, sir, should show your mother all the respect in this world and never, ever raise your hand to her,' he hissed.

'And you should not involve yourself in something that does not concern you,' Mark spat back. 'You are our driver, nothing more, and when we get to the next stop, you won't even be that. When I tell Joseph how you assaulted me, you will be history.' He shook himself free from Karisa and, marching to the Land Rover, wrenched open the back door and threw himself onto the seat.

I felt the hatred from my son hitting the back of my neck as we travelled on. I couldn't believe that he was going to hit me, and the scary thing was that I was sure he would've done so had Karisa not stopped him. But then again, I couldn't believe that I had hit him first. It was the first time I had ever raised my hand to either of the boys; George was the disciplinarian in the family and he was a harsh one. Something was broken in Mark. I couldn't recognise him. He'd always been a sullen and moody boy, angry, yes, but never violent. I had felt a change since his father died. It wasn't Karisa's place to stand between a mother and her son, and his simple act of protection towards me had left him in a difficult situation. What I saw as protection, Mark saw as humiliation.

'We have to find somewhere to stop for the night. This road is not safe after dark.' I could see Karisa was concerned. The episode at lunch had delayed us somewhat and we were nowhere near as far on the road as he would've liked. He thought it best that we headed for a nearby town to try and find somewhere to stay for the night. 'We must choose our hotel very carefully in this town. Some areas are not good for us.'

Even to the untrained eye, this was quite obvious, as the lines of Lorries stopped by the side of the main highways grew. The appearance of shabbily, scantily dressed females increased in proportion with the heavy goods vehicles.

'We can't stop here. We will get murdered in our beds in this place. Fear finally causing Mark to speak.

'I am afraid, sir, that we have no choice. If we continue the journey, we will most likely be robbed or hijacked. We will find somewhere suitable off the main highway I am sure.' Karisa turned the vehicle off the main road and headed into town.

He was right. Away from the make-shift lorry parks and accompanying nightlife, things seemed much calmer as tourists and locals mixed together to do business. The new railway station was very busy and a queue of safari vehicles waited outside for the six-thirty train from Mombasa for visitors to the Tsavo game parks. We headed to a small hotel nearby.

Having parked the Land Rover under the one operational floodlight in the hotel car park, we grabbed our bags and walked into reception. The lobby was small and cramped, the walls covered with dark plush panels. Above the reception desk a photo of the president, sat smiling down like a benevolent father. The place was deserted.

The force with which Mark hit the bell on the desk more than indicated that he was still very angry. There were only two rooms available, Karisa had been insistent on sleeping in the vehicle, but I wouldn't hear of it. He, more than any of us, needed to get a good night's sleep, ready for the long drive ahead. I also wanted him to be nearby. If I was honest, I was afraid of the anger in my son. I needed to feel Karisa was on hand, just in case. I never ever believed I'd feel this way about Mark. George, yes, but not my son.

I arranged with the reception for a meal for us all later and we headed to our rooms. Mark, the gentleman as always, left me to drag my bag up three flights of stairs. By the time I had reached the room, he was already sitting on the bed with his arms folded and a face like thunder.

'Mark, why?' I wheezed, trying to get my breath back. 'Why do you carry this anger with you? Why do you want to hurt me, to hurt Karisa when all he did was protect me? Something he should never have had to do.'

'That man humiliated me, Mother, and you let him.'

'He didn't humiliate you, Mark. You did that all by yourself.'

'Of course, I guessed you would take his side. I mean, you'd never consider taking my side, just for once. It's always Mark's fault, isn't it? Always, always my fault. Ever since I was a kid, I was always to blame. Paul breaks his leg, why wasn't I watching him? Kate gets into trouble after school and it's my fault for leaving her to walk home on her own. And you're darling, precious Josh? Well, it's never his fault for anything. No, everything wrong is down to me. Did it ever occur to you just once, Mother, that someone else could've been to blame?'

My grown-up son had become a twelve-year-old again, as the years flashed back to him being so upset because his best friend Paul had fallen out of the sycamore in the garden and had broken his leg. Nobody had blamed Mark at all; he'd blamed himself that he couldn't stop it. He hadn't even been in the garden when it happened but felt that he should've been, and maybe then it wouldn't have happened at all. The same when his cousin Kate had been bullied in the playground at primary school. Mark was so angry, not only with the bullies, but with himself for not being there to protect her. He was at secondary school a mile away, but in Mark's eyes, that wasn't an excuse. He should've been there, he should have stopped it.

Even the seven years age difference between him and Josh didn't lessen Mark's feelings of responsibility. In fact, he became even more protective of him. He seemed convinced that something awful was going to happen to the new baby. For a while, he screamed and shouted when I made him leave Josh to go to school. No one ever blamed Mark, just himself. I couldn't stop him and I never could understand why he felt this way.

He was sitting very still on the bed, trying to contain his anger. His head was upright and his jaw set firm; he was staring at the wall. Deep down, he was still that little boy in a man's body, and although I was still furious with him, I reached out to put my arms around him. Surprisingly, he let me. Mother and son embraced for the first time in years.

Chapter Sixteen
Karisa

I had bad feelings about the son of Angela. He disrespected his mother, which was not as it should be. I had to step in. I could not let him strike her. I knew this could cost me my job, but I had to do it, and this I would tell Joseph when he asked. Was my courage returning? I thought not, because I now had fear for my job.

My room was a peace from the journey and gave me time to think. I thought of my mother back in the village, her brother passed, and her other son with his own family. This left only me. She was my responsibility. She gave me life. I could never have shown her disrespect the way Angela's son did. He was very wrong and yet he did not show any regret.

My mother wanted me to return home, marry Kadzo, be settled in the village and provide her with many more grandchildren to look after her in years to come. Maybe I could do this... but Kadzo... never! So I did nothing other than see the disappointment in my mother's eyes every time I returned without news.

How would she feel if I told her about the feelings I had for Angela, the feelings that were growing daily? The same feelings that made me turn my head from her when I saw her, in case I showed her my heart. How would my mother feel about a *mzungu* as a daughter, about me having to leave the village for good to be with Angela? Would she be happy then? I knew that would not be the case. She needed me with her to take care of her, as she had looked after me as a child. I could never leave her. Maybe, if Angela's son told on me to Joseph that would solve everything. I would have no choice but to return to the village with no job. I would have to leave Angela. I could then become the man I was expected to be for my mother. Shame on me for thinking it could be otherwise. How could it be? I could never have a life outside my village. It was where I belonged, it was where I grew up and it was where I must return.

So I would not give the son the satisfaction of destroying me. I would speak to Joseph myself and tell him that I could not remain with this journey. I would tell him my mother was sick. This he would understand and allow me to leave with dignity.

Chapter Seventeen
Angela

Mark wasn't hungry at dinner and returned to his room, after gulping down a whiskey and soda, without touching his food. I was relieved.

Both Karisa and Mark had been uncomfortable in each other's presence and I saw Karisa relax into his chair as Mark left. I was glad to be alone with him. I wanted to know so much more about the man in front of me. He intrigued me as well as attracted me. I was trying very hard to accept him only as a friend but it was difficult. I asked him about his life in the village. I had seen a small part of it but I was interested in knowing everything about him. He was reluctant to talk at first and seemed a million miles away.

He opened his mouth as if to speak but then stopped. Finally, he took a deep breath. 'I was unable to finish my education for a long time. My family was the poorest in the village and my mother could not afford to pay my school fees. She used to go and dig other people's *shambas* in order to earn a few shillings to feed us. It was only when my uncle came to help us that I could finish school. People in the village laughed at me without shoes, without books, without food. I wanted to be someone great to show them. I was very brave in those days and used to fight with everyone who laughed. Nowadays, I am no longer brave. I am grateful, though, for the life I have. I can at least help my family.' He looked down at the table.

I reached for his hand but he sprang back.

'Angela, I have to tell you that tomorrow morning, I am leaving my job. I do not want to let you or Mr Joseph down, but it must be me to make this choice, not your son. I said it is past and it is, but the consequences are not and they are mine alone to bear. I just wanted to let you know my decision.' He got up to leave.

'Karisa, stop. Please don't do this. It isn't your fault, you have done nothing wrong. Mark won't tell Joseph anything, I promise.'

'Angela, it is not your promise to give. I did no wrong but your son will not let this pass. He is very angry and I cannot suffer the shame of being sacked. I must leave.' He tried to smile as he walked away, but I knew he was hurting as much as me.

The tears began to fall, silently at first and then in great sobs. Everyone was staring at me, the hysterical *mzungu*. I couldn't return to the room and so I hurried outside into the night air.

The light in the car park hurt my eyes and I found a place in the shadows. I sat on a stone and looked heavenwards. The African sky didn't disappoint in its brilliance, and the romance of this wasn't lost on me. The tears slowly dried up and the anger took over.

'What a bloody mess.'

I guess I must have spoken out loud because a small voice said, 'Are you okay, madam?' I turned round to see a young boy of around ten years old looking at me with the roundest, brightest, blackest eyes I've ever seen. 'You should not stay here, madam, it is dangerous for you. Bad people are about in darkness. They will harm you for your money, for your gold. It is better that you leave.'

I got up and walked over to where he stood in the half-light. 'So why are you here, young man?'

'Me? I have nowhere else, madam. Here I can get scraps from the kitchen. I stay in the light and hide behind cars when the bad men come. I have safety here.'

'But where is your home? Where are your parents?' I slowly edged closer but he backed away.

'Madam, I have none. There is only me, but I am bright. I have been to school for as long as three years. I can manage.' Even in the gloom, I saw determination on his face standing proud, his chin jutting out in defiance. My heart went out to him.

'*Wewe*, what are you doing?' a man's voice shouted from across the car park. 'Stop, you!' The boy was gone.

'What is your name?' I yelled into the darkness.

'Gabriel, after the angel.' He disappeared into the night, with the man and another giving chase.

'Angela?' I turned round to see Karisa. 'Why are you out here? It is dangerous.'

'So my friend Gabriel just told me. Why are those men chasing after him like that? He's just a small boy.'

'Angela, there are some very bad men around here who get young boys and sell them to other people.'

'What like servants to do work in their homes?'

'No, for much worse. Some men, both Kenyan and *wazungu*, like to have young boys to satisfy them in other ways. These children have nothing else. Sometimes they are drugged; sometimes they are beaten, and sometimes even murdered. They have no one who cares for them so they are not missed.'

The Kenyan night sky suddenly lost its appeal and I silently

74

followed Karisa inside and up to my room.

Mark was fast asleep on one of the single beds and I quickly slipped under the mosquito net and between the sheets of the other. I couldn't get Gabriel out of my mind. That poor boy, living the life he had to, without anyone to look after him. Like most people, I'd watched the television programmes about the street children and the like and I'd felt genuine sorrow for them, as I'd sat in my cosy living room in my suburban detached house eating chocolate. But out here in Kenya, it was very different. It was real, as real as the red dust all around. It hit you right between the eyes and you couldn't ignore it. It even had a name… Gabriel, the angel.

I must've dosed off because I awoke with a start to Mark shouting. I could hear him arguing with someone, but there was no one there.

'Stop it! Stop it!' He seemed to be fighting with someone before he calmed down to an incoherent mutter. I got out of bed and went over to him; he was still asleep. Inside his mosquito net, he was wet with sweat. Using a damp towel to wipe his face and arms, he awoke momentarily with eyes full of panic and then fell back into his dream world. Eventually, he seemed to settle a little and so, positioning the one fan in the room directly onto him, I lay down again.

The dawn finally squeezed in through the gaps around the moth-eaten curtains bringing a half-light into the room. Looking over at Mark's bed, I saw that it was empty. The door was slightly open and there was a sound of retching echoing in the bathroom next door.

He turned his head as I walked in. 'This is your fault, you and this God-forsaken place.'

I said nothing and went back to bed. Why was it always

someone else's fault with Mark? Ten minutes later I heard the flush and he slouched back into the room clutching his stomach. He threw himself onto the bed. 'Why the fuck did you make me come here?'

I clenched my jaw. All my life I accepted whatever criticism was thrown at me. All I ever wanted was a quiet life, but I had paid the price with my self-esteem. I thought of Karisa and the childhood he'd had and the wonderful man he'd become, and then I looked at my own son, who'd had everything and felt he was able to treat everyone with such distain. I was trying hard to remain calm; I didn't want another scene. But as I began to speak, Mark groaned loudly and pushed by me to get to the bathroom. Once more, the sound of retching filled the air, drowning the sound of the fan. I left him to his misery.

Karisa sat opposite me at the breakfast table, with a deep frown upon his face as I told him about Mark.

'He will be fine in a while, I am sure,' I said.

'Maybe we should get the doctor to come. He may have malaria.' His concern grew. I liked the fact that he cared, even about someone who had been abusive to him. I wished he was staying.

'Do not worry, Angela. I will not do anything while Mark is ill.' He must have read my thoughts.

'How did you know that was on my mind?'

'It is showing on your face as well as being in your mind. I can see it.'

'I wish you weren't going to do this at all, but I'm grateful that you're staying until Mark gets better. We probably ought to book the rooms for another night at least.'

He promised to arrange that as we tucked into eggs and

some sort of meat. I felt no guilt for having an appetite. Breakfast finished, Karisa went off to reception and then to check the Land Rover and I went back upstairs to the sickbed. Once again, it was empty. I heard a movement coming from the other side of the bed, and it was there that I found Mark, flat on his back.

'Mum, I can't get up,' he wailed, all anger gone. I phoned down to reception to request a doctor. Now I felt guilty.

'Sorry, not possible, madam. Hotel doctor not back until tonight, but local doctor is down the road if you can take him there.'

Mark was listening to the conversation. 'Fuck off, you can fuck right off, I am not going to some witchdoctor. I am staying right here until the proper doctor is back.'

I went to find Karisa.

'We must go to a chemist and buy something to ease his suffering,' he said. 'I will go and search.'

'He will be fine, I'm sure, but he's my responsibility so I'll go take a look and buy something. I need to get some air anyhow.'

'Angela, you cannot go out on your own. It may not be safe for you. I will come with you.'

I was grateful for his company. We got Mark back to bed and left our number with reception for emergencies. I know I should have been worried about my son but I felt little sympathy. All my concern was for a poor boy with the name of an angel. I prayed that he was safe.

Chapter Eighteen
Angela

Karisa grabbed hold of my arm to pull me back as a car headed straight for me.

'You must take care outside; the vehicles do not always stay on the road.'

He was right; I watched in horror as pedestrians jumped out of the way to avoid being run over by whole families on motor bikes, or crammed into the three wheeled *tuk-tuks* as they weaved in and out of the stalls among the rain-filled potholes.

We turned past the police station, with its sentry post and razor-wire fence on top of the high wall. We could see a lot of activity through the gate, probably left over from the previous night in the clubs and bars. Karisa once more grabbed my arm and hurried me along. I sensed his unease.

We were looking for the 'Better Health Pharmacy' recommended by the hotel manager. 'They will not give you rubbish. You will get top western medicine, not something from a witchdoctor. *Mganga* medicine is not for you.' He'd also suggested that we visited the local hospital, as they might be able to help without the need of 'many shillings', so we turned down a slightly quieter road towards the place. Finding it was not a problem; getting into it was another matter.

'Oh my God, we'll never get seen here. Look at the queues.' I looked at Karisa in despair. As we turned in through the iron gates, we immediately joined a line of people winding their way around the building. Some of those in need of attention had given up queuing and were flaked out under the acacia trees dotted in the compound.

'Do not worry, Angela, I will go to the front and tell them that you are waiting to be seen. I will make sure that they see you first.'

'You'll do no such thing. These people were before me, I'm not going to push in. Look at them, some of them can hardly stand. Let's go back to the pharmacy. I have a little money to pay for the medication, these poor souls don't.'

We arrived at the chemist to be told that the pharmacist had popped out for some *chakula,* and as I was a *mzungu* and the patient was the same, then I would need to deal with him only. I was assured that he'd only be a matter of minutes as his home was nearby, but this being Kenya, where time means nothing and minutes could quite easily become hours, we decided to go across the road for a soda at the 'shake it up' bar and restaurant. Thankfully for us, at that time of day there was no 'shaking it up' going on, just a cool, albeit rather dark place to enjoy a cold drink. This also gave us the ideal place from which to watch for the chemist returning, and this he duly did after around fifteen minutes.

I quickly paid the bill for the drinks and, swerving through the traffic, we made it back across the road into the shop. The pharmacist said he was very pleased we'd waited for him as he needed to give our predicament some serious thought. Frowning he made his way slowly along the rows of bottles and packets on the shelves behind him. He carefully selected two packets, handed them to the shop girl, and then disappeared into the back of the shop.

'That will be three thousand shillings, please,' the girl said.

Karisa began to complain but I cut him off. I needed to get back to Mark.

'That was far too much,' he said as we struggled once more through the traffic.

As we arrived back at the hotel reception, there was a tussle going on between a young boy and one of the staff, and as we got closer I saw it was. Gabriel!

'Oh, Mama at last.' He broke free from his captor and ran towards me. 'Where have you been, did you forget the time, Mama?' He threw his arms tight around me. 'Please say yes,' he whispered into my stomach.

But before I could say a word, Karisa spoke. 'We are sorry, son, we did not mean to be late for you.' He grabbed hold of Gabriel by the shoulders and marched him straight passed the bemused staff and up the stairs to his room. Not having a clue what was going on, I gave them my sweetest smile and followed him.

'*Asante Sana Bwana.*' Gabriel breathed a sigh of relief.

'Okay, child, it is time to tell us what is going on. What are you doing here?'

'Bwana, please do not be angry with me. I have nowhere else to go. I hid from the men in the *taka-taka* at the back of the hotel, but they found me and took me. I kicked and shouted, but they hit me hard on my legs and head and then picked me up and took me to a dark room. I was very frightened, Mama. There I knew bad people used to come and take me away and do bad things. Things I cannot speak of because God will strike me down dead. I did not want to go there again and so I bit the man very, very hard on the arm as he came to take me out of the room. And then I ran. I ran so fast, faster than I have ever run before. Faster than the fastest animal in the world.'

'And then what?'

'Then I thought of the lady *mzungu*. Surely she would help me.' He looked at me with those beautiful dark eyes and I felt a rush of love for this boy. I kissed the top of his head and asked Karisa to go and find some food while I found a clean t-shirt for Gabriel to wear. He was very reluctant for me to see him change into the shirt and I could see why. His tiny wretched body was criss-crossed with welts, obviously from previous beatings, and his ribs poked through his very skin. Once he realised that I wasn't going to throw him out, he relaxed a little, and was smiling and chatting when Karisa returned with the food. It took him no time to eat and drink and then, as if the food had taken away his energy, he dropped back on the bed and immediately fell asleep.

'So, Angela, what are you going to do with this boy? He cannot stay here.'

'I have no idea. This was never part of the plan. My son is unwell; my dead husband apparently has another wife, and now this. I can't deal with this. I so want to help but I don't think I can. We'll let him sleep, and then I will give him money to leave. What more can I do?'

Karisa walked over to the window and said nothing.

'Well what do you expect me to do?' His silence was infuriating. 'He's not my problem. It's your country; if you are so bloody concerned then you do something.' I was annoyed at myself for being in this situation. I'd let my emotions run away and now Gabriel thought I was going to help him, and I'd let him believe that.

Karisa remained silent staring out of the window. Slowly, he turned to face me.

'I knew a child like this before, a boy around the same age.

He lived near me. He had no home but sometimes I would give him food. It was before the time I worked for Joseph, so I did not have much food myself, but when I saw him I would share my meal with him. Every time he came he had more injuries, cuts on his back, bruises on his face, sometimes walking with difficulty, but every time I tried to ask him about them, he would just brush them off as small occurrences, happenings, nothing important. Then he would go away again, and when he would return some days or weeks later, there would be more wounds and more excuses. Angela, I did not want to get involved. I told myself I was being a good man by feeding him occasionally. I did nothing else. Then he did not return. I heard they had found his body down the side of a disused shop. He had been burned alive.

'No one claimed his body, no weeping mother or father. Nobody to cry for the loss of his short life. No one to save him. And now, here is another child. I also do not want to get involved, but I cannot just feed him and watch him leave. This time I must do something more. I do not know what, but the thought of that young boy haunts me. I did not even know his name. But this boy, he has a name and he has come to us for help. I cannot turn him away.'

I could see the tears running down Karisa's cheeks and as I looked at the sleeping Gabriel, I knew he was right. We could not walk away.

Chapter Nineteen
Angela

I left Gabriel asleep in Karisa's room and went to see how Mark was. He'd been crying. He didn't want to talk to me but I knew something big was bothering him. I also knew that there was no point in trying to force him to speak; if he had something to say, he would do it in his own good time. I turned and walked back out of the door, leaving him alone. I know that wasn't the right thing for a mother to do, but I'd no idea how to get him to open up to me. It was almost like he hated me.

I went downstairs to get a cup of coffee and think things through. Karisa was still adamant that he was going to leave once my son's health improved. Mark was holding something inside him that he couldn't talk to me about, and now we had Gabriel. My head hurt.

Soon, Karisa and Gabriel came to sit by me Gabriel was wide awake and Karisa sent him to the bar to order some sodas.

'Angela, I have been thinking about the boy,' he said. 'I cannot take the responsibility of him. Soon I will have no job and I will be going to the village back to my mother. There may not be a space for him there.' I was disappointed in his change of heart. Gabriel had returned to the table and I tried not to look at him as I told Karisa that there was no way the boy could come with Mark and I, particularly as he was choosing to leave us.

We both remained with our own thoughts until the waiter

brought the sodas. Gabriel's seat was empty.

'The boy just left,' he said. 'About five minutes ago.'

'You stay here in case he returns,' shouted Karisa. 'I will take the vehicle.' And he too was gone.

'Sod that,' I thought, and ran into the car park and behind the hotel. It didn't take me long to find him. Wedged between the rubbish bins by the kitchen, he was sobbing his little heart out.

'You do not want me. Neither does Bwana. I came for help, but you do not want to give,' he cried, looking down at his feet.

'Gabriel, please look at me. It's not that we don't want to help you, we just don't know how. '

'All I need, madam, is to travel in your vehicle, somewhere, anywhere. Just take me and drop me, that is all. I have to leave this place, it is bad for me. I must go.'

'Okay, come back with me now and we will work something out. I promise.' I took hold of his hand and pulled him to his feet.

When Karisa finally returned we decided that Gabriel would stay in his room for the moment.

The hotel doctor finally arrived to see Mark as darkness was falling.

'Infection,' was the prompt diagnosis after an examination taking less than a minute. 'Has he medicine?' he enquired. Almost before we could answer in the affirmative, he was writing out his bill. 'Eight thousand shilling, madam.'

I was hoping that Karisa might tear him off a strip and argue our case about the cost after his comments in the pharmacy, but this time he remained silent. I counted out eight crisp new thousand shilling notes and the doctor hastily scribbled a receipt.

'Keep him in bed until the fever improves and call me if you need me.'

'Not at your fucking prices,' muttered Mark as he watched him go. I looked at Karisa.

'Surely that is not right?' I said. 'Eight thousand for a five minute consultation?'

He just shrugged his shoulders. 'He is the doctor, we must respect his decision.'

Asking for water, Mark allowed the boy to hand it to him and then get him a cold flannel to wipe his forehead. I saw the confusion on his face as to who this boy was. But for once he didn't create a fuss and settled back on his bed with Gabriel sat by his side.

Karisa and I spent as little time as possible in the dining room without raising suspicion, before retreating to the room with a tray of food for Mark and a handbag full for Gabriel. Mark, still feeling awful, ate very little and then pushed the tray towards Gabriel as a sign that he'd finished. He wasted no time in demolishing what was left.

We waited until the hotel was quiet before Karisa and the boy left our room to go to theirs. I held my breath and listened hard for any sign of a disturbance, but all seemed well. I was more than grateful to hear Mark's gentle snoring and nothing else as I climbed into bed. But after what seemed like only a couple of minutes, I was back wide awake as I sensed, rather than saw, the door opening. I'd forgotten to lock it.

'Angela, me and the boy have to leave. There are bad people about and they want him. I hear then talking outside my window. A few shillings to the *askari* and they will very soon have our room number.'

I shot up in bed to see Karisa's silhouette in the doorway and went to get out of the bed.

'No, you cannot come. You must stay here. Your son is too ill and it will be noticed if we all move now. There is a brother cousin of mine who lives not far from here in a small village. We will find him. It is not a great distance, maybe thirty minutes, but I must take the vehicle. Do not worry. I will return when the boy is safe.'

And before I could utter a word he was off, leaving the door open in his haste.

Chapter Twenty
Karisa

What was I doing, driving off-road with no lights in this darkness? I was scared but I could not show it. The boy hiding beside me was more afraid than I.

'Do not worry, son,' I said. 'My brother cousin will help. He is *Giriama* like me, and he will not turn us away.' It had been some time since I last visited. He would be wary at this time of night and might indeed turn us away if he no longer recognised me. I prayed he would not.

God was with us and we did not attract attention on the main road. Now we were driving the dusty track to his village. There was no light tonight, not even from the moon, and so I drove without haste. I saw a movement to my right. I thought it was an animal but it was not. Staring at the vehicle was a naked man. I knew of these people. They came out in darkness to cast their spells as people slept. People called them night-runners, and they were known to live with the wild animals and tame them in order to cause harm, but he could not see us inside and so turned away into the bush. Because of the vehicle, he would think we were *wazungu* and would not bother us. They did not bewitch the white man.

We reached the end of the road. All around us, I could just see the small dwellings made of the rich red earth and long wooden poles, topped off with *makuti*. This was a poor area and some of the houses were no longer whole where the rains had washed away the walls. There was no sign of life. I struggled to remember which hut belonged to my brother cousin and so remained in the vehicle for a while to see if anyone came outside.

The boy looked at me; I saw only his wide frightened eyes.

'Where are we?' he whispered.

'We are somewhere where we can rest safely for tonight, son. Do not worry.' I tried to sound brave. After some minutes, a man emerged to release his bladder. I saw his fear at the sight of the Land Rover. I slowly opened the door and slid out.

'*Polepole, rafiki* slowly, my friend.' I asked about my relative.

The man nodded and pointed towards a hut some distance away, just visible in the trees. I returned to the vehicle and collected the boy. I was unsure of the welcome we would receive but it was unsafe to leave the boy alone, so we went together.

'*Hodi.*' I gently tapped on the rotten wooden door. 'May I enter?' Nothing happened and so I tapped again a little louder. '*Hodi.*'

After a third knock, a head slowly peered around the door.

'I am Karisa, son of Charo and brother to Katana. I come in friendship and am in need of your help.'

'Enter, my brother. I recognise you from old.' The door was immediately pulled open so we could walk in. This was the home of my brother cousin Bakari and I was thankful for his kindness.

The house was one room, divided by an old cloth hanging from the roof to separate sleeping from seating. I sat on one of the two plastic chairs. Two small sleepy heads popped around the cloth as they heard voices.

'These are my children; their mother is no more. The boy can sleep with them. We, my brother, have a lot to catch up on so I will make some *chai* for us to share as we talk.' Gabriel disappeared behind the curtain; I went to gather what little we had brought from the Land Rover. On my return, we sat to drink and I explained the situation. Bakari had not asked. He had welcomed us, knowing that I would tell in my own time. He understood the perils that young children had to face in the big towns and cities and told us that we must stay for as long as we needed to. But he was concerned about the *wazungu* back at the hotel.

'If they come here, they will attract attention and maybe trouble to our village. Everyone believes that every white person is very rich, and if they come here, they will believe that they have paid me lots of money and will look for it from me. If they don't find it, then they will make many problems. I cannot take that risk with my children.'

I understood his concerns and told him so, but still he agreed to look after Gabriel for a while. He is a good man and would not let his brother cousin down. I got back in the vehicle and drove back to the hotel and Angela. Gabriel would wake up in the morning and find me gone but he would remain safe.

Chapter Twenty-One
Angela

Listening to the sound of the Land Rover pull away, I felt very alone. What if he didn't return? Mark was sleeping soundly and this gave me hope for his health. If Karisa didn't come back, then we would return to England and I would have to put my faith in the solicitor to save my home. I felt foolish for listening to Jeannie and all that rubbish about finding the truth. I knew the truth, that my husband was already married when he met me, and that my whole life was one big fat lie. I began to cry quietly to myself. There was no real reason for me to remain here in Kenya. I'd already made a fool of myself with Karisa and I didn't want him to lose his job because of Mark's pig-headedness. No, it would be better for everyone to just go home and let the solicitors sort it.

After much tossing and turning, I got up to take a paracetamol. I heard a vehicle door bang and rushed to the window just in time to see Karisa entering the hotel. I had to talk to him and was already outside his room by the time he climbed the stairs. As we entered and he closed the door behind us, I sensed his nervousness.

'Angela, we must talk fast. You cannot be seen in my room.'

He explained about Gabriel. 'It would be unwise to remain here for another night, as the disappearance of the boy will bring questions and people may begin to suspect our involvement. There are many bad people here; it is not safe for us. I promised that I would stay until your son is well. He will be much improved by the morning. I will then take you to the station to go to Nairobi. I will return to Mombasa with the vehicle if Mr Joseph agrees. You may get another driver and car in Nairobi. Mr Joseph will arrange that for you, I am sure.'

'What about Gabriel? What will happen to him?' I was stunned that he still intended to leave us.

'He can remain with my brother cousin for a few days, maybe weeks. After that, I cannot answer.' He refused to look at me.

'Please, don't go.' My voice was strangled with emotion.

'I have to. Your son will make trouble for me and I cannot allow that. Also, we both have these feelings and what is happening between us is wrong. It can only cause pain for both of us. I cannot put your way of life at risk. You have your home, you have your family. I have nothing.'

I leaned forward to touch his cheek and he stepped back but this time I was not giving up. I moved closer and before either of us had a chance to think I kissed him. Karisa pushed me away.

'My God, Angela, forgive me.' He sank down on the bed, his face in his hands. 'That, Angela, is why I must leave you. I have no control when I am with you. I beg you, please let me go.'

He was begging me to let him leave and yet I knew I couldn't do that.

'Please, Karisa, I am begging you to stay.'

Mark was awake as I returned to the room.

'Where the hell have you been?' I made up some story about needing air and then rushed into the bathroom to hide my

91

blushes.

'You sound much better,' I yelled, splashing cold water on my face. 'Would you like to come down for breakfast?' He muttered something and when I returned into the room, he was getting dressed.

'The sooner we get out of this bloody place, the better.'

Karisa was already sat at the table as we walked in the dining room and I saw him stiffen as he saw Mark.

Mark ignored him.

'Karisa, I have been thinking about Gabriel. I am very worried about him. How long can he stay at your cousin's?'

'He said he can stay for as long as he wants, but I am not sure whether it would be wise for the boy to remain there. Word will very soon get out that he has someone new in the house. I do not want to bring trouble to him. He is a good man.'

'Can't he come with us?'

Mark jumped up like he had been stung. 'Are you completely mad, Mother? I forbid it. I absolutely forbid it.' Once again he stormed out. I was getting so tired of these tantrums. I stormed after him.

'You FORBID it! You bloody forbid it!' The anger grew and grew as I pushed my son through the bedroom door. The pushes and shoves became slaps and then full-blown punches as I pummelled into him uncontrollably. 'Who the hell do you think you are? You cannot forbid me like some bloody dictator. I am your mother, not some bloody slave.' I was yelling at the top of my voice now but I didn't care who heard me.

Eventually I stopped exhausted and turned away.

'That's it, Mother; turn your back as always. That's what you do, isn't it? You turn away from everything as if it's not happening. You did it to my father, you did it to Grandma and

92

Grandpa and you did it to me. All except your darling Josh. You never turned your back on him, did you?'

I felt the venom in Mark's words and the disgust in his voice. What was he talking about? Did I really turn my back on people? I'd hoped I was a good mother; it had been difficult to be the mother I'd always wanted to be with George around. But I thought I'd done my best but obviously Mark thought otherwise. I turned to face him, still trying to control my anger.

'Tell me, what causes all this rage in you? Am I such a bad mother to you both?' I looked him in the eye; he sat down and hid his face from me. I thought he was ignoring me but I was wrong.

'Mother, I don't know what to say to you. You fed and clothed us, yes, you did, you took us to school and football practise, you even helped us with homework. But you didn't see. You didn't see me or my pain.'

'I don't understand. What pain? All I saw was an angry boy and now I see an angry man. It's like you hate me and I don't know why.

'You didn't help me, Mother, because you chose not to see.' He jumped up from the bed and started to pace around the room; he still refused to look at me. 'I needed you and you weren't there. You didn't care what that man was doing?'

My throat closed as a sudden dread filled me. 'What man, Mark? What was he doing?' I asked him to sit back down but he shrugged me off and continued to pace up and down eyes fixed on some distant place.

'I begged him to stop; he shouldn't be with her. That girl didn't belong with him. She was too young. But he told me it was fine, that I was a good boy and must not tell anyone our little secret. You see, Mother, I saw him; I saw what he was

93

doing. In the end he didn't hide it from me because he knew I would keep his secret; because if I didn't, he would beat me. I was his favourite, he told me, his little soldier because I kept quiet. But you didn't see, did you? You must have known, there were so many, but you just let him carry on his sordid affairs. You let him bully me. When I needed you, you turned away. Whenever any one of them dumped him, he would take the belt to me like it was my fault. Maybe it was, I don't know. But you, Mother, you pretended you never noticed a thing.'

He burst into heart-wrenching sobs as his anger finally dissolved and he sank to the floor, his head in his hands.

I couldn't comprehend what he'd just told me. I tried to understand but none of it made any sense. Was he talking about his father? I sat down on the floor next to my son and tried to hold him but he shoved me away. I watched my son fall apart and I didn't know what to do. My husband had beaten my son in order to hide his secret lovers and I'd let it happen.

We sat for a long time entangled in our own misery until Karisa quietly entered the room. 'If we are leaving today, we have to check out now. It may be difficult for us to stay longer.'

I just shook my head and Karisa got the message. We were going nowhere.

Finally I found my voice. 'I didn't know,' I whispered.

'You didn't want to know, Mother. You wanted to think that everything was rosy, but you knew it wasn't, and in the end, it was down to me to protect the family. You did nothing to help us.'

Was he right... had I known what was going on? I reached out to touch him. He sprang to his feet. 'I have to get away from you,' he said.

'Please don't go... we need to talk about this,' I pleaded.

'There is nothing to say. You can never make it right; no one can ever make it right for me. All the women and now another wife to take away all the money that I deserve, but you'll do nothing, Mother; you'll turn away as always. I'm going back to England. I can't stay here.'

'Let me come with you, Mark.'

'No, Mother!'

Mark caught the lunchtime train from Mtito Andei station to Nairobi. He didn't speak another word to me. How could I blame him?

As I started to pack my things to leave, the one photo I always carried of George fell out of my handbag. The anger was fierce within me. 'I can never forgive you, George. I hope you're burning in eternal fire in hell,' I screamed at the top of my voice. For the first time there wasn't any guilt; I'd done the right thing in letting the bastard die.

Karisa rushed through the door to see me setting it alight. I held onto the photo until it burned my fingers, finally dropping it to the floor and stamping on the embers. The pain in my hand was a welcome relief to the pain in my heart.

'Time to go, Angela,' he said.

Chapter Twenty-Two
Angela

I felt awful. I knew the feeling well. It was my anxiety. I hadn't felt this bad in a long time and I was scared. I slid into the front seat of the Land Rover and concentrated on my breathing as we pulled away. I gulped at the air but my lungs would not accept the breath. My fingers and the end of my nose began to tingle tiny pins and needles and I felt dizzy. I gasped and then gasped again then I felt Karisa's hand on mine.

'Angela, are you okay?'

I couldn't answer him; I didn't have the breath. The panic rose through my body from my stomach. I couldn't stop it. I felt the vehicle stop and then my door open.

'Come, come, Angela, get some air.' Karisa pulled me from my seat. My legs gave way and I sank to the ground. He carried me to the shade of an acacia tree and laid me down.

'Angela, what is wrong? Tell me how I can help you.'

'I am okay,' I croaked.

The look said he didn't believe me. He left me in the shade while he made a phone call. He came back with water and held it to my lips. I thought only of Mark. I wanted to return to Somerset and put things right. But Karisa had promised to stay and convinced me to continue in my search, finding that woman was the only thing I could do now. I knew that but I was falling apart.

'Angela we must let you rest. We will go to my brother

cousin.' Karisa kept his eyes on the ground. I could see the tension set in his jaw.

'I thought he didn't want us there?'

'He will not turn us away when he knows why we are there.'

Bakari greeted us both with a smile but I sensed that behind it there was fear that Karisa had brought the *mzungu*. Gabriel, on the other hand, was ecstatic and threw himself on me.

'Mama, Mama, you came.' He was jumping up and down, unable to contain his excitement. His happiness was contagious and this helped me to calm down enough to drink the *chai* that Bakari had made. He offered to let me use the mattress behind the cloth to rest on; it was a welcome relief to lie down. Gabriel lay down with me. He said he would stay with me to keep me safe from bad dreams. But it didn't work. The nightmares came, and I woke up sweating and feeling the panic rise once more.

Karisa, Gabriel, and Bakari were staring at me wide-eyed. Bakari beckoned Karisa to join him outside. Gabriel, however, was reluctant to leave but didn't come as close to me as before.

'Mama, you are unwell. You say bad things in your sleep about killing someone. Your voice was so loud, it scared me.'

I reached over to hug him but he leapt off the mattress.

'You need *Mganga*,' he said. 'Maybe you have demons inside you. The *Mganga* will get rid of them.'

'I just had a nightmare,' I tried to explain to Karisa when he returned. 'Nothing more than a bad dream.'

'Angela, in Kenya we believe that spirits both good and bad enter through your dreams and that there are many lessons to be learnt in dream time.' His words took me back to Jeannie, she would have probably agreed with him, but I was scared to hear him say these words.

'There's nothing wrong with me. I'm just having a tough time and a few nightmares. Everybody gets them, it is no big deal. Now just leave me alone to rest.' I was beginning to panic again and I didn't want anyone to see me lose control.

'Angela, you cannot stay here in Bakari's home. He is concerned you will bring bad things to him and his children and he cannot risk it. He says there is an empty hut further into the trees where we can stay tonight. You can rest there until morning and then we can decide. We have no choice tonight, you cannot remain here.'

Karisa held onto me as we trudged through the trees leaving the vehicle and Gabriel with Bakari. I felt a little better away from the rest of them and his touch was a comfort to me. The hut thankfully was pretty much intact and he set to sweeping the floor of debris using a few twigs and some cardboard that had been left behind.

'We must make a fire to keep away the snakes and Bakari said he will make food for us to collect. We will be okay, Angela, do not worry.'

Karisa disappeared into the trees and came back presently with a bundle of wood and a couple of coats and a blanket from the Land Rover.

The Kerosene lamp that he'd borrowed from Bakari gave a mellow glow in the hut. In another time, it would have been romantic, but tonight it cast many shadows as he served up the rice and beans that Bakari had kindly prepared for us. I watched him as his eyes closed in a silent prayer of thanks for the food and then started to eat without a word. The hiss of the lamp engulfed the whole room with silence. But I needed conversation. I needed to talk; I didn't dare let my thoughts run wild in a place such as this.

The more he was silent, the more my panic rose. 'You are very quiet, Karisa, is there anything wrong?' My voice seemed to echo through the trees.

'Nothing is wrong, Angela. Where I come from, we are taught not to speak during food. This is the time for eating, not talking.'

I counted my breaths in and then counted them out again.

Karisa went outside to put some more wood on the fire and I lay down on the coats and pulled the blanket over me. He remained outside. The last sounds I remembered hearing were the crackle of the fire and the crying of cats in the distance.

Chapter Twenty-Three
Karisa

I heard the noises in the night. Angela said that they were cats but I knew that this was not the case. Those were the cries of long-dead babies for their mothers. Many animals were able to change into human form at night. This was a bad omen for us to hear but I would not tell Angela this.

Bakari visited at sunrise while she still slept. He was very concerned that we left quickly. He too heard the sounds in the night and he feared greatly. We had to leave; we could not bring bad witchcraft to his home. But first I let Angela continue her sleep. She needed rest. I spent the time in prayer against the evil that was around. God would help us.

I was worried about her. I knew that something big happened between her and her son, but I could not ask. Whatever it was had made her very sick, and if we stayed, they would take her to *Mganga* for a potion and that would not be good for her. We must move from here but I needed to talk to her about the boy. Bakari wanted him to leave with us as other people would soon know that he belonged to the white woman and would think him cursed too. So for his safety, he had to come with us. What would I do with the boy? I was a man alone. Kadzo would never accept him should we ever marry. My mother was too old to look after a young boy, so my destiny and Gabriel's were locked together. If I accepted the responsibility then I must accept the consequences.

I heard Angela stirring as the light from the sun shone through the open door. I went inside to speak with her. She did not reply but looked at me with confusion. I poured out the *chai* and unwrapped the cold chapattis that Bakari had brought with him and offered her a cup. The sweetness of the *chai* was welcomed but I could see that she was struggling to eat.

'Angela, we have to leave this morning. It is not good that we stay and Bakari says that we must take the boy also.'

She looked at me as if she was unable to focus her eyes to see. 'Sorry, what? I was not listening. You said something about leaving, I think?'

I repeated what I had said but she was still not hearing me; she remained lost in her thoughts. After some minutes she said, 'What are we going to do with Gabriel? We can't take him with us, Karisa.'

'I have been thinking about this also. We cannot leave him here and we cannot return him to the life he had before. So what else is there to do?'

She wrapped the blanket tight around her as if she was suffering greatly from the cold and walked outside the hut into the early morning warmth.

I tidied up the hut of all our things. We could not leave a trace. I knew that we had no other choice and I was sure Angela did too, but she could not think with ease at the moment. Her sickness still taxed her. I would have to decide. I went to seek Bakari.

I returned to find her in the same place. 'Everything is in the vehicle,' I said quietly. 'It is time to go.'

She lifted her head towards the sun, took a big breath, and walked towards the Land Rover. She did not seem to see Gabriel sat in the back seat and accepted the hand of Bakari in farewell without response. I said my goodbye to my brother cousin and wished him well. I saw him turn away and lift his hands in prayer.

Chapter Twenty-Four
Angela

I was back in the vehicle. This time sitting in the back seat was not my son, but a little boy who I had no idea what to do with. He, I sensed, was concerned about being with me too. I could tell by his silence.

Only Karisa acted normal as he attempted to sing along to a Swahili song on the radio. The *chai* from this morning churned in my stomach. I felt sick. I asked for water. He reached into the door well by the side of him and produced a bottle. I took a few small sips, trying not to spill it over me on the bumpy road. The sickness eased.

Gabriel remained quiet in the back as we travelled on and finally hit tarmac. As we turned northwards, he sprung to life, grabbing me and giving me a hug. Now I understood his silence. He was worried we would turn south back the way we had come. It had nothing to do with me; it was fear about returning to his old life.

As we drove towards Nairobi, the old Gabriel with all his cheek and energy returned. 'This music is for old people. Put on some modern music, *Bwana Mzee*,' he said, laughing.

Karisa laughed too and turned around in his seat to try and cuff the boy about the head, but he was far too slow and Gabriel quickly moved out of arm's length. 'For that, young man, I am going to make you listen to my music all day.' He turned up the volume full blast, drowning out Gabriel's cries of dissent.

I sensed the pretence was for my benefit and we continued such until we reached a place that Karisa thought would be a good place to stop for food and touch base with Joseph. He'd also dropped some rather strong hints that I should call home. I wasn't so sure that I was ready for that yet but promised him that I'd think about it.

'Mama, where are we going?' Gabriel said.

'We're just going on a little trip up north, maybe even to the city of Nairobi. Or would you like to go back?'

'No, Mama! Not back, we must go on!' I smiled to myself as he grabbed me around the neck from the back seat and planted a kiss sloppily in my right ear. 'We go on Mama.'

The Mountain View Hotel and Restaurant stood newly painted by the side of the road we pulled into the deserted car park.

'Are you sure this is open?' I said.

Karisa leapt out of the driver's seat and ran to the front door. The door opened as he pulled the handle and Gabriel was out of the vehicle like a shot. So, realising I didn't have much of a choice, I swallowed my anxiety and followed the boys.

We were escorted like royalty into the dining room where I was pleased to see a few other people sat at a large table. The minute we sat down, however, they got up and disappeared through double swing doors at the back of the room. Menus were ceremoniously brought to the table and reverently placed in front of each of us. Then a plastic washing up bowl, jug, and towel appeared for us to wash our hands.

Another waiter then picked up the menus from the table, opened them, and handed them to us. He gave a small bow and then took a step back, joining the others who had formed a circle around us.

I inadvertently looked up from the menu and immediately someone stepped forward.

103

'Yes, madam, may I help you?'

'No sorry, that's okay. I was just wondering what my friend here was going to have?'

As if everyone else was wondering exactly the same thing, they all leaned forward towards Karisa, heads tipped to one side awaiting the momentous decision. Realising he was now the object of some considerable attention, he lifted his head in alarm.

'Um, could I just have a glass of water for the moment, please?'

Immediately the crowd deflated with a collective gasp. 'No wine, Bwana? We have a fine collection. Or maybe a beer – we have *whitecap* or *tusker*?'

'No, no thank you. Just water, please.'

The assembled company of waiters melted away, the prospect of a large tip diminishing once they realised that we weren't the big spenders they'd hoped for.

The waiter, who clearly felt he'd drawn the short straw, returned with a glass of water and plonked it down on the table. He turned to walk away but was stopped by Karisa, who grabbed hold of his arm.

'This glass is dirty. I would like a clean one. Also, we would like to place an order, if that is not too much trouble, or maybe the manager would be interested to know why we are taking our business elsewhere,' he said.

The waiter removed the glass and, when he returned, was joined by several other waiters anxious once again to serve. We placed our orders. Karisa and I opted for the biriani, whilst Gabriel, unable to read the menu, decided on chicken, with eggs, chips, rice, greens, tomatoes and onions, and not forgetting the tomato ketchup.

'I have to leave some room for afters, though, Mama,' he said, when I questioned him on his choices. 'I am nearly a man now. I need much food if I am to grow.'

Presently a couple of other people drifted in and like ourselves, sat by the windows to take full advantage of the 'Mountain view', and then proceeded to have, what appeared to be, a huge argument. Seeing my concerned look, Karisa grinned.

'They are talking politics, Angela; a favourite subject in Kenya. Any conversation about such things is never done quietly.'

The food arrived and the portions were extremely generous, possibly a result of Karisa's threat to talk to the manager, and I found it difficult to make much of an inroad. The others, however, had no such trouble and very quickly cleared their plates. Eyeing what was left on mine, Gabriel gave me his best puppy dog look and I gently pushed my plate over to him. Without drawing breath, he finished that too.

Staring out of the restaurant at the view, Karisa explained that the mountains were part of Chyulu Hills National Park. I found myself thinking about a trip to the Lake District with George, not long after we were married.

I was pregnant with Mark and was feeling kind of restless, and so he'd suggested that we got away from it for a while. He'd always wanted to return to the Lake District, having only been there once before on a camping trip with the boy scouts. Looking back, even then we were so different. George always wanted to do his own thing. He hiked and sailed. I was never invited. I longed to do things with him but he said I would slow him down or I wouldn't like it, and so I never got that chance.

'You should ring home.' Karisa's voice brought me out of my daydream and into reality. 'You need to check that everything is okay.'

'Both you and I know that Mark will not want to talk to me, so what is the point?' I snapped.

'You have your last born, Angela, phone him. He will be concerned.'

He was right, of course. I had to phone home. Mark would be back and this would cause concern, especially if he'd told Josh what had happened between the two of us. At the moment, though, this was the last thing I wanted to do. But I could put it off no longer. Josh was quick to answer.

'Mum, thank God you've phoned. What's going on? Mark is back home and refusing to speak to anyone. He's not answering any of my messages and says he just wants to be left alone. What the hell went on out there?'

'Oh, Josh, love, he's been ill and didn't like being here. He told me some things that were difficult for him to say. We had a huge argument and he left to go home.'

'What things, Mum?' Josh was sounding frantic.

'It is not for me to say at this moment. I am okay, but I'm worried about Mark. I need you to look after him for me. He doesn't want to see me or be with me at the moment and that is okay, I understand. But he needs you, even though it may seem like he doesn't. Promise me, Josh that you will look out for him.'

'Of course, I will, Mum, but wouldn't it be better if you just came home? Then we could sort this out together.'

'I don't know. I've tried to think all this through but I can't. I don't even know why I'm doing this but at the moment, I think it's best that I stay away. Please try and speak to Mark, he may help you understand. I love you so much, darling.' The phone went dead; I'd run out of credit. I faced Karisa and forced a smile and then turned to walk outside to get some much-needed air. Gabriel tried to follow, but Karisa held him back.

'Mama needs to be alone,' I heard him say.

The car park provided the space I needed to calm down and

ponder on what Josh had said. Maybe it was better that I went home and sorted it all out, but growing deep inside was a feeling that this would only make things worse. I felt my anxiety rise and my breathing falter. I sank to my knees on the gravel. Karisa rushed towards me. He lifted me to my feet and led me to the Land Rover and sat me in the back seat.

Gabriel ran off and returned with a glass of water.

I tried my best to calm down a little as I sipped. The poor boy looked terrified.

'You must rest, Mama. We cannot go on until you are well.'

I realised the boy was talking sense. Ever since Mark had left I'd felt I was on a precipice, teetering on the edge of some calamity out of control and unable to make even the simplest of decisions. I looked at Karisa. I knew he would make the decision and book rooms for us and I was grateful. I allowed Gabriel to gently lead me back into the hotel.

The bed was luxurious and I snuggled under the covers without getting undressed. Karisa wanted to call the doctor but I wouldn't let him. All I needed was rest. Gabriel was very reluctant to leave and I had to promise him that if I wasn't better by the next day, he could call the doctor.

Sleep came quickly and when I woke up the room was dark. It felt like I'd been asleep for a long time, but checking my watch I saw it was only six-fifteen in the evening. Feeling much better, I got up and headed off to find company.

I could hear Gabriel's squeals before I saw them at the pool table. He was laughing because Karisa had just missed potting the black to win the game.

'Hi there, can anyone join in?' I asked and Gabriel came running to give me a hug. I saw Karisa's concern.

'Mama, you are awake. I thought you would sleep all night.'

'Well, I couldn't very well miss a pool tournament. Could

I?' I laughed. 'Especially as I'm the all England champion.'
Gabriel looked as if he believed me but Karisa's belly laugh
gave the game away.

'Come, Angela, play the boy and we will see.'

So while he went to get some sodas, Gabriel and I messed
about trying to play pool.

'I am fine now,' I said when he asked. 'I don't think I will
need the second night, I am sure that I will be able to carry on
tomorrow.'

'I think there may be a change. Joseph called while you
were sleeping. Your lawyer in England called him yesterday as
you gave him the number of Joseph in case of emergencies.
They have an area for the woman you seek, but it is not Nairobi.
It is about thirty kilometres outside of the city. He is doing some
enquiries of his own. He will get back to us. He said to stay here
until he does; it is easier to change our direction from here. So
we must wait.'

Hearing those words brought a feeling of relief. Despite its
sparseness and many shortcomings, I was feeling more relaxed
here at Mountain View than I had since we left Mombasa with
Mark. The opportunity of at least one more day of rest was very
appealing.

'So let us wait,' I said and promptly potted the white.

Chapter Twenty-Five
Karisa

My concern was great for Angela. Her anxiety was too large for her. I would make her smile again. After breakfast, we would be tourists for the day. We would travel to the Chyulu Hills. The man on reception had organised a guide for us and I had some money from Joseph. She would find peace there, I hoped.

Her tiredness still showed as she arrived in the dining room to eat. Maybe she did not sleep, but I said nothing. Today I would make her well. Today I wanted to take all her troubles away from her, just for a while. The boy knew of my plans and was so excited to tell her.

'Mama, we have a great surprise for you,' he blurted, unable to contain himself.

She looked up from pouring her mango juice.

'Why, Gabriel, this is wonderful. I wonder what it is.'

He turned to look at me as if he would burst. He could not remain seated and rushed to Angela. He looked at me. I let him speak.

'Mama we are taking you somewhere wonderful today with lots of animals. We are taking you to the mountains that you can see from here and we are going to look after you all day,' he told her. 'You must do nothing at all. Today you are the Queen of England.'

Angela nearly choked on her juice and she raised an eyebrow enquiringly in my direction.

'He is quite correct, today is a day just for you.'

I saw immediately the pleasure that these words brought to her and Gabriel was already fussing around her.

I looked on. I wanted her to have happiness, but there was something more in my heart. A feeling that grew stronger that made me want to have her as a man and woman should. Apart from Kadzo, I had never had such feelings. I could not protect my heart from Angela no matter how I tried. I struggled to contain the hardness in my groin when she was around, but I needed to keep control and remain just friends.

Today I would bring her joy. Today she would relax away from her troubles. Tomorrow was another day.

Chapter Twenty-Six
Angela

What a lovely surprise it was to be out in this beautiful place, so unspoilt, so different from life back home. I thought of Josh and my phone call and the guilt stung once again. I tried to pay attention to the guide but I struggled. Gabriel was desperate to see animals and the guide was becoming equally desperate to find some for him.

Karisa was very quiet, much more than usual, and that worried me a little, but every time I turned to look at him, he was smiling back at me and said he was very fine.

After a while we were rewarded with some amazing views and I finally became absorbed in the day. We stopped the vehicle and got out and Gabriel was lifted onto the roof and could barely contain his excitement.

'Look, zebra! And over there I can see *Twiga* , giraffe!' He pointed to the horizon and I was just able to make out a family of giraffe on the tree line.

'These animals are only for tourists and rich people,' he said, 'But now I have seen them with my own eyes.' He couldn't hold back his tears. 'This is a dream, Mama,' he said through his sobs. 'A beautiful dream. May I never wake up?'

I felt my eyes water too as he wiped his tears away to look through the binoculars that the guide was handing him.

'They are so near. I can touch them. Look.' And he thrust his hand in front of the lens pretending to stroke the animals.

What was going to happen to this boy? We may have rescued him from his difficult life, but what now? I couldn't keep him. I'd enough problems with my own children at the moment, plus I'd be leaving Kenya when this was all over. Karisa, although obviously fond of the boy, wasn't showing any inclination towards making him a fixture in his life. So what would happen? My face must have been showing my thoughts because Karisa came to stand next to me.

'You are unhappy?'

'Oh no, not at all, I was just thinking that was all.'

'They were not good thoughts, I can see on your face.'

'I was just thinking of a problem to solve, but today isn't the day to dwell on it,' I said. 'Thank you for bringing me here. It's very beautiful.' He looked pleased with what I'd said and went to fetch some water from the Land Rover.

Watching him as he did this, he seemed different today, like he'd many things on his own mind. He'd been looking at me a lot. Maybe he was concerned about my health and was watching for signs of another breakdown. I wouldn't be surprised; I'd hardly been calm and composed these last few days. Back in the vehicle, the guide explained to us his plans to drive as close as he could to the famous Leviathan Cave. 'This is the largest lava tube in the whole of Africa,' he proudly said. 'It would have been the biggest in the world but I think the Americans cheated with their measurements.' But as we got closer, Gabriel became very agitated until finally, he could remain silent no longer.

'Mama, I don't want you to go into the cave. There may be bad spirits in there and they will make you ill again. I will not let you go in.' No amount of trying to persuade the boy that there were no spirits, good or bad, in the cave would make him change his mind. This was what he believed and not only did he refuse to enter them, he was going to make sure that I didn't either. So, not wanting to cause him any more anguish, I told him not to worry as I'd been in lots of other caves in Somerset and didn't really need to visit these anyhow. Immediately he was back to his boisterous self and declared himself to be 'absolutely starving'. So we stopped for lunch.

The view was breath taking, but it didn't take long for Gabriel to wolf down his food and get the fidgets. The guide took him off to see what they could find in the trees just below us, leaving Karisa and I to finish our lunch in peace. He remained pensive and it was only when we were alone that he spoke.

'Angela, there are some words that I have to say to you and I hope that you will hear me.'

'This all sounds very serious. I hope that it's not bad news,' I said, dreading he was going to say he was leaving again.

'I have been thinking a lot about our friendship. We are friends, I think?'

'Yes, of course.'

'Then I think I can tell you my thoughts and hope that you will accept them. I am feeling more than friendship for you and I think that you may feel the same. I have tried to stop these feelings and protect my heart from you, but it is impossible.'

He stopped speaking and looked away. But before I could even think straight I grabbed hold of his arm and whispered, 'I have feelings too.' He reached for me but this time it was me who pulled away. 'Nothing can happen, we both know that.' I saw his pain. I felt it too.

'You scared away all the birds with your talking,' Gabriel said, coming back up the hill. Karisa set about clearing up the lunch things and got back into the vehicle without another word.

The sun was starting to dip in the sky when we arrived

back at the gate and said goodbye to the guide. Karisa gave him more than a generous tip before jumping into the driver's seat for the journey back to the hotel. Neither of us had received any word from Joseph and so we checked with the reception that our rooms would be available for further nights should we need them, then went to freshen up before dinner. We hadn't spoken a word to each other since lunch.

I hadn't expected Karisa to tell me his feelings today and had reacted without thinking. But now in my room I had time to ponder. Today I felt something I'd never felt before. I'd felt a desire for a man that took my breath away, that tied my stomach in knots and physically made my heart beat faster. But I remembered the sunrise at Tsavo and I felt foolish, who the hell was I kidding? I wanted to believe him more than anything else, but my mind was telling me not to be so stupid, that nothing could ever come of it regardless of what either of us felt or said. But in spite of these thoughts, I dug out the nicest dress I had, did my hair with care and even put on some make-up. Tonight I felt brave.

They were both sitting at the table when I entered the dining room and stood up in greeting. Karisa looked away while Gabriel ran around the table to pull out my chair. 'Please sit down, madam,' he said solemnly. 'Are you comfortable?'

I told him that I was indeed very comfortable and looked for the menu.

'No choice tonight, Mama. This is a special meal, just for you.' He looked to Karisa for assurance and he nodded in agreement.

'First, champagne,' Gabriel said as the waiter arrived with a bottle, looking distinctly unlike champagne but containing fizz none the less.

'Delicious, good choice. The best champagne I have ever tasted,' I said.

Both Karisa and the waiter tried to stifle a giggle but Gabriel was overjoyed.

'I knew you would like it, Mama.'

It seemed so strange and wonderful for me to be here, being treated with such love and kindness by two people I barely knew, and yet for the life of me I couldn't remember a birthday or Mother's Day with my own family where I'd been treated with half as much consideration.

After the meal, we all went to sit outside in the warm night air but Gabriel soon became restless, yawning incessantly so we decided it was time for bed for all of us. I thanked them both with hugs for my wonderful day and went back to my room.

Karisa had held back from the hug. He seemed distant and had turned his head as I embraced him. I rushed away without another word. Had I been expecting too much? I remembered all that he had said to me during the day. I had hurt him.

The soft tap on the bedroom door made me jump. I knew it was him and I dreaded opening the door. Did I want to hear what he had to say? There was a second, firmer knock. This was my last chance to back out and pretend I was asleep. I knew this was the sensible option, but there was an inevitability to it all, and I slowly unlocked the door and let him in.

Without warning, he pulled me into his arms. I could feel him trembling. His kisses were so strong they almost knocked me off my feet. I regained my footing and kissed him back just as strong. He carried me to the bed and gently lay me down. Now the kisses were gentle. I closed my eyes and enjoyed the caress of his lips.

Chapter Twenty-Seven
Angela

When I woke up, he was gone. I knew he would be. Nothing had happened but with the sunrise came the doubts, the doubts of an old woman being taken in by a beautiful young man. Last night I believed he loved me; this morning, I wasn't so sure. I couldn't understand how he could genuinely have the feelings he said he had, and I couldn't get out of my head the thought that he wanted my money as Mark believed. I needed to talk with Jeannie. The signal at the hotel wasn't great but I managed to get connected after several attempts. It was good to see her face. She looked tired but dismissed it when I questioned her.

The lapse in the video call was annoying but Jeannie allowed me to carry on uninterrupted.

'I have real feelings for him, but I think I am being a fool.' I explained to her what had happened between Karisa and I. 'And as for the boy... I have no idea what to do with him. He's become attached and he has no one else in this whole world that he can turn to.'

'How do you know?' Jeannie broke in.

'Sorry, what?'

'How do you know he has no one else? Just because he's told you... He may have a mother and father you don't know, you were just there at a moment in his life. Also, how do you know that Karisa wants you for your money? Do you have any proof?'

Jeannie was not making things any easier for me, but I understood where she was coming from. I was dumping all this stuff on her and she knew nothing about these people, only what I was telling her.

'I don't, I suppose. I'm just assuming.'

'So you believe the boy but not the man, is that it?' she said.

And there was the crux of it. She was right. I did believe Gabriel, but deep down in my stomach, I didn't believe Karisa.

'So what are you going to do, Angela? I'm going to be honest with you; I think you've got yourself into a bit of a mess here. You were supposed to be finding some woman who'd been named on your husband's will, not get yourself a toy-boy and pick up a waif and stray while you were at it. Have you forgotten everything that's at risk? Maybe it's best that you come home.'

I was about to explain to her the reason why I couldn't come home, but something stopped me. I knew she'd never been a fan of George but to tell her what he'd done filled me with shame. So I made some excuse about having to consult the lawyer here before I could make any decision, and promised that I would think about what she'd said before wishing her a tearful goodbye. I knew deep down that Jeannie had my back. She'd promised my mother that she would look after me and had always done so, and I knew that what she was saying was making perfect sense. I was here to find Rose Trippett, not fall in love. I needed to do something before it all went too far. As much as it hurt, I knew I had to go on without Karisa. I could go to Nairobi, see the lawyer and see what would happen from there. He would have to return to Mombasa with the boy. Last night had been a big mistake and I had to stop it going any

117

further.

I couldn't look at him when I saw him in reception and told him I had a headache. I caught a look of concern as I spoke. My feelings were still strong but I knew I was kidding myself to think there might be any kind of future. I knew it would break Gabriel's heart but he would still have Karisa. But first I needed to find the courage to break the news to them and the right time.

I didn't meet up with either of them for the rest of the day. I was a coward and I hoped that tomorrow I could face Karisa. I ordered room service and sent them a message saying I needed to rest. As night came, I lay awake and heard the cries I had heard in Bakari's village. I knew they were only cats, probably somewhere around the back of the hotel in the rubbish, but to Karisa, they were dead babies crying out for their mother. It made me think of Gabriel. He called me Mama. Would he cry out in the night for me when I was no longer with him?

I struggled to get to sleep after listening to the cries but must've dropped off as I was woken up by a gentle tap on my bedroom door.

'Angela, it is Karisa,' he said, from the other side of the door. 'I am just checking that you are okay.'

Now was as good a time as any, I thought. 'Hang on, I'm coming.' I unlocked the door. Mercifully, he was on his own, and so I asked him to come in. He paused before entering. I think he could see in my face that something was wrong and reluctantly walked into the room and sat down.

I felt my heart pounding as I sat as far away as possible from him. I couldn't afford to let my resolve drop and so I needed to be well out of touching distance.

'Karisa, I have come to a decision' – I saw his head drop – 'To carry on the search for the woman without you. You must leave and go back to Mombasa as soon as possible. I'll phone Joseph and sort it with him.' I knew I was being callous but I had to tell him quickly before I began to cry.

'Angela, what have I done wrong?' He got up and walked over to me. I dodged him and walked to the other side of the room. 'Why do you no longer want me? I thought we had feelings for each other. Why this?' His voice broke as he collapsed onto the bed and put his head in his hands. Had I got this all wrong? But I knew I had no other choice. 'What about the boy?' he whispered.

'He must go with you. I can't take him with me.'

He stood to go. 'When are you going to tell him?'

'Karisa, I can't tell him. I'm asking that you do this and for his sake, please do it gently.' The look of hurt that he gave me was one that I'd remember for the rest of my life as he left the room without saying another word.

I had one final thing to do before I could plan my journey to Nairobi and that was to phone Joseph. He was understanding but a little confused, and asked me what had happened to make me dismiss Karisa so abruptly. I made some story up about it being important that we sorted out a place for Gabriel as soon as we could, and that I could happily spend the time catching up with the lawyer in Nairobi. I'd no idea whether he believed me or not but I couldn't think of anything better.

My attention was drawn to the sound of a vehicle door slamming and I looked outside to see Karisa shutting the boot and Gabriel jumping into the passenger seat of the Land Rover. They were leaving this very minute. Gabriel seemed happy enough, so either Karisa had told him and he wasn't bothered or he hadn't told him at all. I hoped the latter. I'd grown very fond of the boy, but I wasn't his mother nor could I ever be. I knew

Karisa would look after him, albeit reluctantly. My tears came as I watched them drive away.

Once I'd pulled myself together, I went down to the reception to book the train ticket and also to pay the hotel bill. It had been paid in full.

My heart ached for him. I had been wrong, but it was too late now.

Chapter Twenty-Eight
Karisa

I told the boy we were going to the market to get fruit for Angela. But he was not stupid and as we drove out of Kibwezi on the road south, he had suspicion. 'Baba, this isn't the way to the market. I am sure it would be in the centre of the town, not this way.'

I did not reply.

'Baba, where are we going? Why are we leaving this town?'

I could not remain silent. 'Gabriel, we are not going to the market. We are going to Mombasa.'

'I do not understand. What about Mama?' He grabbed hold of my arm.

I wanted to be honest with him and tell him about the conversation I'd had with her earlier, but I could not. So I lied to him, and told him that she had to go to Nairobi to meet someone and that she would come to Mombasa soon. I could not break the boy's heart. But I knew that neither of us would see Angela again. He remained peaceful for a while, but as we got closer to where we'd found him, he became restless.

'Do not be concerned son, we are not going to stop here. We will keep going until we reach Mombasa, I promise you. Nothing bad is going to happen to you.'

The boy was now my responsibility alone; there was no one else who would take care of him and I had to plan how I could do this. The place I rented did not have space for two, even one as small as him, and it was also in a dangerous part of town. I could not raise him there. I remembered the boy who died because I did not have the courage to help him; I was not going to make the same mistake again. I could ask my brother if he could help, as his home area was safer, but he had his own family and I could not put any further burden on him. I would go to my village and speak with my mother and those around her to see if they could help.

We travelled quickly and stopped at a roadside *duka* for some rice and beans, before continuing past Voi and onto the outskirts of Mombasa. There the traffic stopped, as the line of container Lorries stretched to the port to drop off their cargo. We would be there for hours and I was anxious to avoid any difficult conversations with Gabriel. He had already asked why Angela had not said goodbye to him.

'Hang on, we are going on safari,' I laughed, as I swung the Land Rover to the left and headed off-road, down the inside of all the lorries and perilously close to the *dukas* and the huts by the roadside. I had noticed that all the *matatus* and *tuk-tuks* were doing this and realised that this was a way to keep moving, no matter how bumpy the ride.

Gabriel loved it, laughing and screaming as we plunged through the huge potholes by the side of the road. 'Let us pretend we are a *matatu*!' He turned up the music full blast as we made our way to the centre of Mombasa and back onto the tarmac. 'That was fun,' he said, turning the music down.

Since I had left the hotel, my thoughts of Angela had been constant. I had great anger in me. I loved the woman and had told her so, but she had rejected me. Now as we headed to Nyali, I had to think what I was going to tell Mr Joseph.

The boy was so excited about being in Mombasa, so before we drove to the house, I took him to the beach so that he could see the sea. I had lived close to the sea all my life, but did not see it until my uncle took me when I was twelve years old. I still remembered the excitement even now, but seeing the wonder in Gabriel's eyes as, for the first time in his short life, he set foot on warm golden sand, hypnotised by the movement of the waves. It made me see the world, my world, in a brand new way.

'Baba, I cannot speak,' he said, holding out his hands like he was trying to capture the view in front of him. 'This is more wonderful than all the animals I saw. This is God's heaven.'

I had to agree. The sky was truly blue, with a few wisps of white like some angel had gently brushed the sky with feathers. The Indian Ocean was a bright turquoise with a curly fringe of waves, and the sand the colour of the crust of the fresh-baked bread that Binty served sometimes. It was perfect and it felt like home.

'We will come back very soon, but first I need to take you to meet some people. Do not worry, they are good people and I am not going anywhere without you.'

I hoped that Angela would have spoken to Joseph and that our arrival would not be a surprise, but I had no idea what she would have said, and so I gave thanks to see smiling faces as we pulled into the driveway of their house. I had only been gone just over a week so much had happened in that time. My heart had been broken.

'Welcome back.' Joseph pulled open my driver's door and engulfed me in a bear hug. 'And who is this little fellow?'

Gabriel was sitting in the passenger seat looking nervous, but a smile and the promise of a piece of cake from Binty put him at ease and he quickly opened the door and took her hand as she led him inside.

Joseph did not ask me any questions about Angela and I was thankful for that. Gabriel went out to play on the lawn overlooking the beach and I went to empty the Land Rover before handing the keys to Joseph.

'What on earth do I want these for?' he said. 'Surely you will need the vehicle again when Angela returns. You might as well hang onto it. Use the opportunity to visit the family. Show the boy your home.'

Gratefully, my puzzled look went unnoticed and I gave a quiet thank you and put everything back in the vehicle. I did not know what Angela had said, but Joseph believed that she would return to Mombasa. I would tell him the truth at some time, but first I had to make arrangements for the boy.

I had planned to travel to the village immediately, but the roads were very busy with people driving home from Mombasa at the end of their working day, and the daylight had quickly come to an end. It would be foolish to travel at this time. I did not wish to cause inconvenience to Joseph and Binty, so I told them that we would pass the night at my brother's in Mtwapa. For the third time today, I had lied. We would spend the night in my room in town, where we could at least rest and I could finally think hard about what the future held for us. I paid some shillings to leave the Land Rover in a secure area. It was unwise to take the vehicle near to my room, it would have been stolen without a doubt, and so paying the money was the only thing I could do. As we caught a *matatu* for the final bit of the journey, I felt the fear in Gabriel's body increase the further we went along.

'This is just like where I was,' he whispered into my ear. 'I am afraid, Baba.'

'Do not worry, son, I will take care of you and I promise you that we are staying here for one night only. Tomorrow, I will take you to meet my mama.'

'But will Mama Angela be able to find us? We have travelled far and she could be looking for us and not know where we are.' He grabbed hold of my hand tight. His usual smile was absent.

'Mama will find us when the time is right,' I reassured him as we got out of the *matatu* and walked the short distance to my room.

I was relieved to see that the large padlock was still on my door and that all was quiet round about. Once we were inside, and the kerosene lamp was lit, Gabriel began to relax.

'I used to live in such a place with my real mother once my father left, until the sickness got her. We had to leave because we could not pay. We lived with an uncle until she passed and then I was pushed out of his home. He was a bad man.'

My heart went out to the boy. In his short life, he had known nothing but sadness. Inside me, the anger grew against Angela. I still did not understand why she had sent us away. The rejection of us both hurt me greatly. The anger gave me determination to look out for Gabriel and to find him a home where he could be happy and get an education.

We did not delay in leaving the following morning. I tried not to think about the honest conversation that I would have to have with Joseph at some point and concentrated on the road ahead. This was a road that I knew well but it felt brand new travelling with the boy by my side. He was so excited to be out of the city and into the rural areas, and had so much to say about every palm tree, mango tree and hut that we passed. The

125

closer to Kilifi, the more questions were asked.

'Baba, how old is your Mama?'

'She does not know. She has no certificate of birth to mark the date.'

'I do not have one either, but my mama said I was nine before she passed, so I can add nine to the one year since and I know that this makes ten.'

'You are very clever, son.'

'How many brothers and sisters do you have?'

'Just one brother.'

'Are we going to a nice place, Baba?'

'It is a wonderful place, especially for little boys of ten years,' I laughed.

'So will I be happy?'

'You will be very happy. I would never take you anywhere where you will not be happy. I promise you that, Gabriel.'

As we turned off the main road, a feeling of peace came over me as I drove towards my home village. This was where I belonged, where I grew up and where I would pass away in the future. This was the land of my ancestors and, stopping the Land Rover by my mother's *shamba*, I knew that this was the place for Gabriel. If that meant that I had to be here too, then so be it.

My mother was surprised to see me, I had not had chance to contact her to tell her of my arrival. I could see concern on her face as she rushed out of her hut to greet me.

'My son, why are you here? You should be upcountry with the *mzungu* lady. What has happened?'

'Mother, I thought you would be missing your son and so I came to see you.' I tried to laugh but she could see behind the smile.

'No matter, son. I am indeed pleased to see you. And I see that you have brought another guest to greet your mother?'

'This is Gabriel,' I said, pushing him forward. 'He is a very fine young man and a great friend of mine.'

'*Shikamoo*, madam,' he said, using the correct Swahili greeting to show great respect.

'*Marahaba, mtoto*,' my mother replied, and held out her arms to acknowledge his greeting. Taking his hand, she led him into her hut. 'Come child, it is time to eat.'

She began to share out her meagre meal amongst the three of us. I knew better than to refuse this small offering. Sharing food together was important to the people in the village, and no matter how little they had; it had to be divided amongst visitors and those in need.

The sweet *chai* and leftover chapattis from the previous evening were quickly finished by Gabriel. I sent him to get water. I said the words that I had to say. My mother listened very carefully. I spoke the same story I had told the boy and Joseph, so that I did not become confused. I was not sure that she believed me as she continued to look troubled.

'So the *mzungu* will be coming back to Mombasa, yes?'

'I do not expect so, Mother,' I said, 'Although I have told Gabriel otherwise. I cannot tell him at the moment that he may not see her again, as he calls her Mama. I want to settle him first and then speak with him. I hope you agree that this is the best way forward.'

'I believe that is so, my son. You have done the right thing returning to your home. We will arrange a meeting of all the uncles, brother cousins and neighbours to see what can be done.'

The meeting was organised for the morning and Gabriel and I spent our first night together in the village. He settled in well with the other boys; it was only I who was troubled.

I took my place in the meeting the next day and prayed to my God. It fell to the Elder of our village to bring the meeting to order.

'We are thankful to welcome our brother Karisa back home safely, but we have a problem that needs to be considered, concerning a young boy that he has rescued from a life of crime. It is our duty to take this boy to our hearts and help him to find the true light.'

I shook my head. Gabriel was not to blame for the life he had been forced into, but I could not contradict the words of the Elder. I saw my mother whisper into his ear and he paused. He coughed gently and looked my way.

'But let us hear from our brother first.' He motioned for me to stand up and speak.

I stood in front of my relatives and my neighbours, people I had known all my life, but today I felt like a beggar. I did not mention Angela; it was of no concern to them. But I told them of the life that Gabriel had been living when I had found him, and was strong in telling everybody that he was not a bad child, that he was not a criminal, but a victim of a bad life. They understood, they had known it many times.

When I was seated again, many people began to talk and the Elder had to give everyone who wished to, a chance to speak. Everybody wanted to help in whatever way they could, and so he organised for each to contribute what they could to help the boy.

I felt a deep gratitude to these people who had nothing, nothing at all, putting their hands in their ragged pockets and bringing out the few shillings that they had. This was true charity and I felt ashamed.

Chapter Twenty-Nine
Angela

Many times, I wanted to call Karisa, but what would I say? Whatever I said he wouldn't believe me. All he knew was that I had forced him to go and take the boy with him.

Nairobi was too noisy for me, causing my head to ache. So I stayed in my hotel room. It was one of those corporate rooms that looked the same whichever city you were in. I'd stayed in a few of them when we were first married, but once Mark was born I stayed at home. It was a welcome relief.

I'd been reluctant to contact Joseph so when the phone call came, I was unprepared and far from calm. I told him that I was travelling across the city and couldn't talk to him, but he wasn't put off easily and over the next hour or so he called me five times. I answered none. Eventually I phoned him back. He wasn't in the mood for pleasantries.

'What is going on, Angela?'

'I've been with the lawyer most of the time. Sorry I missed your calls, but I was so busy.'

'And what did the lawyer have to say?'

'Oh, you know this and that… not a lot to be honest. He doesn't seem to be that interested. It was a bit of a waste of time.' I hated to lie to Joseph.

'So you will be coming back to Mombasa, then?'

'Not for a few days, Joseph. He says he might have some news soon, so I thought that I might as well hang around here for a little bit. It seems a bit pointless to come back just yet.'

'Angela, is everything all right?' Joseph asked, his voice almost a whisper.

'Yes, of course, never better. You know what it's like though, with all the travelling. Just feeling a little jaded, must be my age!' I laughed.

I hadn't slept well and was feeling very anxious. I'd dreamt of Mark last night. He'd taken me on a journey to a very dark place full of young boys being beaten, and I'd woken up sobbing, determined to leave Kenya within the next twenty-four hours and return home regardless of the consequences.

'Angela, I'm going to ask you just one thing and I want you to be honest with me. Why have you been lying to me?' He sounded hurt.

I'd told so many lies to so many people recently that I wasn't sure which one he was talking about.

Thankfully, before I could put my foot in it any further, he said, 'I know you haven't been to visit the lawyer because he's been phoning me to try and get a message to you. I don't understand why you did this. I thought you would at least be honest with me.' I was so grateful that he hadn't found out about Karisa.

'I'm so sorry that I did this, but I just needed some time on my own to deal with some family matters.'

'Are you sure that everything's all right? There's nothing that you want to get off your chest, dear? I am a good listener.' How could I tell him that after all his help I was afraid to speak to the lawyer?

I reassured him that I was fine and told him that I may just go home for a while to see my children as I was missing them, but that I'd be back within a week or two. I was trying to buy myself some time to breathe, and to maybe mend some bridges, I made two phone calls, one to the lawyer to make an appointment and one home to Josh.

'Ah, Mother, you're still living then?'

'Please don't be harsh with me. I know I haven't been in contact much, but I do have lots to think about.'

'Of course. We don't have any issues of our own; we're only dealing with the sudden death of our father and with the equally sudden departure of our mother. No, everything is tickety-boo with us. No problems at all.'

I said nothing.

'Mother, does it ever occur to you that I've been worried sick about you? You know that I'm on your side, but I knew that something was wrong the minute Mark came home. He still hasn't returned my calls and refuses to meet me. I think you owe me an explanation at least.'

I desperately wanted to tell Josh the truth, but I knew that would only make matters worse between Mark and I. 'I'm sorry, Josh, I know it must be very difficult for you to understand what's going on. I don't understand it myself. But Mark has been through a really tough time and he'll tell you when he is ready. If I tell you, it will do more damage. I know you're very angry with me, but I can't tell you.'

'Okay, Mother, if that's the way you want to play it. Then that's fine. Don't forget to call again when you can spare the time.'

'Please, Josh, it's not like that at all...' The line was dead! 'Fuck it!' I threw the phone across the room.

I wasn't looking forward to meeting the lawyer, but I knew this was something I had to do after the conversation with Josh. I still didn't know whether I would continue with my search or just go home. I could imagine what Mark would say, though, if I returned without having a conversation with the man who might have at least some of the answers, if not all.

The minute I saw Mr Daniels sat at his desk, I knew that I was wasting my time. He looked like something from a Mickey Spillane movie with a small greasy moustache that was curling at the edges. He constantly ran his thumb and finger over it to smooth it down, but it had little effect other than annoying the hell out of me. The office was small and humid and he was squeezed behind an old wooden desk under a barely opened window. The seat he offered me was facing directly into the sun. I felt beads of sweat appear on my top lip. He peered over his classes and seemed to be looking over my shoulder. The dislike was instant and, I think, mutual.

'I have no idea why you felt the need to come to Kenya, madam? We could've handled this much easier without you getting involved. We get this all the time, the natives trying to get their hands on our money.'

I'd met his kind before. They still believed the white man was king in Kenya. George had been the same. Joseph was different; typically British definitely but colonial never. His attitude angered me and I found it easy to challenge him.

'So what exactly have you found out since my husband's death? Absolutely nothing, it appears. Surely, as you're dealing with my money, I have every right to be involved.' I could feel my temper rising as I looked at his pale sweaty face.

He removed his round wire glasses, revealing his tiny piggy eyes, and continued to look straight past me. 'Your husband's, actually,' he said.

'What?'

'It's your husband's money, not yours, and that's why it is

better for us to be left alone to get on with the job we have been given. In this case, by your husband.' He smiled a smile that deserved to be hit with a brick.

'And now they know you are in the country, they'll see this as a sign that you're desperate and will use that to their advantage. If you'd only remained in England and done as you were told, then it would've been much simpler to negotiate with them.'

'Negotiate? Why should I negotiate? I'm not here to strike a bloody deal, I'm here to find out who the hell this woman is.' I'd thought to be honest with him about my dire financial situation but swiftly changed my mind. I didn't trust the man.

'Your husband chose to leave this woman fifty thousand pounds of his own money freely. She's now claiming that she's his lawful wife and therefore is entitled to much more. Until we're able to prove otherwise, then I can't say whether she has a case or not. Indeed has it ever occurred to you, madam, that you may not be legally married to your husband? This Rose Trippett could very well be his first and therefore his legal wife.'

The exertion of this speech caused him to sweat profusely and he rummaged in his trouser pocket for a grubby handkerchief and proceeded to mop his face frantically. For the first time since I walked into the room, he looked me square in the eye, triumphant.

'And it could take some time to locate this lady. I hope you have the sufficient funds to see this through to its conclusion. Things like this in Kenya may take years. But don't worry, madam, we will be in touch the minute we have any news.' I was obviously dismissed.

I found a quiet place outside and phoned Joseph.

I sensed his relief. I explained to him everything that the lawyer had said and I also told him of my mistrust of the man.

133

He felt that it may be better if I came back to Mombasa to stay with them to work on this together. He knew a guy in the city that may be able to help us. This all sounded very sensible; there was just one problem. Karisa was in Mombasa. How on earth was I going to cope with seeing him again?

Chapter Thirty
Karisa

I had been called to Joseph's. He was my employer so I had to go. Gabriel was happy to stay in the village, as long as I promised I would be back by the time darkness fell. Although he slept in my mother's hut, he spent most of his day out visiting everyone else in the village. They all wanted to share him.

I had decided to tell the truth with Joseph, even if it put my job at risk. There had been too many hidden stories; I owed it to him, to tell the truth. He was a good man. But first I had a meeting to attend.

My mother believed that Gabriel deserved a real family and her solution was for me to fulfil my duty to the families of Kadzo and myself and marry her quickly. In her eyes, it was the only way. She had spoken to the father and they were in agreement to add something to the 'bride price' for the boy. I doubted this plan but I would not bring shame onto both families. I agreed to meet with Kadzo, as she attended a university conference in Mombasa. My feelings for Angela were still strong, but she had rejected me and I needed to provide for the boy. I had a promise to fulfil.

'She will agree,' her father said. 'She is a good girl. She will not let her family down.'

I remained with hope.

I arrived early for our meeting at a small cafe near Fort

Jesus and started to look through the menu board on the wall to hide my nervousness. Within a couple of minutes, I could see Kadzo walking through the door and making her way to the table. She sat down and immediately lit up a cigarette.

'When did you start smoking?' I was horrified.

'Oh, I have been doing this for ages. It is not a big deal.'

Within a couple of minutes of finishing her cigarette, she lit up another, sucking on the tip with her red painted lips and tilting her head back to blow her smoke high into the air. She looked out of place in the small cafe, like a ruby among charcoal. The place was too small to hold her.

'Karisa, I have a new boyfriend,' she blurted out, 'And I love him.'

My face could not hide my feelings.

'For goodness sake, why the look? I want you to be happy for me. I am in love.'

'But what about our promise?' I thought of home.

'Karisa, there is no promise. There never was one. You must have realised that. That was just what the village and our parents wanted – childhood stuff. Surely, you did not take it seriously.' She laughed loud and people began to look around at us. I was embarrassed.

'Kadzo, what about your parents? I spoke to them just the other day, they expect a wedding.'

She lit her third cigarette and blew smoke in my face causing me to cough. 'It is nothing to do with them. They know nothing other than their tiny village. I want to travel; I want to live in a big house, not a mud hut. I want a car of my own and a career and Vincent can give me that.'

'Vincent?'

'Yes, that is his name. He loves me and I love him. That's

it. I am only telling you because you are my close friend. There was a time when I thought that maybe you and I could be together in Nairobi. But you would not come. You are never going to be anything other than a chauffeur to that white man and I want more.'

I stared at this woman in front of me. I did not know her. I could no longer recognise the Kadzo from the village.

Before I could say anything, she stabbed out her cigarette. 'I need one last help from you. I need you to come to the village with me to tell my parents. I need them to understand that there is no hope of the two of us ever marrying and then maybe, in time, I will be able to introduce Vincent to them. Please, Karisa?'

For the first time today, I caught a glimpse of the Kadzo I knew. The girl I had grown up with, the one I was prepared to marry to give Gabriel a home. She had let her mask slip. I did not want to be a part of this, but I could not walk away. As the man, I had to play my part. I owed it to my mother, so I agreed to accompany her. But first I had to go and see Joseph in Nyali and we arranged to meet on the main highway near his house later. We could go to the village together in the Land Rover, providing I still had a job after our conversation.

Joseph was waiting for me; he opened the door immediately when I stopped the vehicle. 'Ah, Karisa. I am glad that you could make it.'

I followed him through to the garden overlooking the beach. He asked if I should like tea. I declined and we sat down to the business in hand.

'I believe that both you and Angela aren't telling me the truth,' he said. 'That, of course, is a woman's prerogative; however, you are my employee as well as my friend. I'm paying you to accompany Angela on her search and the very least I expect from you is honesty. Or am I wrong?'

'You are not wrong, Joseph; it is I who am wrong. I have not lied to you, please believe me. I have just not told you everything. I am sorry. Will you permit me to put this right now?'

And so I told him all that I had to tell, I omitted nothing. He listened closely sometimes shaking his head at the things I was telling him.

'I know you must be disappointed in me, sir, in my behaviour to your friend, but please believe me I did not plan it this way. If you wish, I will hand in my resignation this very moment.'

'Now, now, old fellow, not sure that it needs to come to this. After all, we have been together for many years and I think I know you pretty well. I knew something was going on and I needed to get to the bottom of it. But I'm not sure that you've told me everything. When I spoke to Angela, she seemed very sad, as if something was weighing her down. I would've thought with what you've told me that if she'd wanted to 'Get rid of you' as you say, then she would've left the country immediately. But she hasn't and I can't understand why.'

I told him what I had witnessed between her and her son and that this was probably the reason she remained in Kenya. He seemed unconvinced.

'I need to think about this, Karisa, and speak to Binty. One needs a woman's viewpoint on this, I think. Leave it with me for a couple of days and I shall get back to you. By the way, what's happening with the boy?'

He was delighted to hear that he was settled in the village and so I took my leave, grateful to still have a job. I half-hoped that Kadzo had changed her mind and would not be waiting for me, but as I turned out of Joseph's road, I could see her leaning against a tree, cigarette in hand.

'Thank God,' she said, as she swung open the passenger door. 'I thought you were never coming. Oh my goodness, Karisa, you drive so slow. Why do you not go faster? Vincent has a very big car and he says that one day I will be able to drive it – when I have passed my test, of course, ha-ha. He has a very important job with the government. I do not know what he does exactly, but I know it is very important.'

'How do you know?' I could not resist asking the question.

'I know because he has this big car and he has many friends and also he carries a gun,' she said proudly.

'How does that tell you that he has an important job? Many people have many friends and many criminals carry guns. That tells you nothing about his work, but surely tells you a lot about who he mixes with, if he feels the need to carry a gun.'

'Vincent says all important government officials carry guns, some even have bodyguards. He says that he is brave and strong enough to not need one.'

I concentrated on the road ahead. As we got closer to our turn off towards the village, Kadzo began to bite her immaculately painted nails, the broken nails thrown on the floor by her feet.

'What do you think that my parents will say?'

'What do *you* think that they will say, Kadzo?'

She did not speak; she already knew the answer. She was not a fool. Before we got to the village, I stopped the Land Rover and explained to her about Gabriel and the conversation that had taken place between my mother and her parents. She was very upset.

'Why did you do this to me? You knew that we would never be together and yet now you have given my parents hope that not only will there be a wedding, but that I will take on this boy. This cannot be, Karisa. This is your mess, you must put this right.'

'Please listen, Kadzo. I did nothing for your parents to expect such a marriage, but they have wanted this to happen for many years and we have not spoken the truth to them. Now they are in need of your bride price to survive and we are going to have to tell them that this is not going to happen. I did not know that you had a boyfriend and neither did they. The only thing that we can do now is tell the whole truth and explain that although there is not going to be a wedding with us, that you now have this important government man, that they can look forward to a very big wedding and they must meet him very soon.'

I started to drive off but she grabbed my arm to stop me.

'Karisa, there will not be a big wedding.'

'Surely if you are in love as you say, then he will wish to marry you?'

'Oh, yes, he does, very much, he tells me all the time. But I will not be his first wife, you see.'

'But a good bride price can be paid for the second wife also.'

'But Karisa, I am to be number four. The bride price will be very small, he has already said that. He does not need me to bear him children; he already has many. Too many, he says, for him to afford an education for all of them. He loves me for me and wants me for himself alone.'

Then I knew in my heart, that this man was just using her to look good, and when her looks started to fail then he would discard her. I had known it many times with men who wanted to feel important. But she could not see this for herself and so I gently squeezed her hand and told her that everything would be okay. What else could I do?

Gabriel rushed to meet us when he saw the vehicle pull up

and was tugging me out before he spotted Kadzo. He stopped pulling; he had hoped for Angela. Outside the hut sat my mother with Kadzo's parents. Two empty chairs were waiting for us.

'Welcome, daughter,' said her father, taking her hand and guiding her to one of the empty chairs. 'Please sit, we have much to discuss.'

My mother nodded to me in greeting as I sat down and her father began to pray. He had only just started when Kadzo spoke.

'Mother, Father, I have to tell you that I respect you very much and love you as a daughter should, but I cannot do as you ask with this marriage.' The loud gasp came from my mother alone. Kadzo's parents remained quiet. 'I have grown up with Karisa and I love him dearly, but as a brother and a friend. I could never be his wife.'

Her father stood up to face his daughter. 'Daughter, the choice is not yours. The choice is mine alone and I choose that you marry the man you have been promised to. You will marry Karisa.'

She turned to me and then back to her father. She was defiant. 'The traditional ways may say this, but I do not. It is not for me to stay in the village. I want freedom to live my life as I choose. I am grateful for everything that you have done for me but the traditional ways are not for me.' I was proud of her strength and grasped her hand tight.

'We did not do this so that you could defy us. This is the way of our ancestors, our forefathers, and so you not only go against your parents, you go against everything. I will not allow this shame on our family. The marriage will go ahead.' Her father's anger was deep.

Kadzo went to walk away but her father restrained her, forcing her back down into the chair. I could see Gabriel hiding behind my mother's hut and my heart was filled with sadness for him. He did not want Kadzo as his mother, he wanted only Angela, and if that could not be then it would be better for him to have no mother at all. I got to my feet.

'I would be thankful if you may let me speak.' Her father nodded. 'I have known your daughter, as she has said, all my life, and I always believed that one day we would marry and have many children and make our parents proud. But I have to tell you here and now that this will not happen. This is not only Kadzo's decision, it is mine also. We do this not to disrespect you or our ancestors, but because we believe that for a marriage to succeed, the two people must love each other as man and wife, not as brother and sister. We have known each other too long for that to happen.'

I saw the shock on the faces of all those present. They did not expect me to speak as I did. Her father stood to face us.

'Then from this day, I no longer have a daughter. She will never be welcomed back into the village again. My daughter is dead to me,' he roared.

'That is fine by me,' Kadzo yelled back. 'This village is nothing to me. I am happy to leave it all behind.'

I felt her shame, for it was mine also.

Chapter Thirty-One
Angela

I was thankful it was Joseph that met me from the airport. As we drove through the city traffic, he told me all about the conversation he'd had with Karisa. I was relieved that everything was out in the open and he wasn't judging me, and it was good to be back in Mombasa.

The following morning, Joseph was in town to see 'his man', so I took a walk around the garden. The frangipani was in its full waxy bloom, and even though the heat hadn't risen, the fragrance from the flowers was already overpowering. Away on the edge of the reef out to sea, I could see a dotted line of small boats stranded on the coral, waiting for the returning tide to free them. A refreshing cool breeze drifted in from the ocean and, lost in my thoughts, I absently picked a flower.

'Penny for them, dear?' I spun round to see Binty lying on a sun-lounger. 'Sorry. I didn't mean to startle you, but you look miles away, like you have the whole world on your shoulders. Why don't you come and sit here by me?' She took her straw hat from the seat next to her and patted the cushion.

I wasn't really in the mood for company, but felt it would be rude for me to say so. Binty seemed to read my thoughts and turned back to the book she was reading, and I lay back on the lounger and closed my eyes. Undisturbed, the same old questions came rushing into my head. Why was I still here in Kenya? As the sleazebag lawyer in Nairobi said, I'd probably made things more difficult for everyone by getting involved. But something had made me get on a plane and it wasn't just jealousy about my husband leaving money to another woman, or even that she might take everything I had. It was the truth, and this was more important than ever now Mark had spoken. I felt as if my whole life was a lie, none of it being the reality that I thought it was. I was still lost in my thoughts when Binty closed her book with a thud and looked straight at me.

'I know you may feel you're on your own, dear, but you aren't, you know. Joseph has told me about what happened with you and Karisa and I expect that you think that I'm shocked, but believe me, I'm not. He's a good, kind man and I'm sure that he would never do anything to hurt you.'

Mention of Karisa confused me. I'd been thinking only of George and I must have shown my confusion.

'Angela, you're not the first white woman of a certain age to lust over a young Kenyan man and you certainly won't be the last. Over here, age doesn't have the same meaning as it does in the UK. Oh, I know some of the beach boys are looking for the rich *mzungu* to marry – some even go to the witchdoctor to get a supposed love potion to make the woman fall in love with them – but not all of them are out for money. Sometimes our feelings don't come out in the way you'd expect them to. Your husband may be dead, but you, my dear, are not.' She gave my hand a squeeze and went back to her book.

I hadn't expected Binty talk to me about Karisa and I was grateful that she hadn't asked me any questions about my feelings, because I didn't have any answers. I knew though that soon I would have to see him and I wasn't sure whether I felt fear or excitement.

When Joseph finally returned, Binty and I were just

finishing a delicious lunch of avocado salad and freshly baked bread. He wandered in, sat down and helped himself to some of the remaining bread and butter.

'Well, how did you get on?' Binty was speaking before I had chance to. 'Don't keep us in suspense.'

'To be honest, ladies, there's nothing really to tell at this moment. My man is working on it and will contact me when he has something. In the meantime, all we can do is sit back and wait.'

Joseph was pouring himself a gin and tonic when the door burst open and I was swamped in a huge hug.

'Mama, Mama, you are back!' Gabriel threw himself on me.

'I am sorry, but once he suspected that I was coming to see you, he would not get out of the vehicle. He must have overheard myself and my mother talking and he was determined to come.' Karisa stood in the doorway in his crisp white shirt and black trousers. The sight of him took my breath away but thankfully I was able to bury my reaction in Gabriel's neck.

Joseph and Binty were laughing loudly at the boy's antics.

'Drinks for everyone?' Binty jumped up. 'Joseph, Gabriel, would you give me a hand?'

'But I want to stay with Mama,' he wailed.

'I have chocolate.' Binty said as she left the room, and he was off like a gazelle, leaving Karisa alone in the doorway watching me.

I wanted to rush to him, but I stayed where I was sat.

'We are like strangers with each other,' he whispered.

'Not strangers, Karisa.'

'But not friends either, Angela.'

'I don't know what we are any more, but it is good to see

145

you.' I slowly stood up and walked a little way towards him. 'I don't want to be a stranger to you.'

Binty came bustling back into the room almost immediately, maybe she'd been listening at the door, and I swore that she gave me a little wink as she rushed past me with the drinks. Gabriel sat himself down on the sofa, chomping his way through a bar of *Cadbury's Dairy Milk*, and Joseph helped her to dish out the drinks.

'Come on then, you two, sit yourself down and make yourself comfortable, no standing on ceremony here.' I sat back down on the sofa and Karisa sat on the other side of the room.

'No, Baba, you must sit here next to Mama and me.' Gabriel moved closer to give him room and he hesitantly changed seats. 'Now it is good, Mama is back with us.'

As we had to wait for news, we had time to kill, and Gabriel was keen for me to go with him and Karisa to the village. With strong encouragement from Binty, I reluctantly agreed. I didn't want to rush things but I was looking forward to seeing his mother again. She'd been so nice to me at the uncle's funeral and I wanted to repay her by taking her a gift. Gabriel decided on a new cooking pot.

'Her old one has holes in it that you can see the sky through.' I also bought some *Ugali* flour, sugar and tea and Gabriel was so excited when we set off to the village. He found it impossible to sit still, pointing out every little thing that came to his notice along the way. The sisal fields stretching for miles, the cement works, the clothing and maize factories and of course the little gathering of huts and *dukas*, I had to be shown them all.

Karisa was pensive. But as we were driving past a group of

school children he spoke. 'He must be educated.'

'Sorry, Karisa, I don't understand you. Who must be educated?'

'The boy, he needs to attend school.'

I was silent. 'Do you not agree, Angela?'

'Of course, I was just thinking, maybe it would be better to have this conversation when we are alone,' I said, casting my eyes to the back seat where the boy had suddenly quietened. This, at least, gave me some time to get my thoughts together before we would speak on this again.

Gabriel remained quiet for a while – he'd heard us talking – but it didn't last for long as he caught glimpses of the sea as we drove along the main highway.

'Baba, can we go to the sea. Look it is so close.'

'Mm, I am not sure. Maybe today the beach is not open.'

The poor boy's face dropped. 'Oh, I wanted to take mama.'

Karisa smiled for the first time on the journey. I'd missed that smile. 'Of course, we shall go the beach. It never closes. But I am going to take you to a very beautiful one today.'

We passed the road that would lead us to the village, crossed Kilifi Creek and turned towards the coast. We eventually drove into a small hotel. Karisa spoke to the security on the gate, the barrier was raised and we continued down the drive to the reception. The building had seen better days, the white-painted front cancerous with dark patches and the signage faded to the point of illegibility by time and the weather. But through all the neglect was a building of some magnificence, and as we walked into the reception there were many old photos on display of the landed gentry of Europe taking the waters here. Once we'd made our way through the hotel down to the beach itself, I could fully understand why. It was simply breath-taking. The sand was pure white and completely deserted and the sea was the colour of blue topaz and as clear. I stood enthralled at the sheer beauty of the scene before me. Not so, Gabriel. He was racing down the sand towards the water.

'Gabriel, wait!' I ran after him, kicking off my shoes. Karisa quickly overtook me as I soon stopped to put my shoes back on, the sand was scorching. I could hear both of them screaming out loud as they fell in a heap, Karisa catching up with him before he plunged headlong into the sea.

In the short time it took me to catch up with them, they were down to their underclothes and running towards the waves.

'Come in, Mama!' Gabriel shouted. 'It is very wonderful!'

'Mama does not have a swimsuit,' I shouted back.

I could see him looking questioningly at Karisa. He said something to him and whatever was said brought understanding onto his face. So I sat on the beach near to the water's edge and watched them having great fun and enjoying the peace of being in this paradise. I could've stayed at this beach for the rest of the day but time was going on and I didn't want to be too late returning to Mombasa.

'Time to go, gentlemen,' I said as they continued to jump in and out of the waves, Karisa holding on tightly to Gabriel.

'Mama, it was wonderful. I did good, didn't I, Baba? I will soon be a very good swimmer.'

Grabbing hold of the boy Karisa carried him back up the beach where they dried off the best they could.

We resumed the journey to the village, and soon we were driving into the gathering of huts. As before, a crowd came to greet us, but this time instead of it being Karisa they were excited to meet, it was Gabriel. He was soon out of the vehicle and heading off into the trees with his friends. It brought a lump to my throat to see him so settled and happy.

I watched him disappear without a backward glance.

'It is not always the same. He has suffered greatly in his short life and many times the pain shows, but he will not let his mama Angela see that.'

Karisa's mother stood in the doorway of her hut, stony-faced.

'*Jambo Mama, habari*?' I held out the new cooking pot for her.

She gave a short grunt and then turned back into her hut. I felt the snub.

'What is the matter with your mother?'

'I do not know, but please wait here, Angela, and I will go and find out.'

I found myself a plastic chair, still clutching the pot filled with provisions, and waited. After a while, there were raised voices coming from inside and people from close by started to gather. I felt conspicuous as the gathering crowd turned to look at me from time to time; it was obvious that I was the subject of the argument going on. After about ten minutes of shouting, the hut went silent and a very angry Karisa stormed out.

'Come, Angela, it is time for us to go.' He caught hold of my arm and flung open the door of the Land Rover. I left the pot on the ground.

'What on earth is going on?' We bounced down the dusty road at high speed. 'Why did we have to leave? I didn't say goodbye to Gabriel.'

'I have something that I need to tell you, Angela, but we need to get to a place that we can talk. So let us drive and then we can find a place to sit.'

149

We travelled without speaking until, eventually, we found a small cafe. It was empty. So, grabbing a couple of sodas, we made our way to a corner of the small room where we wouldn't be overheard.

Karisa was obviously troubled by what he had to say and spoke very quietly. 'My mother was not happy to see you today.'

'That was very obvious even to me. What I don't understand was why, unless you told her what happened between us?'

'Angela, I have not told her, believe me. But she is not a stupid woman; she knows her son well and can see things also. But that is not the main reason that she is angry. A few days ago I broke her heart and the hearts of some good friends of hers by breaking off my promised marriage to Kadzo.' He paused to look into my face; I looked away. He continued.

'It was not only my decision; it was Kadzo's as well. Her family was very angry, as this arrangement had been in place for a very long time, since we were children together, and they were expecting the bride price very soon. But she has found a new man, a rich man, in Nairobi, and she no longer wants to fulfil her promise to her family. I supported her decision and this is why my mother is angry. She feels that we have let both families down. Bringing you to the village today was a mistake. It is too soon afterwards, and my mother feels I am shaming her by bringing a *mzungu* to the village after rejecting Kadzo. I tried to tell her that we are just friends, the same as we were the last time that I brought you home, but she does not believe me. She thinks that you are going to take me away from her to England and she will never see me again and that she will have no one other than my brother to help her as she ages.'

I fully understood the mother's concern. But I was overtaken with jealousy at the thought of another woman with Karisa. One he was prepared to marry just a couple of days ago. As much as I felt for him, I didn't belong in his world, but Gabriel did. It made me realise that no matter what my feelings were for this man, we could be nothing more than friends.

'Take me back to Mombasa, please, Karisa,' I said quietly putting my hand on top of his and giving it a gentle squeeze. 'It is time to move on.'

Chapter Thirty-Two
Karisa

Today I did something for the very first time in my life. I was disrespectful to my mother. I have not done so before and I have upset her greatly, but I could not stand and listen to the words she spoke about Angela. That she had bewitched me to take me away from my homeland and that was why I no longer wanted Kadzo. She believes in witchcraft and was not able to understand any other reasoning and so when I knew that Angela was not welcome in her home, I left. I knew my actions would confirm everything that she believed but I had to do it? I could not let either of these women know my true feelings and so I lied to them both.

The journey back to Nyali passed quickly and in silence. Joseph was very good to me and had given me a small room at the back of the house in which to sleep. He understood that I could no longer afford the room in town while I was paying to keep the boy. So when we arrived at the house, Angela went to her room and I to mine. I saw the look on Binty's face as she watched us; she knew that things were not well. She is a wise woman.

I was thankful to close the door to my room and lie down on the bed alone with my thoughts. I did not know what to do. My feelings were very strong for Angela but I had already frightened her away and I did not want to do the same again. This was crazy for both of us. Even if she had the same feelings for me, I did not know how we could be together. My mother was right; I could not leave my family and Angela could not leave hers. We had no hope for the future. All we had was now.

I barely heard the first knock on the door, but the second one brought my mind awake.

'I hope you don't mind me coming to see you?' Binty gently pushed the door open to enter the room. 'I am concerned about Angela. It may not be my place to talk to you about it, but I can't keep quiet. You must know that she is very fond of you and I think that you may feel the same. But what I can't understand is how two people who feel about each other as you do can make each other so unhappy. You left this morning full of the joys of spring and yet you return like there's been a death in the family. What has happened?'

I did not reply at first as I did not know what to say. But she did not move and so I had no choice but to tell her about the arrangement there was between the mine and Kadzo's families. I told her that I would have married Kadzo even though I did not love her as a man should his wife, but that she had found someone else. I think she struggled to understand why I would have done so. The *wazungu* will always find it difficult with our tribal ways. But I know she saw into my heart.

'Go and talk to her, you must tell her how you feel. Then at least you're being honest with each other.'

My courage failed me I told Binty it would be better to leave things as they were.

'Nonsense, you two are going to be honest with each other and you, my man, are going to do it now.' She pulled me to my feet and I followed her to Angela's room. She gave my shoulder a squeeze and walked away.

It took me some minutes to knock on the door. My heart

was beating too fast.

'Come in.'

I did as I was asked. I could tell by her face that I was not the one that was expected and she quickly rose from the bed.

'Angela, I have come to talk to you. I feel we must speak the truth with each other. And so, as the man, I will speak first.' She sat back on the bed. I was strengthened by that, at least she was not angry with what I had said so far. I went on, 'I think you know that I have strong feelings for you and I hope that you believe that they are true. You made me leave once and I do not know why. I am so very afraid that you will want this to happen again. But I cannot be silent and I must tell you how I feel. If this is causing you pain then I will leave now but I do not believe that this is the case.'

I let out a loud breath at the end of this speech. I had been holding it for a very long time. I felt relief for saying the words in my heart, and fear in waiting for her reply.

'Karisa, as we're being honest with each other, then I must tell you that I too have feelings for you. But I have to ask you a difficult question... are you with me for my money? I need you to tell me the truth.'

'Angela, I am very sad that you feel that. This is not in my heart at all. If I wanted money, I could get a job in the Middle East and earn many times more than I earn here, but I do not go because I value my freedom and I love my country. I am a proud man. I could not live off a woman. When you look into my eyes, do you not see the love I feel in my heart? Or do you see greed? You must tell me now.'

She walked towards. 'I see love,' she whispered.

I took her in my arms and held her tight. Finally, we were together. But the togetherness was not for long, as she pulled away from me.

'But there is no future for us, Karisa. Your mother's right: as she gets older, she'll need you more. And what about Gabriel? You're his father now. He's settled in your village and he needs to go to school.'

All my hopes were crushed with these words. 'So what do you want me to do now?' I said.

'Nothing, I don't want you to do anything. We've been honest with each other and we know we have feelings for each other, but we mustn't act on them.'

'Do you want me to leave?'

'No, please, don't. I want us to try and be friends first, just friends, and if that gets too difficult we need to say and then we may need to part. But I want to give it a go first. What do you think? Do you think you could just be my friend, knowing nothing further could happen?'

'I am willing to try and I believe that I can do this. I am sure that I can be a great friend to you and only a friend.' The lies spoke easily.

Chapter Thirty-Three
Angela

What on earth made me suggest that Karisa and I could just be friends? Who was I kidding? But I was desperate. I couldn't contemplate losing him again but I also wasn't naive enough to think that we could ever be in a proper relationship; there were too many barriers. I was just not ready to let go yet. So we hung around, not knowing what to do with ourselves. In the end, Karisa decided that he needed to return to the village to check on Gabriel and to make amends with his mother.

'It is very likely we will be travelling upcountry again soon, and I need to reassure the boy that *I* will return,' he said. His words pricked my conscience.

While he was away, Binty suggested that we had lunch in her favourite restaurant. I readily took up her kind offer. The *mojitos* were delicious as we sat watching the small fishing canoes cast their nets into the creek in the hope to catch something to sell for a few shillings. Across the water lay the city of Mombasa, with its uniform of blue and white, and if you stretched out to your left you could just catch glimpses of the large ships moored where the estuary met the sea. I hadn't felt very hungry until I took the first bite of the delicious red snapper I had ordered, and then my appetite returned with a vengeance and I polished it off at lightning speed. Poor Binty had hardly begun before my plate was clean.

'Would you like something else dear?'

'Oh, no, Binty, I couldn't... well... maybe a little plate of bread and olives to keep you company. I'm sorry for being such a pig, I didn't realise I was so hungry.'

It had been such a long time since I'd had girlie time. Back in Somerset, I used to visit Jeannie whenever George would let me, but that seemed in a different lifetime and so I was very grateful to spend this time with Binty. It was only when we were munching our way through dessert that the subject of Karisa was raised.

'Oh, that's all sorted now. We've had a long talk and decided the best way to go forward is to be just friends.'

Binty looked up, astonished. 'And do you think that is possible, Angela?'

'Oh, yes, it's what we both want. After all, we've only just met and it's crazy to think that we could be anything more. I think I might actually be old enough to be his mother. Could you ever imagine that working out?'

'You'll be surprised what can happen out here.' She stopped eating, put down her knife and fork and looked far out to sea. 'Did I ever tell you about William?'

'William? No, I don't think you did.'

'William was a *fundi,* a workman that we had when we very first bought the house. We knew we were going to retire here, but at the time Joseph was still working up in Nairobi. So I came down here to sort the house ready to live in. William was beautiful, I mean really beautiful. I know you shouldn't say that about a man but in his case it was true. He used to tell me to *'pole pole'* all the time, to slow down, when he saw me running from one place to the next worrying about curtains. You see he couldn't understand my need for all this stuff. He was a Rastafarian and not interested in possessions. He used to tie his dreadlocks up with string.' I could see tears in her eyes and she struggled to carry on. After a couple of minutes, she regained her composure.

157

'While Joseph wasn't around we were able to spend such wonderful times together, talking and even sometimes just sitting together in complete silence, no words needed. Of course, he used to disappear at the weekends when Joseph travelled down from Nairobi. But I missed him, Angela, I missed him so much.' She paused again and swallowed hard. 'Obviously, one thing led to another, the talking became the most delicious kisses, and from there we ended up in bed together. He made me feel so special.'

'So what happened?'

'I had to make a choice, William or Joseph. Joseph was due to retire in a month and the relationship with William was getting stronger. But he had to go. I couldn't risk my marriage for him, what would we have done? I was a middle-aged woman with no means of income and he was a beautiful young Rasta man. Don't get me wrong, I seriously thought of leaving Joseph, but this was all happening at the wrong time in my life. So I had to let him go, but let me tell you this, Angela, had I not been married I would've gone with William.' She was serious again. 'Life is too short, my dear, for regrets. So before you give up what you have with Karisa, think very hard, very hard indeed. You're free and so is he. What other people think doesn't matter. Now, you can ignore my advice if you want, but let me tell you one last thing.' I waited for the pearl of wisdom. 'This place does the best strawberry daiquiris in the world!' We ordered two large ones.

By the time Joseph picked us up, we were very merry and giggling like school girls.

'Not sure they will let us back in there in a hurry,' said Binty as she clambered into the car with more than a little assistance from Joseph.

'Steady on, old girl.' He struggled to prise her substantial hips into the back seat of the Land Cruiser.

'Did you know that the Kenyan men definitely prefer a bit of meat on their women? They can't understand why white men like them skinny. That's true, isn't it, Joseph?'

He smiled indulgently at both of us. 'Yes, dear.'

I wondered if he ever knew about William.

While we'd been enjoying life to the full, Joseph had been to see his contact in Mombasa to get further details for us before we set off on our journey.

'I was hoping to have more definite news for you before you set off, but all I have is hearsay. You know the sort, somebody knows someone, who knows someone else, who might have heard something from someone who's Great Aunt Fanny might have once met someone who said they worked with somebody called Rose. So to be honest Angela it's up to you. You can set off on something that may or may not be a wild goose chase or you can hang around here waiting for more news not knowing how long that will take.'

I felt more than a little discouraged by what he had to say, but I could hardly blame him or his contacts, everyone was doing their best to help me.

'What do you think Joseph; I could do with some advice on this?' I said.

'Let's wait until Karisa returns and then we can all have a conflab about it.'

This gave me the opportunity to take to my bed for a nap and hopefully to sleep off the raging hangover that was threatening. Making my excuses I escaped to my room.

It was dark when the knock awoke me and it took me a while to work out where on earth I was. My mouth was bone dry from the lunchtime binge. I told them I would be with them presently and gulped down a whole bottle of water as I attempted to make myself look human again. Everyone was already in the lounge when I made my entrance.

'Drink, dear?' asked Binty, helping herself to a gin and tonic. That woman had the constitution of a horse.

'Not for me, thanks,' I said and sat down in the seat she had just vacated. The only other seat available was next to Karisa and I wanted to be able to look him straight in the eye to gauge his reaction to the conversation.

'Okay, Angela, while you were sleeping, me and Karisa had a little chinwag about the situation so that he was up to speed as it were with the developments. So as I said before, it is your call.'

'Karisa, what are your thoughts?' I said, looking straight at him.

'As Joseph says, it is for you to decide, Angela.'

Everyone was looking to me to make the decision and I didn't have a clue what to do and I told everyone that.

'I have an idea,' said Joseph. 'Let's toss a coin. Heads you go, tails you stay.'

'Don't be silly,' snapped Binty. 'This is a very serious matter, you can't just decide on the flip of a coin like that.'

'Why not?' I said. 'It's as good a way as any to make this decision. Go ahead, Joseph. Let's do this.' And so, on the flip of a coin, I found myself packing my case once again for the journey northwards. It was a simple as that. Heads had called it.

Chapter Thirty-Four
Angela

'Today the rains will come.' Karisa was concentrating on the busy road ahead.

It was the first of April and I asked him if he was playing a joke. The sky was the deepest blue, and there wasn't a cloud to be seen.

'No joke,' he said, confused.

I tried to explain to him the tradition of April fool's Day in the UK, but my explanation did nothing to alleviate his confusion. He merely repeated his first sentence and then informed me that the rains in Kenya were nothing to joke about. Suitably chastised, I asked him how he knew it would happen today.

'Trust me, Angela, today the rains will come. That, I know.' He was right, of course, for within the hour the heavens opened and the downpour began. Karisa pulled the car into the side of the road and we took refuge in a small cafe full of truck drivers. 'It is very dangerous to travel in such weather. We must sit here and wait for the rain to stop.'

While we waited, we ordered a bowl of *pilau* each, and continued to wait. The rain showed no sign of easing and so we made ourselves as comfortable as we could on the hard bamboo chairs.

We were certainly attracting our fair share of attention from the other customers, but Karisa seemed oblivious to it and ate his rice without concern. I, on the other hand, was feeling a little uncomfortable. Not only was I the only *mzungu*, I was also the only woman. A group of small boys gathered outside the door, happy to stand in the pouring rain to take a look at the white woman. Karisa, spotting my discomfort, began to laugh.

'They mean no harm. They have come to see the ghost! Some of these children will have never seen a white person before and will think because of your colour that you are dead and therefore a ghost. Let them look, Angela, it will give them something to tell their friends, maybe even their children, ha-ha!'

Finally, after an hour or so, the rain eased and Karisa decided to get back on the road.

'We will have to be careful though, it will still be dangerous.' The boys had disappeared by the time we made it outside.

'They do not want to be too close to the ghost.' He laughed, as he threw our stuff into the vehicle. 'Now, me, I do not mind at all.' He helped me into my seat. The touch of his hand on my arm and the closeness of his body brought a flush of heat to my face. So much for being just friends, I thought. The man was flirting with me.

He was right about the road ahead. Progress was very slow. The water had collected into the large potholes, making them impossible to spot before we dropped into them, jarring your back and neck. Many vehicles had decided to go 'off-road' to avoid the holes, but were now stuck in the bright red mud that glued them to the grassland. Karisa was using all his concentration on the road and we continued in silence.

Was I reading too much into his words? Normally, I would've dismissed it for the harmless banter that it probably was. A particularly deep pothole brought me back to my senses as I shot forward towards the windscreen, saved abruptly by my seatbelt. We'd made reasonable headway but were barely halfway when the rains began again.

'Kibwezi is just up the road and I think this rain is not going to stop today. We will rest there for the night,' he said.

'Oh, is that really necessary?' I felt uneasy about being in a hotel with Karisa. 'Can we not just go on a little bit further?'

'Yes, we can if you wish, Angela, but the road will only become more dangerous. My advice is to stop. But it is your choice.' He was right, and I was being stupid putting both our lives in danger. Surely nothing was going to happen?

'The Mountain View it is, then,' I said.

We were greeted like long lost friends. Bookings were moved so we could have the same rooms and tables were changed so we could sit at the same table. Karisa could see that I was on edge.

'Angela, we promised we would remain just friends and this is how it will be. I know you feel discomfort at being back at this hotel, I too feel this, but it was wise to rest here. Please do not worry; nothing will happen between us again.'

I wish I could say that these words brought me peace and comfort but they only brought me sadness of what we'd lost.

I spent the night feeling anxious and sleep wouldn't come. By dawn, I was in a rush to get back on the road. Thankfully Karisa felt the same and was already in the dining room when I arrived for breakfast.

'Let us get some more water and things to eat as we travel.'

'Good idea,' I said. 'The sooner we find this woman, the sooner I can go home.' His face dropped but he said nothing. I changed the subject. 'You didn't say how it went with your mother?'

'I am not sure I want to talk about it. Both my mother and the boy are very angry with me. But I cannot change what has happened. I promised Gabriel that I would return, but he talked only of you. He is not a fool. He knows that you will not return with me and so do I.'

I had no answer for him. The sun was beginning to dry up the water-filled potholes and so, as we journeyed on, it was easier to spot these hazards and save ourselves the pain of a twisted spine. For the first part of the day, the new railway ran alongside and it was strange to see something so modern in such an ancient landscape. The acacia trees providing shade for goats, cattle and herdsmen alike. Something they would have done for hundreds of years. I started waving back to children by the side of the road as they waved to me. It gave me so much joy to see them bursting into laughter as I stuck my arm out of the window. I felt at ease until it reminded me of Gabriel. Then I stopped.

We turned off the main road to Machakos a couple of hours later. Karisa felt it would be wise to phone Joseph so we stopped outside a small bar on the way. He answered within a couple of rings and was happy to know that we were safe after the heavy rain. He told us that the information he had was scant, but he'd been reliably informed that there was a man who could help us. I quickly wrote down the name and telephone number as Karisa repeated it and, phone call finished, we sat to contemplate our next move.

'We must phone this man.' Karisa took the paper from me dialled the number. 'We meet him tomorrow,' he said.

He was very quiet for the rest of the journey and I left him to concentrate on the road. But the minute we booked into a hotel, he said he had a headache and needed to go to bed. He said it was because of the driving but I didn't believe him. There was something else.

Chapter Thirty-Five
Karisa

I did not have a pain in my head, but I could not face Angela. I did not want her to see my fear. So I made my excuse. The man I spoke to called himself Wambua and told me he would help us. But I could not be sure that he was telling the truth. Joseph had great faith in his friend in Mombasa but did not know this man in Machakos. He told me I must trust him. I was not sure I could.

I could not talk of my fear to Angela because then she would know that I was a coward. Once upon a time, I was not, I was a brave Kenyan man, but the police beat my courage away with their blows to my body and my broken bones. Today I felt afraid, as afraid as that time alone in the prison cell. I had a feeling inside me that told me of danger.

I tried to rest but many thoughts were in my head, so I went downstairs and out into the street. I had never been to this town before and it was very large. I feared that I would get lost and so travelled only as far as the bar across the road. It was full of office men in their smart suits, having finished a day at work. I felt out of place in my t-shirt from the market and my dusty trousers, and I took my *tusker* outside and sat beside the busy traffic. I nodded to the man on the wooden seat next to me. He seemed to be watching something or someone, because his eyes stared at our hotel alone. He made me feel uncomfortable and so I left. He paid me no attention and I was thankful.

I thought the alcohol would have calmed the trembling in my hands, but it had not and so I hid my hands in my pockets to hide my weakness. It was mine alone to bear.

Chapter Thirty-Six
Angela

We had arranged to meet Mr Wambua at the university. He'd said it was unmissable and indeed it was, being only one hundred metres from our Hotel. I watched people come and go from the balcony of my room and wondered which one was likely to be him when Karisa knocked on my door. I felt nervous but it was obvious that he was in a much worse state than me. I touched his arm in solidarity and followed him down the stairs and out of the Hotel. It had crossed my mind how Mr Wambua would recognise us until I realised that mine was likely to be the only white face around. Immediately, a man approached. I tried to estimate his age but that was impossible, putting him at somewhere between thirty and fifty. He wore a baseball cap and as he removed it to introduce himself I caught sign of a wide gash across his forehead, florescent pink against his jet black skin. He smiled widely at us but there was no warmth. His struck me as someone from the military uncomfortable in civilian clothes, his eyes darting around us as he spoke. He involuntarily touched his head.

'Car accident,' he said. 'I almost went through the windscreen but I was saved by the front mirror. I thank God for this scar; it has taught me a great lesson.'

'What is that?' I asked.

'To always wear your belt even when you are in the back seat.' As his face creased with laughter, a trickle of blood seeped from the wound. He wiped it quickly with the back of his hand, winching at the pain. His laughter was hollow and I was afraid. He showed no inclination to talk further and set off down a small, bustling side street. We followed without question. Karisa, I could see, was shaking; he glanced at me and then pushed his hands into his pockets. What had I got him into?

Wambua scanned the surroundings as we walked. Karisa followed the man's gaze wherever he looked.

'If you wish to meet this man, then we must hurry. He will not wait for us.' I stumbled on the uneven ground as Wambua surged ahead. Karisa took hold of my arm to steady me; he was still shaking. Wambua made no concession for our lack of speed and several times we lost sight of him for a minute or two until we caught up. The place was a labyrinth; each alleyway narrower than the previous one until we stopped in front of an entrance. Where there should have been a door, there was a paper sack nailed to the surround on the top and the left side. We entered into pitch dark.

'This is Nzoka. He will be able to help you to find your lady, but this will come at a price. I have brought you here to negotiate.' Wambua removed his jacket, his bright white shirt shone in the gloom.

The man they called Nzoka got to his feet slowly and moved into the light. He didn't smile or greet us but looked us up and down in a lingering appraisal. He nodded to Wambua and then sat down again.

'So, madam, how much are you going to pay this gentleman to help you?'

I looked to Karisa for support but he turned his head away. This angered me. Now wasn't the time to be timid I took a deep breath…'Nothing,' I said. 'I'm not going to pay him a thing.'

'That is not the way it is done in Kenya. We have to negotiate. So you must tell me how much you will pay and then the negotiations can begin.' I sensed Wambua's impatience as well as feeling my own indignation.

'I'm not here to negotiate with any of you. I'd hoped, and in fact believed, that you had information for me and were going to help me, Mr Wambua.'

'I am helping you, madam, by introducing you to this man. But this man has his price and so if you want the information that he has, you must pay.'

Karisa continued to ignore me. 'He is saying one hundred thousand Kenyan shillings for the information.'

'Time to go,' I said, looking at Karisa for support but none came. 'I will not pay this price. You're wasting my time. How do I know that the information that you have will help me? Maybe it would be better if I went directly to the police.' I turned to walk out of the door.

'Wait, madam, as I said, there is always room for negotiation. Let us begin.' Wambua caught my arm and whispered, 'If you leave now, you will never find the woman you want. Only this man knows this woman, you must come back and play the game with us.' I hesitated before turning back to face Nzoka.

'Okay, let us start at a sensible price,' I said, looking him straight in the eye. My panic remained and I struggled to keep control.

The conversation with Mark still rang around my head. He expected me to turn my back and walk away. I had no intention of giving in that easily.

We agreed on half the sum originally asked and to meet with Nzoka again the next day. Wambua left us at the university.

Karisa hadn't spoken a word either to me or Wambua since we'd met him and I needed to know why. But he didn't give me chance to ask him as he once again made an excuse and went to his room. Leaving me in the foyer of the hotel, all eyes on me. I too went to my room.

We'd arranged to meet for dinner but as I sat waiting in the dining room I was worried he wouldn't show. I felt guilty that I'd got him involved, but I depended on him now and was concerned about his behaviour. Finally he arrived. Smiling weakly he sat down.

'Angela, I need to apologise,' he began, fiddling with his napkin. 'I did not support you when we had the meeting. I was very wrong. It will not happen again.'

I wanted to know more of his reasons why he hadn't spoken, but I could see that this was not the time and so accepted his apology and we ate in silence. He didn't stay long.

I wished him goodnight and, once out of sight, began the eight flights upstairs. I couldn't think about Karisa too much tonight, my thoughts were on home and Mark in particular, I decided to call. The phone was answered immediately.

'Marcus Trippett speaking.'

'Mark, it's Mum… please don't hang up.'

There was a long pause before he replied, 'What do you want, Mother?'

'I want to talk to you, that's all. You are my son, and I know that you maybe don't like me very much at the moment and think that I let you down badly, but we have to talk.'

'Do we? Why on earth do you think that?'

'Because if we don't try to talk to each other, then things will only get worse, and I love you too much for that to happen. Please, Mark… just give me a chance.'

Another long pause. 'Go on. What did you want to say?'

'I haven't thought about what I want to say to you. I just want to hear your voice and know that you are okay.'

'Mother, you know that I'm not okay and I'm not sure that

I'll ever be okay. But to ease your conscience, I'm coping and, yes, I'm getting some help. Your favourite son, Josh, stepped in after your chat with him and has been arranging weekly sessions with some kind of shrink. But don't worry; I haven't let him into our little conversation, so your reputation as a perfect mother is still safe.' The line went dead.

He hates me… my son hates me. I lay on the bed, watching the ceiling fan go round and round. The anger that I felt for George came flooding back. This was his bloody fault. Why was I even bothering to search out this woman? Let her have the money and let me get on with rebuilding my life, I thought. But then what? Spend the rest of my life wondering who this woman was, or what had happened between her and my husband? I couldn't let her take away everything I had. I would prove Mark wrong and see it through to the bitter end, whatever that might be.

Amazingly, I managed to get some sleep and woke up feeling more determined than ever. The luxury of a comfortable bed and the silence that the triple glazing afforded me had a remarkable effect on my mood. But I still didn't know what to do about Karisa. My initial reaction was to head off to the meeting on my own. It was my problem and I knew being here caused him great anxiety. But I also knew that it would be a very foolish thing to do. I rang his room. He wasn't there, or in the dining room when I went downstairs. I asked at reception and they said that he'd left the hotel early but had told them that he would be back within a couple of hours. So I wandered into the dining room to breakfast alone. I was enjoying a rather decent cup of coffee when he came in and sat at the table.

'Sorry that I was not here when you came down. I needed to clear my head and went for a walk near where we met that man Nzoka yesterday. I do not trust him, he is a bad man Angela and I think we should leave. He will not be honest with you.'

'Karisa, I know you're very scared, so am I.' I saw him flinch. 'And I won't force you to remain here. If you want to return to Mombasa, then you must do so, but for me, I have to stay.' I couldn't tell him what I stood to lose if this woman truly was 'the wife'. I had to meet these men even if Karisa chose to leave. There was no other choice.

I didn't contact him when it was time for the meeting, leaving the hotel alone.

'Where is your friend?' Wambua asked when we met. I made some excuse about him being ill and that I hadn't wanted to let Mr Nzoka down. He seemed happy with this explanation and grabbing hold of my arm, led me away down the route we had taken yesterday. This time, however, we didn't go to the same place but entered into a seedy bar on the way. A strong, sweet smell pervaded everywhere in the gloom and once I could see a little, it was obvious what most of the occupants were enjoying.

'Fancy a smoke, do you, woman?' A sour-faced man thrust a joint in my face as I walked past.

'Leave her alone, she does not want your drugs, old man,' Wambua put himself between me and the man as he stood up to face him. He gently pushed him back down onto his chair. 'Get on with your smoke, we are not interested.'

I was thankful for his intervention and reassured that he at least was on my side. We continued to walk through the bar and out into the fresh air at the back. Nzoka sat with another man deep in conversation, but on seeing us approach sent the man away and pushed the spare chair towards me with his foot indicating that I should be seated. Wambua found himself another chair and sat facing the doorway that we'd just come through, clearly a little on edge.

'Do you have the money?' Nzoka said. I'd had no idea that he was able to speak such clear English. He picked up on my surprise.

'I am not uneducated, madam, I have learnt many things, but circumstances have not been kind to me. But do not think for one minute that I am stupid.' Once again, Wambua intervened.

'Nzoka, we are here to do business. Now are you able to help us or not? I am sure that there are many others who would like to do business with this lady if you do not want to.'

The men looked each other squarely in the eye and I sensed that Nzoka was not used to being challenged. 'Let me see the money first.'

I showed him the notes, but if I'd hoped to be taken to meet Rose immediately, I was disappointed.

'We shall meet here again tomorrow at the same time, and I will have the woman you want to speak to with me,' he said as he got up to leave.

But before he had chance to walk away, Wambua gripped his arm. 'Make sure that you do, my friend. I am not someone that you should mess around.'

There was a brief nod between them both and Nzoka was gone. I finally let out the breath that I had been holding and felt the fear rise.

Chapter Thirty-Seven
Karisa

I let Angela down yesterday and felt her pity for me. This shamed me greatly. I am a Kenyan man and yet this woman showed more courage than I, and this could not remain the case. I needed to find a way. I found a *mganga* that may be able to help me. I would not normally use the services of these people, but I was filled with desperation.

I left the hotel and the man behind the reception desk, the man who gave me the name, nodded to me and smiled as he handed me the directions of where I must go. He had organised the meeting for a few shilling and it was only now that I received the instructions. Everyone in Africa believed in witchcraft whether they spoke of it or not. I myself have denied my belief may times, but today I had to believe that it would help me with all my heart.

The directions were clear and I arrived at the home of the man in good time for my meeting. The people around looked at me with suspicion; I was new. The *mganga* was waiting for me and took me into his small hut, hidden behind a row of *dukas*. The hut was dark and, coming in from the bright sunlight, I was blind. I struggled to sit down on a small mat on the floor as requested and tried to ease the fear inside. As my eyes got used to my surroundings, I saw a bowl in front of me containing what looked like powdered chalk, and by the side of it was a dead chicken. There were many coloured bottles on the floor and dried leaves on the ground beside me. The *Mganga* asked me why I wanted his help and I told him, although it was not easy and I trembled very much inside.

'I can help you, my friend,' he said when I had finished speaking. 'But the cost will not be small.'

I had expected this. 'I have money,' I said.

He disappeared outside the hut, saying he had to make a brew for me, but it had to be made in the sunshine. Making it in darkness would increase my fear, he explained. I was left alone for some time but he returned carrying a small brown bottle.

'You must put ten drops of this potion in your water and you must do this every thirty minutes for this day. Tomorrow, you must do the same every hour. By the end of tomorrow, your fear will have gone and your courage will begin to return.' He put some of the white powder in his hand, told me to close my eyes, and then blew it into my face. The meeting was over. I paid my charge of seven thousand shillings, much of my savings, and left.

It did not take me long to get back to the hotel. I thanked the man on the reception desk and asked if Angela was at the hotel. She was not.

Chapter Thirty-Eight
Angela

When we'd first arrived, we'd driven through a beautiful, affluent neighbourhood, full of gorgeous detached houses set in luscious greenery. I'd been convinced that was where we would find the woman I was looking for, but now I wasn't so sure. Meeting Nzoka and visiting his house didn't make sense. I'd imagined that the woman would be an expat after all, those were the people that George hung out with but the lawyer had used the word 'natives'. I disliked that word as much as I disliked him. Wambua had told me that I needed to trust him and I had no choice. So against my better judgement, I set off for another meeting with Nzoka alone. I knew I should have waited for Wambua but he was late and I didn't want to miss my chance. Where my courage came from I didn't know. I just knew that I had to give it my best shot to try and find this woman. What I would do once I'd found her, I hadn't a clue. I knew that Karisa was reluctant to be a part of this and I didn't want to put him through anymore anxiety. He was obviously scared, so was I, but this was my problem and I thought it best to keep him out of it. This was something I had to do on my own.

We'd arranged to meet in the same bar as yesterday and I found it easily. All eyes were on me as I found a table opposite the door where I was unlikely to miss anyone entering or leaving. The confidence I'd started the day with began to fade and I felt my throat tightening. I tried to breathe deeply and put it out of my mind. I had to do this if I wanted to meet the woman. I couldn't back out now.

Right on time Nzoka arrived and spotted me immediately. He wandered over and sat down; I was disappointed to see that he was alone.

'You do not think that I would bring her here, do you?' he said. 'I wanted to make sure that you kept your word first. Now I see that you have, I will arrange the meeting. But it will not be here.' I felt uncomfortable that we were going somewhere else to meet Rose. I thought about calling the whole thing off but knew I might not get another chance to do this. I slowly nodded, picked up my bag and followed him. The minute we were outside, we were joined by a couple of other men.

'Meet your shadows,' he laughed. 'They have been keeping a close eye on you, Mrs Trippett.' They gave me the creeps.

Without waiting for any further introductions, we walked quickly along the thin passageways. I vaguely recognised the route we'd taken to Nzoka's home, but when we came to his door we carried on. I tried to pick up landmarks along the way to remember, but it was difficult. Yet again I questioned my decision to come. Eventually we turned a sharp right into dead-end and entered a door.

He left his men outside the building, which consisted of eight doors opening into a small passageway that was blocked off at the far end. Along the passageway, washing was strung like gaudy prayer flags and a couple of women were crouched down over large plastic bowls full of soap suds. The women immediately stood up as they saw Nzoka and watched us intently as we entered the door chosen by him.

'She is not here,' said one of the women. 'She has gone to

deliver some washing.'

'Who asked you?' He walked up to her and grabbed hold of her throat.

The two of them locked eyes for a minute, then the woman whispered some words that sounded like an apology. Nzoka let go of her and went to speak to the men outside.

'Find her!' he yelled. 'I do not have time to deal with silly women today.' Grabbing my arm firmly, he took me inside the room. We sat and waited in silence.

My eyes soon became accustomed to the darkness in the room. Gradually I could see a small thin mattress propped up against a grimy wall and in the corner, there was a pile of metal pots that I assumed were used for cooking. They reminded me of the pots in Karisa's village. Just by the doorway was a small charcoal burner, positioned, I expect, to let as much of the smoke as possible out through the door. There was an old calendar stuck on the wall with sticking plaster, showing Jesus ascending into heaven in full glory. Underneath someone had written 'God is good', in crayon.

The two women outside had disappeared and all around was very quiet until I heard one of the men shout, 'She is here! We have her,' and an older woman was pushed into the room.

'Where have you been, whore? I have been waiting for a long time for you to bother to come back.' Nzoka pushed her against the wall and she slid to the floor, not once taking her eyes off him. He raised his hand as if to hit her and she lowered her eyes immediately. 'This, madam, is the woman you seek. This is Warudi,' he said.

'I am sorry, but you must be mistaken. I am looking for someone called Rose.'

'Madam, do not take me for a fool. This is the woman you

wanted. In Swahili, her name is Warudi; in English, this translates to Rose.' He pulled her to her feet. 'Speak to the English woman.'

'He is correct,' she whispered, her eyes never leaving the floor. 'My name in English is Rose. My father worked for a large flower farm near Athi River that is why he named me so.'

'Do you not mean our father?' Nzoka snapped. 'I know you were his favourite, but he was my *baba* too.'

'Do you mean to tell me you two are brother and sister?'

'That is so,' said the woman.

'We do not have time to spend chatting today, ladies. This madam is to prove to you that she does exist, and that if you play the game with me, then I will deliver what you ask. You two have now met, but it is time to go.'

'But I thought we'd be able to spend time together. I have a lot of questions to ask her, you promised me time.'

'No, madam, I promised that I would allow you to meet and so you have. Now we must go.' He was already out of the room and heading back down the path.

'Mr Nzoka…' I began, but before I could say anything more I was ushered out of the room and back into the bright sunlight. We walked back the way we had come.

'You will meet again, do not worry. However, the price has risen. The money you paid was for a meeting. You have now met. If you ladies want to get to know each other, the price is higher.' I sensed his change of mood.

'Madam, I am not playing games and I expect to be paid in full for the considerable effort I have gone to on your behalf,' he said.

'What effort? She's your sister. There was no effort. I've already paid you some money and when I've had my next meeting then I'll pay you the balance.' I'd no idea where my courage came from but it inflamed him even more. He reached out to grab my wrist, but one of his men stopped him.

'This is not the place,' he whispered into his ear, 'And this is not the time.'

Nzoka moved up very close to me without laying a hand on me. 'You must be very careful, madam, in this town. Very careful. Many bad things can happen to people who do not know the way of this place. Sleep well and I shall be in touch,' he said, under his rancid breath. 'Take great care.' And he walked through the doorway into the bar, leaving me in the company of the two men.

'You would be wise to listen to him. He is very powerful and you are just an old white woman.'

I walked away as quickly as I could my throat tightening with every step. What was I playing at? I was getting into a very dangerous situation and I'd been very lucky that things hadn't got nasty just then. I needed to get myself together. It was extremely foolish to meet Nzoka on my own again, but I wasn't sure that I'd have much choice if I was insistent on meeting with the woman again. There was still huge doubt in my mind that this was the woman in the will. I couldn't get out of my head that she was the other Mrs Trippett.

I was glad to get back into the more public space of the university again and was relieved to see that neither of the men were following me, but in my haste to get back to the hotel I stumbled over a raised stone. As I fell to the floor, many students who were milling outside the entrance came running to help me and managed to lift me back on my feet and guide me to a safe place to sit.

'Excuse me, *pole*.' I heard a voice that was instantly

recognisable. 'Allow me through, please, this is my friend.' Karisa pushed his way through the students and knelt at my feet. I was so pleased to see him. I tried to stand but the pain was too much.

'Angela, please sit, we must go to the hospital.'

'No please, no hospital.' I was embarrassed at the crowd around me. 'It's only twisted. Just get me back to the hotel; I have a bandage in my luggage that will help it.' And so, with the help of many students, I was carried across the road to the hotel.

As we entered, the porter and receptionist came to help and I was laid gently on a sofa in the reception, while a rather noisy conversation took place as to what should be done with me. Thank goodness, Karisa listened to me and insisted that for the moment we did nothing, but if there was no improvement by the morning then medical treatment would be sought. Unfortunately, there was no way that I would be able to make the four floors up to my room via the stairs and so I had no other choice but to face my fear and step into the lift. Once again there was no shortage of help and four others crammed in to assist me, making my panic increase. I kept my eyes closed and concentrated on breathing.

Once in my room, I was able to lie down, propped up with many pillows and cushions obtained from empty rooms. Karisa was fussing round me like a mother hen and insisting that he got some ice from the bar to put on the now very swollen ankle. I was glad to get him out of the room for a while and so gladly accepted his offer.

'If you're going for some ice, can you please make sure that it's surrounded by a large gin and tonic?' I yelled. I was feeling very angry with myself and a little stupid for tripping over. This would complicate everything if I wasn't able to get out and about tomorrow. I was deep in thought when the door opened and Wambua marched in.

'You, madam, have been very fortunate today.'

I feigned innocence. 'I have no idea what you're talking about.'

'Do you think I am an idiot? That I am not able to do my job, even when silly women think that they are better at it than me. Is that what you think, madam? I know exactly what you have been doing today and where you have been. If my man had not stopped Nzoka outside the bar, you could have been badly hurt. This man is very dangerous. If you mess with him, he will hurt you, of that have no fear. He would have waited for us. You were very foolish to have gone alone.' I looked behind him and there was Karisa clutching my drink, eyes wide open. 'It was me who suggested that your friend perhaps head over to the university. I told him that you could quite easily get lost. That is how he came to be there when you fell.'

The look of concern on Karisa's face belied the feelings that he was trying to hide. 'Angela, you must listen to this man. You put yourself in grave danger today and I am grieved that you have lied to me so much about this. I believed everything you said because I thought we were friends. But you do not trust me, why?'

I looked into his open face and started to cry. Immediately he put his arms around me and held me tight. It felt so good. Wambua discreetly left the room and stood by the door while I continued to blubber uncontrollably. Eventually, I calmed down enough to wipe my face and to take a very large gulp of the gin and tonic and he re-entered.

'Now that you are calmer, I want you to tell me exactly

what happened today, piece by piece, and please do not miss anything out,' he said. 'It could be very important.'

And so I went through everything, as best as I could with Karisa holding the ice wrapped in a towel on my ankle. By the time I'd finished the ice was all but gone, along with the G&T. I asked him to get me another while I put the bandage on my ankle. Once he had left the room, Wambua said, 'Your friend is very concerned about you but he is also very afraid of the people we are dealing with. He is wise to be afraid. I am not sure how useful he will be. Had you not fallen and injured yourself then I would have not included him at all, but now you will be unable to walk far for the next few days and you will need him to accompany you. How do you feel about that?'

'You do not need to worry about me.' Karisa's voice sounded from the doorway. 'I will not let Angela down again.'

I believed him. There was something different about his manner. He was the man I'd met at the very beginning. He was strong and confident. Whatever had been troubling him seemed to have disappeared.

'Angela, you must understand that I have not been well, but now I am better. Something in my past had turned me into a coward, but I have seen someone and I am now cured,' he said once Wambua had left us for the evening, promising to be in touch in the morning.

'What someone?'

He looked a little sheepish. 'A *mganga*. He is a very well-known person and has helped many people. Now he has helped me.'

'You sound like Gabriel,' I said, and for the moment we both knew we were thinking about the gorgeous little boy that called us Mama and Baba and was waiting for us back in the village.

183

'I think I want to go back, to Mombasa,' I said. 'I've had enough of all this. I don't care about that woman; I don't care about the money. It's not worth it.'

Karisa smiled and took my hands in his, 'Whatever you want to do, Angela, we shall do.'

Chapter Thirty-Nine
Angela

It was obvious that my ankle hadn't improved during the night and I'd have to visit the hospital for an x-ray. I remembered my conversation last night with Karisa about wanting to go back to Mombasa, back to Gabriel, and stop all this nonsense. How did I feel now? I felt guilty, that's how I felt. My own children needed me and if I was going anywhere it should be back home not to Mombasa and a boy I hardly knew. As if he could hear my thoughts, Karisa arrived.

'So, Angela, do you still want to return to the coast? We will do whatever you want to do.'

'To be honest, I'm in so much pain that I can't think of anything other than my bloody ankle. Can we get this sorted first and then have another think?' I needed time.

I felt the warmth of the sun enter the room as he pulled back the heavy curtains. The dawn was just showing over the building opposite. Even though it was very early in the morning, there was plenty of noise from the street below. Like all things in Kenya, it had a rhythm all of its own. My parents, my brother and I had lived in London for a short while, and there, the noise from the street was just that: noise. But here, you heard the sound of people first and then the sound of traffic. In London, it had only been traffic, like people did not exist outside their vehicles. Here, the street sellers, the *matatu* conductors, the children going to school and the pedestrians walking to work all came together in a beautiful symphony of sound. Even though my leg was hurting, I found it relaxing, listening to the voices and, yes, admiring the silhouette of Karisa as he wandered around the room. I could get used to this, I thought.

This thought was very short-lived. There was a loud rap on the door, followed by the voice of Wambua. I caught a quick glimpse of surprise on his face as Karisa answered the door and I felt the need to explain his presence. It was only when I saw both of the men trying to stifle a grin that I realised that my explanation had served only to make things worse. At least my comments had lightened the atmosphere, as Wambua began to laugh.

'Madam, it is no concern of mine what you get up to in the privacy of your own room. But you may wish to take great care of your leg, whatever you are doing.'

'Okay, okay, I get the joke,' I said. 'Now would you kindly tell me what you are doing here at this ungodly hour in the morning?'

'First, I wanted to check on your leg. Secondly, we need to get together to sort out the plan for when Nzoka gets back in touch, and he will. Of that, I am certain.'

'Well, first of all, my ankle hurts like hell and I may need to get an x-ray on it. Secondly, I don't think that there's going to be any plan. Karisa and I talked it over last night and I'm seriously thinking of leaving. You were right; yesterday I could have got myself in real danger. I'm scared of this Nzoka and I don't want to see him or that woman again. I shall just let the lawyers deal with it and get on with my life.'

Wambua scowled. 'Madam, I do not think that it is a good idea for you to leave. You must continue your meetings with

Nzoka; you must speak to the woman further.'

'But why? Surely it's my choice. I understand that I've put everyone to a lot of trouble for this, but I'm scared, really scared. As you say, this man is very dangerous. I do still have a family back in England and I want to see them again.'

'I understand that it is your decision, and I cannot force you to stay if you should wish to leave. I would just like you to consider it for another twenty-four hours, maybe visit with them both one more time, and then you can make your choice.' I hesitated and he saw his chance. 'But first, let us have an English breakfast before we take you to the hospital.'

I burst out laughing. 'But we're in Kenya, Wambua, where will you find an English breakfast here?'

As if on cue, the door opened and two waiters walked in, carrying bacon, sausage, fried eggs, mushrooms, baked beans and orange juice.

'No hash browns?' I said jokingly, scanning all the dishes.

'Hash browns… what are those?' Turning to the waiter, he said, 'Hash browns, have you forgotten them?'

The waiter shrugged his shoulders. 'I do not know what they are, Bwana, these hash browns.'

I told the waiter not to worry and that everything looked wonderful, and gave them both a hundred shillings. Karisa arranged my pillows so I could tuck in without dribbling the food down my front; it was delicious.

Wambua had organised for a wheelchair to be brought to the room and so, although I still had to use the lift, it took considerably less people to manhandle me in and out. I was a little concerned what would await me at the hospital, but was pleasantly surprised as we entered. The staff were wearing clean, brilliantly white gowns, and the waiting areas and consulting rooms were modern, bright, and pristine. There were very few people.

Wambua must have noticed my surprise. 'This hospital is a private hospital. It is for rich people only.'

My stomach lurched, how much money did they think I had? I was dreading the bill, but had no time to voice my concern as my name was called.

Both men piled into the consulting room with the nurse who'd very kindly pushed me through the door and settled me on the bed. The doctor looked at them and Wambua said something to him in Swahili, which caused both him and Karisa to smile and nod. As it was obvious that no one was going to leave the room, I made myself comfortable on the bed. Apart from when the doctor wandered over to me and gently examined my ankle, I wasn't acknowledged. Eventually, I was helped from the bed back into the wheelchair and carted off down several shiny corridors to the empty x-ray department.

Once done, I was wheeled straight back to the doctor's room and, within two minutes, the results were being looked at by the doctor, Karisa, and Wambua. After lots of pondering the diagnosis was made. There was nothing broken; all that was needed was rest, heavy strapping, and a supply of strong pain killers. Once I'd been bandaged, I was free to leave. This was the part I was dreading, but to my utmost surprise, I was pushed straight past the receptionist and out the door into the morning heat.

'*Err,* haven't we forgotten something?' I said, 'Like paying?'

'No need, madam, it is all taken care of,' said Wambua.

I looked at Karisa questioningly.

'Yes, that is the case, Angela.'

'I don't understand who has paid my bill?'

'There is no bill to pay, madam, this, I promise,' Wambua replied. 'So please do not worry about these things.'

Yes, I was suspicious, but who was I to complain? I'd just saved a fortune!

I was glad when we arrived back at the hotel and I was able to rest my ankle. I'd forgotten to take my phone with me and had no idea if Nzoka even had my number, but I noticed I'd had a missed call and when I played back the voicemail, the unmistakable voice blared out.

'I am disappointed that you did not return my call and that I have had to leave you a message,' he snarled. 'You must realise that I will not be calling back.'

'Well, I didn't want to speak to him anyhow,' I said, as I put the message on loudspeaker for everyone to hear.

'Madam, you must ring him. It is very important that you meet again. You do not want to hand over money without any real proof that this Rose is the person you seek,' Wambua said. 'I know you said that you wanted to leave, and you can do that, but surely you want to know the truth before you do.'

And that was the rub. I did want to know the truth and I did want to save my home, but I also wanted to save my neck. I knew Karisa wanted me to return with him to Mombasa, but there was something that was niggling inside the pit of my stomach and I knew what it was. It was the fact that if I didn't see this through, then George would win again. I'd had enough of that in my marriage. Mark's words came back; everyone expected me to walk away, and that was why I couldn't.

'I thought that you knew she was the right person,' I said. 'After all, we're here because of information from Mombasa. Why would I mistrust that information? Joseph said that the person could be relied on entirely and I assumed that it's the same with you too. If you've led me to her why are you now casting doubt?'

'I am not casting doubt, madam. I just believe that, although we have every reason to trust that this is the Rose that you seek, you need to find out for certain before you hand over the money in your husband's will. They are unlikely to agree to meet with anyone else on your behalf. Now my suggestion is that you phone Nzoka and explain that you have injured yourself and that you were at the hospital this morning. Give him the details so he can check up should he wish. Tell him you wish to meet again, but that you are unable to walk unaided and will need to bring somebody with you. Then you tell him that you will bring Mr Karisa. He will not be happy but will accept him because he wants to secure the money. If you do nothing then this woman will receive the money without question. Is that what you want?'

The easiest thing for me to do would be walk away, but then they would win; George would win and Mark would be proved right again. No I couldn't do that so I made the phone call and a meeting was organised for the following day.

Chapter Forty
Angela

I could tell when Karisa came to my room that morning that he was scared, so was I. Nzoka and I hadn't parted on the best of terms last time and I was worried how he would treat me when we met in an hour or so. We went for breakfast but neither of us was hungry and so decided to set off early, to give us plenty of time to negotiate the rough pathways, Karisa had never pushed a wheelchair before and found it difficult. The meeting had been scheduled for the same bar and Karisa was surprised that I found my way so easily. I brushed it off as having a good sense of direction, I hoped he believed me.

Even though we were early, they were both waiting for us, and I took this to be a good sign. Rose got up to greet me and seemed genuinely concerned that I'd hurt myself. Nzoka remained seated and silent. It was obvious that he was unhappy that I'd been unable to come alone and was considering his options. Finally, he spoke.

'We shall go now to Rose's house and you women can speak. But your friend here is not able to come with us.'

'I am not leaving her side.' Karisa held on tight to the wheelchair.

'Then the conversation will not take place. Madam, the deal was always to meet alone, and even though you are hurt, the deal remains the same. Your friend can remain here. Rose will help you. Otherwise, we both leave now.'

I sensed Karisa move towards Nzoka but I grabbed his hand and slowly shook my head. It wasn't ideal, but having come this far, I felt I had very little choice. Wambua was right, I needed to know for sure that this was the woman mentioned in the will and then work out how I could stop her from getting the money. The only way I could do that was by spending time with her.

'Okay, I agree, but every thirty minutes I'll contact my friend here to confirm that all is well. If I don't call, then he will phone the police. Do you understand?'

'If that is what you want.' Nzoka nodded his agreement.

Karisa was far from happy with this arrangement. 'Angela, it is very foolish to go alone. I must go with you.'

'I'll be fine,' I said, sounding much braver than I felt. 'Please don't worry.'

But I could see the fear on his face as I was pushed out of the bar and down the road. He came outside to watch me go but was barred from coming any further by one of Nzoka's henchmen.

We followed the same route to Rose's room, but it took far longer, as the road was very uneven and she found it difficult to push me in the wheelchair. I wasn't surprised; there was nothing of her. I could see that Nzoka was becoming impatient and ordered the man with us to take over. Whereas Rose, lacking in strength, had chosen her way carefully through the potholes, this man had no such compunction and almost tipped me out of the chair immediately as he rushed down the road. I caught a smirk on Nzoka's face as he saw my discomfort. He was obviously unhappy that I'd refused to pay any more money to him and knew that he had to go through with this meeting to get the rest of the fee agreed and to stand any chance of anyone receiving the fifty thousand pounds. But he wasn't going to make it easy for me.

Eventually, we arrived at the same building as before. This time the women were nowhere to be seen and neither was their washing. The place was deserted. I was helped out of the wheelchair which was deposited outside and plonked in the same plastic chair I had sat in previously. Nzoka apparently had no intention of staying and said that he'd other business to attend to and would leave us women to talk. We weren't going to be left alone, however; his man would be standing guard by the doorway of the room.

'When will you come back?' I asked.

'Sometime.' He laughed and continued on his way.

Rose visibly relaxed as he left. 'Would you like some *chai*?'

My first thought was to refuse, but then thought it better if I accepted her kindness. The man was obviously going to relate back everything that we'd spoken about to his boss, so I had to be cautious.

She poured some water into a small pot and set it on the *Jiko* to heat up. I took this time to observe her. She was terribly thin, and the kaftan she was wearing was faded and ragged. She was tall, much taller than her brother, but she hardly lifted her head upright, rounding her shoulders, and she continued to avoid standing up straight as she made the tea. I'd rehearsed this moment many times in my head, but for the life of me, I couldn't remember any of the questions I wanted to ask. I sat watching her until she finally handed me the plastic mug full of the sweet tea, and sat on the floor nursing one herself. She hadn't offered our doorman a cup, I noticed, and I could see that he wasn't pleased.

'So you are the wife from England?' She said.

'And you, supposedly, are the wife from Kenya.'

'Do you doubt that?'

'I doubt it very much. Look where you're living. This is a slum, and as far as I know, my husband never even came to this town. He would never have met you. I don't know what you expect to achieve by your actions, but it won't work.' My pity had dissolved the minute she'd spoke. There was no way, even with all his sordid fantasies, that George would've got mixed up with a woman such as the one who sat opposite me.

'Do you think that I have always lived like this?' she said. 'As I said to you, I was born in Athi River, to good parents who raised me well and educated me. I took full advantage of this and worked hard. The woman you see before you is a college graduate, madam, not some street whore. I worked my way up to a good job in Nairobi and that, Mrs English Wife, is where I met your husband. I was a young girl then, not the tired old woman you see before you now.'

'I don't believe you,' I said. 'This is all one big lie. You could be anyone.'

She slowly raised herself off the floor and started to move some of the metal pots. She pulled out a small wooden box and brought it over to me. 'Look in there. You will find your proof.'

I slowly opened the box, and there on the top was a black and white photograph of George, with his arm around a beautiful young Kenyan girl. They were in a restaurant and they were gazing into each other's eyes with a look of pure love. I'd never known that look. I couldn't speak. I tried to swallow some *chai,* my eyes fixed on the photograph.

'Are you trying to tell me that this is you? It could be anyone,' I croaked.

'I knew you would find it difficult to recognise me or to believe that it was me and so maybe this might help?' She snatched the box from my hands and pulled out a battered document which she said was their marriage licence.

I couldn't breathe. I needed to leave and stumbled to the door, pushing the startled guard aside. But he easily caught hold of me as I dragged myself down the corridor. 'Stop. You cannot leave.'

He grabbed me round my waist and lifted me back into the room. I kicked him hard with my good leg and started to scream. He held me tight, but my panic was out of control and I fought with him with all the strength I had. He held me tighter and pushed my arms behind my back. The room was spinning.

'Leave her alone,' I heard a voice say. Even in my panic, I recognised it as Rose's. 'She cannot breathe.'

The man loosened his grip on me and I slumped to the floor. She held my hand as I gulped at the air.

'You will be better soon,' she whispered. 'It will pass.' She passed me a cup of water. 'You are ill?'

I was shocked at her concern for me, but I couldn't let that cloud my judgement. She was trying to con me and my family out of a lot of money.

'Give me that piece of paper. I want to see it again,' I croaked.

This time, she very gently handed it over. There was no trace of malice or triumph. There was almost a sadness that she had to do it. And there in my hands was the proof. A shabby piece of paper that proved that George had married this woman. I felt the tears stinging my eyes and I swallowed hard to stop them overflowing. All my determination, all my bravado, all my faith in the world collapsed.

'I want to leave now,' I said.

'Madam, you cannot leave,' the guard said. 'I have my orders to keep you here until Mr Nzoka returns.'

'And when the hell is that going to be?'

'He will be back in the morning, madam.'

'I want to speak to him!' I shouted at the man barring my exit. 'Get him on the phone now!'

'I am sorry, that is not possible. You are quite safe here; no harm will come to you. You told Mr Nzoka that you wanted time to speak with this woman. He has done as you asked and you have many hours to talk.'

'If you don't let me leave, I will phone my friend and tell him what's happening,' I said.

'Madam, you will not be able to phone your friend in the same way that I am unable to phone Mr Nzoka. There is no signal in this area.'

I looked to Rose and she nodded. 'That is sometimes so,' she said.

'No one is here but us, madam. You have no choice but to stay here until you are collected. It is best that you make yourself comfortable.' He laughed.

Chapter Forty-One
Karisa

I was concerned that I was not able to go with Angela and told the man so.

'They will be back soon. Do not worry, your woman will not come to any harm,' he said.

I was unsure. This had not been the plan at all. Angela was unable to walk without help and was at their mercy. I did not like that. I had to wait here until I heard from her. The man guarding me like a prison officer was sat with his back to the door.

'That way you can be the first to see when they return,' he said.

I knew he was trying to show kindness to me, but I could not be thankful. My phone remained silent and my fear grew. 'It is time for me to call the police,' I said after one hour.

'That is not a wise thing for you to do. Mr Nzoka would not like that at all.'

'I have no interest in what that man likes. My concern is only with Angela. She is my dear friend and she has not contacted me as promised. Therefore I must do as she asks.' I tried not to think of the worst, but my heart was beating hard as I took the phone out of my pocket. The guard stood up quickly and knocked it out of my hand.

'There will be no call to the police,' he said, picking up the phone up off the floor.

My fear was very large now. Even if she phoned, I would

not be able to speak to her or follow her wish to phone for help. Another hour passed by, and still, they did not return. I could see that my guard was impatient also so I offered to buy him a drink.

'I should not do this,' he said, taking a long look at his bottle of *Tusker*. 'If Mr Nzoka finds out, he will be very angry.'

'But he is not here, is he? We do not know where he is, do we? We are sat here like a couple of old village women waiting for a man to return to us. I for one do not see this as the role of a Kenyan man.'

He picked up his beer and took a long drink. 'You may be right, my friend, but I do not have any choice. For watching you today, I will get a few shillings to take home to my family. My boy is sick, he is always sick, he is not a well boy, and I have to pay many shillings to get medicine for him.'

'I am sorry to hear that, my friend. It is very difficult if you have a sick child.'

We sat together drinking our beer in a more companionable silence, both deep with our own thoughts. When the beer was finished, I ordered another one and the same when that one was finished. My thoughts were of escape to find Angela.

'I should not continue to drink with you. I am tasked to watch that you do not leave this place.'

'How can I leave, my friend? You watch over me as a sea eagle watches a fish. I cannot go anywhere. You are too good at your job, but that does not mean that we have to be strangers to each other. My name is Karisa.'

'You are correct, my friend, my name is Samson.'

We bumped fists in greeting.

My plan was that I would escape when he had to go to the toilet. But I had not considered the strength of his bladder, and the determination he had to stay with me throughout. Eventually, nature had its way and he rushed off, giving me the chance to run.

I am not a runner; that is for the Kalenjin tribe. Giriama people do not produce good athletes and I soon found myself out of breath. Even with the head start, Samson was able to catch up with me easily.

'Why do you put my life in peril?' he puffed, as he grabbed my arm behind my back. 'If I do not keep you, Nzoka will kill me, of that I am sure.'

'But my friend, the lady that I was with, is in grave danger herself. If you say he will kill you, whom he knows, what will he do to a *mzungu* once he has the money he has been promised?' I could see that Samson was giving this some thought so I talked on. 'Are you going to spend the rest of your life getting a few shillings from that man when he chooses to give them to you? What happens if he decides to stop giving these shillings, what will you do then? How will your boy receive his medicine? Come, my friend, let me buy you some food. I will not run from you again.' I saw the hunger in his eyes, this man would welcome food.

'I would very much like that. I cannot remember the last time I had a full stomach, but we must return to the bar. Many people will have seen you run out and I have to prove to them that you did not escape from me. If we do not return, they will inform Nzoka and I will be finished.'

The pity I felt for this man was real and I returned to the bar with him so everyone could see that I was a prisoner again. Then we could go somewhere else to get something to eat. I wanted to talk further with this man, but not in that bar. Samson agreed; he was concerned in saving his face and once that was done, he was prepared to take a risk in order to fill his stomach. I felt that if I could get this man to trust me then I might still be able to make my escape. My thoughts were only of Angela, alone and in danger while I could do nothing.

I insisted that we went somewhere that was very public. I did not want to go down back streets where dangerous things could happen to me and so we headed back towards the university. This was only a short walk from the bar should we need to return quickly, and so the mind of Samson was at peace also. I ordered large plates of *pilau* for us both. I could see by the speed that he was eating that it was some days since he had eaten and so I let him finish mine too.

When his hunger was satisfied, the questions began. He wanted to know why we were there and why we were involved with someone like Nzoka. I told him a little of the will and the search for this woman. I did not mention Wambua or Joseph and his contact in Mombasa; I said that we had been directed to this place by the lawyer in Nairobi.

'And you know that this woman is the one that you are looking for?' he asked.

'This is what we are trying to find out. The lady I am with has lost her husband and she is trying to do the right thing as is stated in her husband's will, but we have to make sure that this is the Rose that we search for. I have to tell you, I do not trust a man like Nzoka.'

'You are right to do so. He is not a trustworthy man. I wish I could help you and this lady friend of yours; you seem to be good people. But I cannot.' I could see the tension on his face at the mention of Nzoka. This brought me more fear for Angela.

'I do not expect you to put your life or that of your family's in danger; I just want you to give me the chance to search for them. It is many hours now and I have not heard from them as promised and I have great concerned. I just ask that you give me a few minutes in private to make a phone call to someone I know who may be able to help. I promise you that it is not the police. Surely that is not too much to ask of you?' I watched as he considered my request.

'Make your call friend. I will wait outside,' he said.

Thankfully Wambua picked up the call almost before it rang and his concern was also great when I told him what had happened.

'I should have expected this and planned for this,' he said. 'Any idea where they have gone?'

'I have no idea; I was prevented from following them. I have tried to run away from my captor also, but he caught me. But I do not think that he is a bad man, not like Nzoka.'

'Do you know the name of the man that is with you?' he asked, and when I informed him that it was Samson, he breathed a sigh of relief. 'That is good, Karisa. I am now confident that we shall soon find out where your friend is. But we must hold our time, we cannot rush into this. We have to be very wary of Nzoka at this moment. He is desperate to receive the money, but I do not think that her life is in any real danger until the money is handed over. Leave things with me and I will try to call you in one hour. Stay with this man and continue to be nice to him and if you are set free then return to the hotel and phone me from there. Do not try and find Angela yourself. If you try that, then you will put her in more danger than she already is.' He hung up.

I put the phone back inside my left sock – I hoped I could keep it – and went outside to meet Samson. He was very agitated that we had been away from the bar for some time and so we went back quickly to wait. 'Thank you, *Rafiki*,' he said. 'You are a good man.'

Chapter Forty-Two
Angela

I was angry with Rose and Nzoka, but more so with myself. I'd got myself into this situation, no one else. I should've returned home and not listened to Wambua. How could I've been so stupid? I wondered how Karisa must be feeling and what he would be doing. I hoped he'd called the police, but even if he had, where on earth would he direct them? That, I suspected, was the reason Nzoka hadn't stayed with us. If the police found him, he'd be nowhere near us and could deny everything. There would be no proof. There was little sympathy from Rose.

'There is no point in anger, English wife. We are stuck here together and we have to make the most of it. Do you think I want that thug stood outside my door? Do you think my neighbours want this too? Have you noticed none of them are around? This is his doing. They have been frightened from here and will not return until we are gone. So from this, I will lose my home. They will not welcome me back when this is all over.'

'But if you are the person you say you are, then you will be very rich,' I said. 'You'll have a lot of money.'

'Do you not believe that I am the woman that you seek? Do you think that I am lying to you?' For the first time she looked me straight in the eye, the challenge obvious.

'I don't know you at all and I'm being held here against my will. At this moment, I don't trust anybody. Until I can get verification of who you are and you can give me much more information about your life with my husband, then no, I don't believe you. Surely if you were who you say you are, you wouldn't need to keep me captive here.'

'Am I holding you here?' The defiance grew. 'Is it I who is stopping you from leaving? I would gladly push you all the way back to Mombasa rather than have you stay here, believe me. This may be my own home, but I too am held captive.'

Suddenly there was the sound of a phone ringing and the man outside quickly moved away from the door to answer it.

'I thought he said there was no signal here?'

'You are more trusting than you think, English wife. You believed without doubt that there was no signal. You are a very foolish woman indeed.'

I would have gladly put up with twice the pain in my ankle if I could've got up to slap away the smirk on her face. But I needed to go to the toilet.

Rose helped me to negotiate my way to the back of the building. Our guard was still on the phone and just nodded when she explained to him where we were going. She stayed outside in the fresh air whilst I shuffled my way into a small enclosure surrounded by plaited grass panels. The smell of the communal hole in the ground was overpowering, and I tried not to look down into the depths as I struggled to undo my trousers. It was impossible for me to balance and I had to ask for her help. My degradation was complete as she held me as I crouched down, holding my breath for as long as I could. I found it hard to hide the tears.

'Message your friend now,' she whispered. 'This is your chance. Our guard will not enter. Let him know that you are safe.' The surprise must have shown on my face.

'Your friend will be worried about you, and if he calls the police and Nzoka is arrested, then all of us will pay.' I sensed real fear in her words and so did what she suggested, hoping and praying that Karisa would get the message. I only had time to type '*Karisa*' before there was a loud voice from outside telling us to come out now. Rose popped her head outside the sacks and told the guard that I was just pulling up my underwear, and if he didn't believe her he could come and help me do it himself. That did the trick, and I was able to check that the message had gone before I gratefully stepped back outside and into the fresh air.

Why had Rose suggested sending the message? I still didn't trust her and half expected her to tell the guard what I'd done. But she remained quiet as she helped me back to the room. She smiled as she took my arm and settled me back in the seat. My ankle was more painful than ever and she used the wooden box for me to rest my leg on. She said that she would've offered me some food if she had any but she did not. I smiled back. I didn't want to make an enemy of this woman, at the moment I was dependant on her. I thought of the message I had tried to send Karisa; all I had been able to write was his name. What would he make of that? I could have been writing anything, it was hardly likely to send out alarm bells. I'd turned the volume off on my phone so that if I got a reply it wouldn't be noticed, and it was now safely tucked away in my bra.

I thought about my family and Jeannie, and how scared they'd be if they knew where I was and what was happening. I took comfort that they were oblivious to everything. My life in Somerset a long way off and I yearned for that simple life again. It wasn't that I felt in any danger. Surely Nzoka was not stupid enough to do anything while I still had the money. I just felt lonely I missed my home so much. I pictured Jeannie with her elderberry wine, her crystals and her garden, and literally ached to be back with her. But my home and my life in Somerset was the very reason I was here and I had to see it through. I couldn't hide the sound of my stomach rumbling. I felt embarrassed and said I was sorry.

'Do not be sorry,' Rose said. 'We are all hungry and if we had known what Nzoka had planned for us we could have got provisions, but I have nothing. Had my neighbours been here, they would have given us something. But their doors are locked and I am not a thief. Regardless of how hungry I am, I will not steal from others.'

My stomach continued to groan. 'I have money.'

The guard moved inside the door. 'Woman,' he said, speaking to Rose. 'If she has money to burn, then find someone to go and bring some rice and beans, and she can buy us chapattis and drinks too.' She slipped out of the door and down the corridor to shout to one of the young children nearby. They would go. She soon found one and told the boy what he had to get and that someone must help him to bring the food back. He ran off quickly to do his errand, leaving me wondering whether I would see my change or food anytime soon.

Within ten minutes, the boy returned with his older sister, carrying three plastic bags of food and several chapattis wrapped in newspaper. He could not carry the sodas, he'd said, and so was going to rush back for them. Rose dished out the food in plastic bowls, giving the guard the largest portion by far, and we settled down to eat. The boy returned with the sodas and handed Rose the change, she turned to hand it to me but I refused it, telling the boy to take it to his mother for food. She looked at me, nodded in agreement and the boy ran off clutching his shillings.

The guard was still sat on the floor outside the room, finishing off his food, when the unmistakable voice of Nzoka was heard. He jumped up. Rose grabbed the plate from him and rushed around the room trying to hide the evidence of the meal. It was too late.

'I can smell food. Who has got food?' He barged in through the door, almost knocking the guard off his feet. Rose dropped to the floor, looking only at her feet, as I had remembered at the first visit.

'You left us here,' I snapped. 'We didn't know how long you were going to leave us. We were hungry.'

'You, idiot,' he said, grabbing Rose by the shoulders and dragging her to her feet. 'I told you, sister of mine, that you were not to leave. You defied me and you will pay.'

'We did not leave,' she said, continuing to look at the floor. 'We shouted a boy to come and help. Ask anyone around. We did not go to get our own food.'

'So you shouted? Well now you can do some more.' He grabbed her hair and pulled her out of the door. I shuffled to help her but the guard stopped me. I could hear the blows but she didn't make a sound, then the door was opened and she was flung inside. I lowered myself gently to the floor and crawled to her to comfort her. It was obvious that he'd beaten her, blood poured from her nose and lip.

I felt my phone vibrate in my bra. I needed to get another message to Karisa, assuming it was him. The situation was getting more dangerous. Nzoka was now taking out his anger on the guard, who was doing nothing to defend himself against the punches. He was very much someone to be feared. Would I be next, I wondered?

'Now, madam, you have seen that it does not pay to lie to me and to defy my orders. I hope you understand.'

I remained silent. I was afraid that if I opened my mouth, my anger would get the better of me, and I didn't want to make things any worse than they already were.

'I had come to take you back. I thought that you would be in need of food, but I can see that you are not. My own sister went against my orders and I now know that none of you can be trusted, and so, for tonight, we will remain here in case your friend has called the police and they are waiting for me to return. Tonight they will be disappointed.'

Rose dapped at her mouth, where a steady flow of blood was pouring; she winched with the pain, but would not look up. Nzoka insisted on having the only mattress in the room and she searched for a blanket to cover him. The rest of us had to make do as we were. Rose and I helped each other onto the two chairs in the room and she offered me a *kikoi* to wrap around me to take away some of the night chill. The guard remained on duty. Before I settled, I asked to visit the hole outside again. It was obvious that Rose would not be much help and so, reluctantly, Nzoka agreed that the guard would help me.

I managed to get myself up to standing and the guard placed his right arm under my shoulders and we made our way slowly and gingerly round to the enclosure. The guard attempted to come in with me but I pushed him outside. Once more I held my breath and didn't look down as I pulled my phone from my bra and read Karisa's message.

'Where are you Angela? I am very worried for you?

'At Rose's danger Captive,' was all I could reply before the guard pulled a panel away. I quickly stuck the phone back in my bra, pretending to lose my balance and fall into his arms.

'Whoa, madam, you were lucky I was here to catch you.' And leaning close, he whispered in my ear, 'I know Wambua.'

Immediately he carried me out of the toilet and put me down gently outside. I was convinced I'd misheard, particularly as he said nothing else. He didn't even look my way as he half dragged me back over the rough ground to the room. He pushed me through the doorway and then quickly shut the door.

'I hope you were well taken care of?' Nzoka sniggered, turning over and pulling the blanket tight around his neck. *'Lala Salama.* Sleep safe, my friend.'

Chapter Forty-Three
Karisa

I was happy when I received the first text from Angela, but this new one concerned me greatly.

'*At Rose's danger Captive,*' I read once more.

Samson had remained with me since we returned to the bar and had said few words. Luckily he did not wish to accompany me to the toilet, but I did not know whether I could tell him I had received messages from Angela or not. He might contact Nzoka to inform him and that would make things very much worse for her. But I could not do anything without his help. The man behind the bar told us it was time to move as he wanted to close, and I saw confusion on Samson's face.

'I do not think that they will be returning tonight, friend, what are we to do?' I said.

'I am thinking the same thing also. This was not expected and I cannot think of anywhere that we can go.' I could see his fear.

'Let us think about this together. The bar is closing and so Nzoka will not expect to find us here. I do not expect that he will come looking for us tonight at all. So I think from now until sunrise we can rest wherever we want. I have a nice hotel room not far from here with two beds. Surely this is the place to go?'

'What if Nzoka does come looking for us? He will expect to find us.'

'So where shall we go? Maybe you can take me to your

home if it is nearby?' I said.

'I cannot take you there. I am sorry, my friend, but I need to protect my family. I do not want Mr Nzoka to know where I live; it will put them in danger.'

'So it seems that my room is the only option. If this man is as dangerous as you say, then no one will open their doors to us tonight. You are known to work for this man and they will be afraid to offer us shelter. At least at the hotel, there is an *askari* on the door, and reception will inform us of anyone asking for me. What do you say?'

Samson, I could see, was thinking hard about this decision. 'If we go there, we must return early tomorrow,' he said. 'We must be back at this place at sunrise.'

He looked behind us always on the way to the hotel to check that we were alone, and we walked in the shadows. Thankfully the reception to the hotel was empty and we were able to walk to the room without difficulty. I opened the door with gratitude.

'I have never seen such luxury.' Samson did not move from the doorway, I had to push him inside quickly and close the door.

I ordered some chicken and rice to be delivered to the room. We could not be seen in the dining room.

While he was lying on the bed I went into the bathroom to send a message to Wambua. Angela needed my help and I needed Wambua's. The signal was very weak but I hoped that he would receive it. The food arrived and Samson ate very quickly remaining on the bed while he did so. A knock on the door startled him greatly.

'It is probably the waiters come to take away our dishes,' I said, and went to open the door a little to see who it was. The door was flung against me and Wambua rushed in with another man. That man grabbed Samson before he could move and held him face down on the bed.

'Do not hurt him!' I yelled. 'He is a good man.'

I was still not sure whether that was the truth, but I did not want any harm to come to him. Wambua told the man to release him.

'I am glad to see you, my friend,' I said. 'I am very concerned about Angela; I believe that she is in some danger.' I took out my phone to show him the messages I had received.

'Nzoka is a nasty man indeed, but I do not believe he will cause any harm to your friend until he has received the money. The money he is expecting from Madam today for the meeting is very small compared to the amount he will take from Rose when she receives that from the will,' he said. 'So for the moment she is safe.'

I was not convinced but his words eased my mind a little.

'Who are you?' Samson had found his voice.

'Who I am, does not matter to you. All that matters is that you do exactly what is required and then you may see your family again. Nzoka will not be happy that you have failed in your task and will be looking for revenge. You do not have the security that Madam has at the moment and it is you that is in the biggest danger, my friend.' Wambua stood close to him and I could see the fear strike him like a thunderbolt.

'You are wrong about the woman. If Nzoka does not get all that he wants very soon, he will cause harm to her, trust me. He is not a patient man and he enjoys the drugs many times. You cannot reason with him when he is angry. The reason your friend is not with you now is because the deed has not been accomplished. That is not a good omen for her,' Samson said.

I asked Wambua and his man to leave the room for a few minutes. He was not pleased to do so but I needed to have a conversation with Samson alone.

'My friend, I greatly need your help and in return, I will do

211

everything I can to help you too. I care deeply for this woman as you do for your family and I will do whatever I am able to make sure that she is safe. I know you have a good heart and would not like the blood of this innocent woman to be on your hands and so I am begging you to help me.'

Wambua could wait no longer and rushed back into the room. 'What is going on?'

'You must ask Mr Samson,' I said.

He got up from the bed and walked over to me. 'Mr Karisa, my friend. You are right, I am at a cross pathway now, and I thank you for this opportunity. But as much as I would truly like to help you in my heart, I have a great fear of Nzoka. My head tells me I cannot betray him. If I do he will kill me and my family. I ask for some time to pray to my God for guidance.'

He sank to his knees in front of all of us and began to pray silently. I felt for him. The choice before him was a difficult choice, not one that I would want. All three of us moved to the other side of the room and left him in peace.

When he had finished, he stood up. 'I feel that my God has spoken to me. I know in my heart that I should do what is right but my fear is great. I do not know whether my life will be spared, but I have to put my trust in God. I pray that he will spare my family also, because Nzoka will not. I will help you to free your friend and to find out the truth,' he said, looking me straight in the eye.

'This is good news,' said Wambua. 'Now we have plans to make.'

Chapter Forty-Four
Angela

In the darkness, I heard Rose moaning. I felt sorry for her, Nzoka was a bully and her life must be a torment having a brother like him. They were so different. Of course, I still didn't trust her one bit, but deep down there was a kindness to her, and I suppose in different circumstances I might even have liked her. But I realised it would be very foolish to let my emotions take over. The reality of the situation was that this woman could destroy my life. I couldn't feel sorry for her. I had to remember that she was able to take everything from me. I couldn't afford sympathy.

I dozed a little throughout the night but was too nervous to fall asleep totally. Nzoka seemed to be fast asleep for most of the night. I didn't dare move at all to see whether the guard was still there and so I sat in my plastic chair waiting for any signs of the dawn. There wasn't any natural light in the room; the only sign of the sunrise was around the door. It had the effect of an alarm call on Nzoka and therefore on everyone else.

'Wake up, woman,' he shouted to Rose, kicking out with his feet and making painful contact with her legs. 'It is time to go. We must move on.' She got up without a word and opened the door so she could see enough to tidy up the room. She didn't question Nzoka at all, but I did.

'What do you mean it's time to move?'

'If your friend has phoned the police, now that it is coming to daylight, it will not take them long to track us down. I cannot afford to take you back if your friend has done this and so we cannot remain here. There is another place that we must go.'

'But I can't walk, and after your treatment of your sister last night, she's not strong enough to push me in the wheelchair.'

'She is stronger than you think. She is not a weak *mzungu*,' he laughed. 'Come, it is time to go.'

'Do not argue with him,' Rose whispered. 'At the moment we cannot do anything other than what he says.' And so we gathered what could be piled on my knee in the wheelchair and she helped me into the fresh air. My request to go to the toilet was forbidden by Nzoka and so my chance to contact Karisa passed by and we set off in a new direction.

It didn't take long before it became obvious that Rose didn't have the strength to push me over the rugged ground, and so this task was once again given to the guard.

'This is the job of a woman,' he grumbled under his breath as he pushed. But with him pushing me, we were able to move much faster. Nzoka's mood improved and he allowed us to stop at a *duka* for me to buy breakfast for everyone. Before I would pay for the food, I insisted that I visited the toilet and he told Rose to arrange for me to use the one belonging to nearby rooms. Once again, I wasn't allowed to go on my own and she was detailed to accompany me.

'Do you have your phone?' she barely whispered. I nodded that I had. 'Good, then you must tell your friend that we have moved.'

'But I don't know where we are going.'

'Tell him that we are passing the "Jesus loves me" church, that will help.'

214

I did as she said and sure enough, as we returned to the *duka*, by the side of it was a small corrugated iron building proclaiming that message. I still wasn't sure whether she wanted us to be found because of my safety or her own. But either way, I was very grateful for her help. If only I could get the photos and that marriage certificate out of my mind.

Chai and *mahambri*s finished, we moved on. I noticed that every so often Rose would greet somebody very quietly. Nzoka was oblivious to this and was almost cheerful as we went along.

'I hope you appreciate all the trouble I am going to for you?' he said. 'I am making very sure that you have many hours to spend together. That way you will know for sure that she is the person that you seek.'

My anger rose and I was about to snap a reply when the guard pushing me laid a hand on my shoulder. I swallowed my words and kept my thoughts to myself.

A little further on, we turned into a small school and entered a tatty brick building by the entrance of the compound. It turned out to be the home of their uncle and Nzoka was greeted warmly by the owner. Rose was ignored. The man immediately left and we were alone in a room with a battered old sofa, a small table in the centre and a kerosene lamp hanging from a hook in the roof. Other than that, there was nothing until the man returned carrying a couple of dusty chairs, presumably from the school next door. Nzoka explained to us all that we were going to be here for a while and for us to make ourselves comfortable.

It was obvious that the uncle and him were well acquainted; however his sister continued to be ignored. Nzoka was quick to spread himself out on the sofa, leaving no room for anyone else, and so Rose and I took the chairs to the small window and went to sit down.

'Move away from there,' Nzoka shouted and jumped up to close the ragged piece of cloth that served as a curtain. 'Sit over in that corner where no one can see you.'

The guard took his position on a chair outside the building. The uncle did not return.

I was suspicious of this man and wanted to know why he had ignored Rose.

'So what is your uncle's name? Does he work around here?' I immediately saw her fear.

'Umm, yes, he works locally,' she said and stopped.

'But what is his name?' Her eyes darted around the room.

'Why do you want to know?' Nzoka boomed. 'It is no business of yours what the man is called, but if you are really interested, he is called Uncle. Is that okay with you?'

Rose was obviously uncomfortable with this conversation and so I let it go for the moment. I didn't want to make things more difficult for us all. But without conversation, there was nothing else to do. I was unable to look out of the window at the surroundings and there was little to occupy my mind within the room. Nzoka was dozing and so I took the opportunity to examine my ankle. It was still very painful although movement was a little easier, but still nowhere good enough for me to make a run for it, even if I knew where to run to.

My thoughts drifted back to Karisa, dear Karisa. I hoped he'd got my last message and in my mind's eye, I could see the anguish on his face when he realised that I was in trouble. It seemed a lifetime since I first met him as he picked me up from the airport and I could remember his face clearly when I told him why I was in Kenya and how eager he was to help me. I didn't expect he felt the same way now. The feelings that I'd been trying to keep hidden since Mombasa resurfaced so real that I heard myself gasp.

'Are you in pain?' Rose whispered to me.

'Yes, I am a little,' I said using this excuse to bring my thoughts back to the present. 'But don't worry, its easing now.'

Nzoka snored loudly. He obviously didn't think either of us were a threat.

'I need to ask you one question and I would like you to answer me honestly. Do you know the man whose room this is? Do you know this Uncle?' I said as quietly as I could.

She started to speak, then shook her head. The answer was obvious. 'Then I must ask are you and Nzoka really brother and sister?'

There was no time to get an answer, because the guard entered to allow the uncle in with some food. He was followed by a young boy, carrying a plastic jug and a washing up bowl for us to wash our hands in. Nzoka woke up with a grunt.

We ate in silence but my mind was racing. I was sure now that they weren't brother and sister and so one or both of them were lying. Rose had documents and Wambua had brought us to Nzoka. None of it made any sense and I was scared of who these people were: all of them. There was no way I was handing over money to these people and that put me at risk. I thought of Karisa and wanted him more than ever before. Even at a time like this, in a place like this, my love for him shone through.

Chapter Forty-Five
Karisa

Wambua trusted us enough to leave Samson and me alone to sleep. I awoke to Angela's message.

'Where is this church?' I showed him the message I had received as we ate breakfast in the room. 'Do you know this place?'

'I know the place.' For the first time, I felt hope. 'Then you must take me there immediately.'

'That, my brother, I cannot do. If I am seen with you then Nzoka will know that I have let you free and my life will be in danger. I am sorry. The barman will be suspicious that we have not returned this morning and may have already called Nzoka.' I was left with only one choice; I called Wambua. He was with us within half an hour.

Samson explained very carefully where he believed the church was and the best way for us to get to the area without attracting attention, and promised that after he had visited his home and his family to let them know that he was safe, he would return to the hotel. I doubted greatly that this would be so, but I remained silent. Wambua, myself, and his companion decided to split up and approach the church from different directions rather than travel together. Wambua set off alone and I was accompanied by his man.

The journey we took was no different from other journeys I had taken in Kenya. The *dukas* were the same, mostly painted bright green emblazoned with adverts for *Safaricom* phone network or a deep red, the colours, and lettering of *Coca-Cola*. The homes were the same also, mud on a wooden frame with *makuti* roofs or blocks badly cemented together to provide shelter. The very poor made their homes out of sacks and plastic sheeting, they had no other choice. But the churches were always full of people praising the God that left them in such poverty. Hope was a very strong drug and the 'Jesus loves me' church was no different; the voices of many people raised to heaven met us before we were able to see the building.

Wambua was already waiting for us, a cup of *chai* in his hand, and we walked up to him and greeted him like old friends casually meeting each other in order to not raise suspicion. But we were not fools; we knew that we would be recognised as strangers in the area and so it was important that we did not wait too long. We did not know whether Nzoka was nearby or not. Wambua finished his *chai* and returned the cup to the woman who had served him. I saw him lean to her and speak. He gave her some money and then he returned to us smiling.

'The message was true; she remembers the *mzungu* in the wheelchair being pushed by a large man and being escorted by a thin woman and Nzoka. He is known in these parts but he is not liked, which is much to our advantage. They stopped here and then went straight down the road. They must have turned off because when she looked again they had disappeared. So let us move down the road and see what we can find,' he said.

The three of us kept our distance from each other, looking in and past every home, shop, or alleyway as we moved. We walked for a long time down the road until we came to its end and we were at the very edge of the scrubland.

'We must have come too far. You said the woman believed

that they had turned off soon after the church as she could no longer see them,' I said, turning to Wambua.

'You are right, we must turn back, but this time let us go down the small paths leading from this main road. I will take one side of the road and you and my friend must take the other. Do not stop, do not do anything, just look and listen to the sounds around you and we will meet back at that church from where we started.'

And so we parted and began to search once more. I tried very hard to tune my listening for Angela's voice but could not hear it anywhere. People stared at us as we walked, fearful of the strangers among them, and so we did not linger as we moved through the area. We tried to approach someone to ask them about the *mzungu* but they backed away from us and so we left them alone. It took us some time, even though we walked quickly. There were many alleys and I insisted on checking every one and so by the time we reached the church and Wambua, he had been waiting for some time and was showing his impatience.

'I think it is time for us to leave now. We are beginning to be noticed and, although Nzoka may not be liked in these parts, we cannot be sure that he does not have some friends around.'

'We cannot just leave. Angela is around here somewhere, I know, and she is in much danger. I cannot walk away back to my beautiful hotel room and leave her here.'

'Mr Karisa, you need to keep your emotions and feelings of love under control. I, like you, want to find them and to get your lady friend back safe, but by remaining in this area we are putting her life in more danger. I do not want to arouse suspicion and then they move her to a different place. You are indeed right, she is probably still being kept around here, but at this moment in time, it is not easy to find out where, and so we need to leave now and return another time. Do not worry, my friend, we will find your love.'

Wambua was able to see straight into my heart and he was right, I must control how I felt. I was very concerned that we were leaving but I knew that it was the only thing to do, so taking one final look down the road hoping to see a something we had missed, we returned the way we had come each along our separate ways back to the hotel.

Surprisingly, Samson was in the reception waiting for us on our return and looked as sad as I was that we were not returning with Angela.

'She was not there?' he asked.

'She is there, my friend, that I believe, but we were unable to find her,' I said and went to reception to get the key to my room.

'Madam has left the room?' the man on the desk asked. 'I have not seen her. But the housekeeper says that her belongings are still there.' I told him she had gone to see friends for a couple of days and that she would return soon. I was not sure that he believed what I was saying was the truth.

Darkness was falling quickly and we had not eaten since breakfast and so Samson and I left the hotel straight away to find food to fill our stomachs. He was still very wary, but his need of food was greater than his fear. Even though I did not have much of an appetite, I managed to eat some *pilau* and he happily finished off what was left. I was very happy that he had returned and this increased my trust in him. He said his family were well and had told them that he may be away for a few nights but they were not to worry.

'I did not tell them anything about what I was doing or who

I was with, that way they could not tell anyone anything if they are asked and this may keep them safer. I told them if they felt in danger they were to return home to the *shamba* and my father's family upcountry. I left them all the money I had and then I came straight back as I said I would.'

Wambua and his friend decided to stay in the room with us for the night and so I got the key to Angela's room to sleep in; I told them she had asked for me to look for something for her. They did not question it and handed me the key. I needed to feel close to her, and the moment I opened the door, I felt her presence like a spirit come to give me hope. I lay down on the bed and wrapped my arms around the pillow next to me that held her fragrance and closed my eyes. My thoughts were only of her.

Chapter Forty-Six
Angela

'There have been some strangers spotted in the area.' Nzoka was not happy. 'This is not good news. We must leave now.'

The mention of strangers raised my hopes that they might have something to do with Wambua and Karisa, and so I knew I couldn't move too far from the 'Jesus loves me' church. I whispered to Rose that we must not move that the strangers may have been my friends.

She nodded her understanding. 'We do not have to be enemies. I will help if I can, but Nzoka is very angry and will want to leave.'

I was beginning to like Rose and this was making me even more confused. I still didn't know whether this woman was trying to con me out of fifty thousand pounds or not. Maybe she was playing the role of a downtrodden sister to gain my sympathy. I needed to toughen up.

'So, Nzoka, it seems that you are in a bit of a mess.' I felt rather than saw Rose's surprise as I spoke.

'Who asked you, woman? You need to shut your mouth; you are not safe with me.'

'Why am I not safe? I still have my money and that's what you want and I can't do anything more until you let me go.' I gave a small laugh; I was trying to be brave. But I could tell by the look on Rose's face that she thought I was being foolish and whispered to me to keep quiet. But I couldn't, the anger was boiling over.

'I'm a big fat cheque to you, Nzoka, nothing more, and I won't be giving you one single shilling until I am free. So we're at a stalemate. You have me but no money, I have the money and no freedom, and so I ask you again, how are you going to solve this mess we are in? You can keep moving me around but nothing changes. My friends are onto you and they will find you wherever you take me.'

I could see that I'd hit a nerve. He remained quiet and Rose, I saw, breathed a sigh of relief.

The guard outside the door, on hearing our exchange, moved to just inside the doorway and raised his eyebrows in my direction. I'd no idea what this meant and stared blankly back at him.

'Keep an eye on her,' Nzoka said, and rushed out of the room, leaving the three of us alone.

'Do not anger him please?' Rose pleaded. She knew as well as I did that if Nzoka lost his temper it was more likely to be her that suffered rather than me. I tried to explain.

'We can't carry on as we are. He has us all prisoner here, and if this continues, then he'll get more and more desperate. I know you're not his sister and therefore not the person who is in the will. I won't be giving any money to that man and as soon as he realises that, then all our lives are in danger.

I looked to the guard to see any reaction and he nodded in agreement and whispered, 'It is so.'

'Nzoka,' I shouted. 'I need to speak with you.' The guard went outside to summon him.

'What do you want, woman, screaming like that?'

I knew that he was rattled, but my patience was worn and I continued to yell. 'I need to speak with you. You don't scare me and if you lay another finger on your sister here then I'll scream even more.'

I saw a glimpse of anger flash across his face before a tight smile appeared. 'I am here now, so what do you want to speak to me about?'

'It's time I went back to my friends. I've been away from them far too long and you know as well as me that they'll have called the police now. You know that once the police get involved, then the British Embassy will be too. It's a very serious crime to kidnap someone and you could go to prison for a very long time. As far as I can see, you have two choices. You can carry on as you are, moving me around until the police catch up with you, and they will. Or you can let me go and get the money organised with the lawyer and the bank. Without my okay, nothing further can happen. The choice is yours. But without me speaking to the lawyer and letting him know my agreement, nothing will change, and we'll just wait here until the police arrive and take you to prison.' My bravery was growing and for the first time in a long time, there were no tremors of a panic attack or even nervousness.

Nzoka was silent and stepped outside once again.

Rose collapsed onto the sofa and was holding her head in her hands. 'He will be very angry,' she said and when a short time later Nzoka came back into the room, she involuntarily put her hands over her head in preparation of the expected blows. But none came.

Nzoka walked calmly over to me, told Rose to leave and sat next to me on the sofa. 'What you say has some truth in it, but you did not include the choice I have to hurt you both. Your courage may be showing now but I think it would not be there should I start to beat my sister.'

225

'Why would you beat her? Without her, you have no claim on the money. She's the person who is mentioned in the will. It's to her that the money will go, not to you. So if you hurt her then there'll be no money from me, be assured I'll make sure that you don't get one single shilling.'

'Why do you care what happens to this woman? She was married to your husband; she slept with him while you were at home. She has the proof that she was his before you were, why does her safety matter to you?'

I almost told him that I knew the truth to wipe the smug smirk off his face, but I bit my tongue hard. 'It was my husband that did wrong, not her, and if she's entitled to the money then she must have it.'

Once again Nzoka left the room. I was concerned that Rose hadn't come back as I wasn't sure what he would do. But all remained quiet and I was left to gather my thoughts on what my next plan of action was going to be.

'You must be mindful of this man and woman,' said the guard as he entered the room. 'They will trick you if you do not watch them.'

Looking over his shoulder through the doorway, I could see them walking towards me. The guard quickly went outside. Nzoka had his arm around Rose, looking very happy as he entered. She, on the other hand, was looking very nervous as she came back into the room and sat herself on the floor near the door as if she might bolt at any time.

'My sister and I have discussed your conversation from earlier and feel that what you say offers us some very clear options. I am glad that you have finished your investigation into my sister here and believe her to be the woman that you seek, and so all that is left now is for you to give the all-clear for the money to be released to her. I believe that is right?'

'There is just one thing that she will have to do in order to get the money, and that's to come with me to the lawyer's in Nairobi and sign some papers. You see, Rose may have all the documentation concerning the marriage, but we need to make sure that the signatures match up with the ones on record.' I was lying through my teeth. I didn't know whether there was any such thing as a signature on record, but what I did know was that this woman, whether she was called Rose or not, was definitely not the sister of Nzoka and therefore he wasn't getting his hands on any of the money.

I saw the glance between them but Nzoka quickly regained his composure. Rose's face told me otherwise. He told her to leave and settled himself at the other end of the sofa demanding that *chai* be brought for both of us.

'Well, this is a pleasant change, you and me having tea together, very civilised.'

'Do not think that you are winning. I still have you prisoner, and I do not see any police running to save you. Maybe your friends do not care for you as much as you think they do.'

A vision of both Karisa and Gabriel came unbidden into my head and I couldn't help but smile. I knew they both cared for me with a love Nzoka would never understand or would never know and I told him so.

He looked away. Once again I'd hit a nerve. 'If you think that I have never known love, then you are mistaken.' His words caught me off guard.

'I am sorry, I did not mean…' I began but he put his hand up to stop me and remained silent for some minutes.

'I may not have known the love of a good woman in the

way that your friend loves you,' he said. 'You think that I did not see the fear and concern in his eyes when I took you away? You think I do not know that look? I too have felt that fear and I know that it is love.'

I took a sip of the sweet milky tea to calm me before I spoke again. 'Tell me about it?'

'Why should I do that? That was a long time ago and it is of no consequence now. What happened cannot be undone, it is all past now. But you, woman, can help to take some of the pain away, by giving my sister what is rightly due to her and to do it immediately You may think that I am an evil man, but sometimes things happen in our lives that change us beyond our knowing and we find ourselves doing things that we would not want to do but that are necessary to make amends.'

I didn't reply to him. I didn't know what to say. I knew he was revealing something to do with the situation I was in, but I couldn't understand it. There'd been a great pain in his life but what did it have to do with me? I hadn't a clue what he was talking about. The *chai* finished, he didn't give me a chance to find out more. He stood up and walked to the door.

'We will speak again,' he said.

Chapter Forty-Seven
Karisa

I had a bad dream last night about Angela. She was in great danger and I could not get to her. I tried to go towards her but my legs would not move. She was shouting for my help and I could not give it. This morning I wanted to visit a wise man to explain to me my dream, but I was too afraid to do so. What if it meant that something very bad had happened to her? I went back to my own room. I was going to tell the others of my dream but I could not, I did not know why. I felt that if I spoke it then it would come true. That was what they believed in my village.

Everyone was already up and leaving for breakfast as I arrived and so I followed them, but I had no hunger. The dream played on my mind. Why had we not called the police? Should we have done so? Angela had been taken away from us and now this was the third day without her return. It was time to call the police and I said so.

'No, no, that is not a good idea,' Wambua said immediately. He did not even stop to think.

'But Angela is in great danger and we do not know where she is. I cannot understand why we have not done this before. Surely we must speak to the police.'

The more I thought about it, the more I realised how foolish we had been not involving them before but Wambua was so certain that this was a bad idea.

My anger overflowed. 'You must tell me your reason why.'

He called for me to follow him outside the hotel and took me to a place behind the building.

'We do not need to inform the police,' he said in a whisper, 'Because they already know of the situation.'

'How do they know that? I do not understand.'

'I am a member of the police force and so is my companion. The man that your friend contacted in Mombasa is also a policeman. He is very high up and he arranged for our meeting when you arrived here. Once your friend spoke in Mombasa, we knew that the woman you sought was connected with a man that we wanted also and so we helped you to come to this town with the hope that you would help us.'

I could no longer control my anger. 'So you knew that we were in danger and yet you allowed Angela to be taken like this and you did nothing?'

'We did not expect this to happen; we thought it would be very simple. But I do not believe that she is in any danger at the moment. Nzoka will not do anything to her until he holds the money.'

I decided to phone Joseph. I was scared for Angela. My voice was small when he answered the phone. It would not say the words that I wanted to say; the words that were in my heart. But he is a wise man and he heard my pain.

'Remain calm, Karisa, I'll go to see my man in town and see what he can tell me about the situation. I don't think he's been entirely honest with me and I'm not very happy about this. Keep your phone with you and I shall be back in touch as soon as I can.' He rang off before I had chance to say anything in reply.

Wambua was in deep conversation with his companion

when I returned to him and told him of the conversation I had just had with Joseph.

'Your friend speaks wisdom. Now I think we should return to where we were yesterday. Hopefully, if there has been any movement in the area people will have noticed. Will you join us in the search for your friend?'

I told him that, of course, I would be joining them and asked why would they think otherwise. I was still very angry but knew the only option we had at the moment was to continue the search.

This time Samson said he would come with us. 'I may be able to get more information out of the people in the area.' I was thankful for his help. I knew he was putting himself in great danger.

We left the hotel but the dream would not leave my head and I wished that I had been able to speak to the wise man. My mother always believed that dreams are messages from the spirits and, if this was the case, then they were telling me that Angela was in trouble and we needed to find her very soon. This time Samson insisted he remained with me and so Wambua travelled one way to the church, his companion another, and Samson and I a new way that we did not search yesterday.

'I have had calls from Nzoka,' Samson said as we walked. 'I did not answer the first one, but then I thought he would send people to find me if I did not answer when he rung again. I told him that I was still guarding you but that we had moved to a friend's house. He did not ask where this friend was. He asked if you had phoned the police and I was able to confirm that you had not. He was relieved at this news and told me I was doing good work. I think he is not far away and he will feel that he is safe knowing that you have not called the police.'

The search for Angela came to an end the moment I received a phone call back from Joseph. He told me that his contact in Mombasa had said that we were putting her in more danger by being seen to be searching for her and we were to stop immediately. So our search went no further. We met outside the 'Jesus loves me' church, sat down for a soda together, and then returned to the hotel the way that we had come.

I was very concerned about this change of plan. But once Wambua had spoken to Joseph's contact, he agreed that it would be foolish to continue the hunt at this moment and so all we could do was to remain at the hotel until we got further instructions.

Wambua was happy to let Samson return to his family should he so wish, but he wanted to stay, saying that it was very important to him that the lady was found safe and well and also that Nzoka was arrested and punished for what he had done. I was very grateful to have him remain with us. I was still not sure whether I trusted Wambua completely or understood what was happening. Samson was someone that I could talk to and voice my fears and know that he understood.

The day dragged on and I was losing hope of anything happening when there was a knock on the door and I was very surprised to see Joseph accompanied by a much taller Kenyan man.

'It's good to see you, old chap.' He gave me a big hug. 'I couldn't stay away. I spoke to Mr Munga, my friend here, and we decided it was time we travelled to you.'

It was good to see him again. His presence gave me comfort and hope. Mr Munga and Wambua disappeared into the corridor to talk, and this was my chance to introduce Samson and explain his part. Joseph said he was very pleased to make his acquaintance and was grateful that he had turned to the right path and decided to help. He seemed to be overwhelmed by what had been said to him and simply nodded and shook his hand when it was offered. The two men came back into the room and asked us all to sit down.

'First of all,' Mr Munga said. 'Let me tell you that I believe that your friend is safe and well and being kept not far from where you have been searching. But it is just as well that you did not find her as Nzoka could do something that would have been dangerous to your friend. You may wonder why finding someone mentioned in a dead man's will in the UK has become so difficult and potentially unsafe for you all. I will try to explain all that we know in the hope that it will give you further understanding of the task ahead.

'Rose is not the person that is mentioned in the will; she is not even the sister of Nzoka. She is an old prostitute who works for that man and owes him a lot of money. We suspect she agreed to play the sister in order to help to get the money and to have her debts removed. Also, we believe that Mr Nzoka is not the person behind the cheating of your friend. He, like Rose, has, we think, been promised money to pay off a considerable debt that he owes to another man. That man is the man we seek and although we have our suspicions we are still not one hundred per cent certain who this man is and this is why we have to allow the whole transaction to happen. If we interfere at this moment in time, all that will happen is that Nzoka and Rose will be arrested and sent to jail, but these are just small players in this game, but if we let the situation continue then we will find out who is behind it all and stop him.'

We all remained silent and I tried hard to control my emotions and to understand what Mr Munga had said. His certainty that Angela was safe was not enough for me. I wanted her back here with me. Joseph, I could see, was also having difficulty understanding what had been said.

'I didn't realise that Nzoka was not the man that we sought,' he said. 'Had I known this was a police investigation into something larger, I wouldn't have involved you, Mr Munga, and I can't say that I'm happy for Angela to be caught up in this sordid little affair. This is not sporting at all!' He stormed out of the room and I followed.

'You have to believe me Karisa,' he said, once we were alone. 'I had no idea anything like this was going on. Munga told me he could help me to find the woman and I believed it was only that. Why didn't you contact me sooner, surely you didn't believe I knew this would happen, for God's sake?'

'I did not think to contact you because I did not understand myself what was going on. I had to find the courage to support Angela; she was determined to meet this woman. Even when she hurt her ankle that was not going to stop her. I was frightened to contact anybody else in case it put her life in danger, and also Wambua told me not to speak to anyone and now I know why. I feel so foolish.'

'We've both been foolish, my friend, that, I can tell you. But now we know the whole story, we have little choice but to help them and pray to God that Angela is kept safe. Let's go back into the room and listen fully to what they have to say and what their plan is. It's important that we know exactly what's going on from now on. We can't let them have any more secrets from us.' We turned and walked back to the room.

Nothing more was said of the situation for a while and I

accompanied Joseph and Mr Munga to the reception to organise a room for them to stay in.

'Your lady friend still does not return from her trip?' the receptionist asked. 'That is the only room that is not being used. If you want to stay here, then you must take that room. Your friend stays away for a long time?' We decided that myself and Joseph would move into Angela's room for the moment and that would leave Mr Munga and Wambua to share my room with his bodyguard. As for Samson, should he choose to stay, he could share with us.

Night was drawing on and so Joseph, Samson, and I went for a walk. None of us were hungry but Joseph said he needed a drink.

'So tell me everything,' he said, taking a large mouthful of his beer. 'Do you believe, Samson, that Angela is safe with Nzoka?'

He, I could see, was shocked at being addressed so directly by Joseph and struggled to answer at first. 'Nzoka is not a good man and is much feared in the area. He is also a clever man and a very greedy man. He will not do anything to your friend until he has the money, I believe. But if he finds out you know the truth, he will become nervous. That will be the time that it will be dangerous for your friend. So we must pray to Almighty God that he is not aware of what is known by you people.'

'Amen to that!' Joseph said.

I was grateful for the time away from Wambua and the opportunity to be totally honest with Joseph around my fears for Angela. He cared for her deeply as well, and would do everything in his power to make sure she was returned to us safely. So with this assurance in my heart, I quickly fell asleep once I got back to our room. I gave Joseph the clean unused bed in the room and I happily slept in the one that had been used by Angela. I could still smell her perfume on the pillow. Samson declined a bed even though I offered him mine, saying he would prefer to sleep on the floor as he did so at home and he would be very comfortable. It felt like I had only just closed my eyes before I was woken by banging on the door. Mr Munga entered the room. It was dawn.

'Time for us to plan forward,' said Wambua following close behind. I pushed the covers away and prepared to listen.

'Mr Munga is not known in the area that we have been searching and would attract some attention if he wandered alone. So we propose that he goes with Samson to the area and, if there is a church service going on, that they both attend this. I know that it will be obvious to everyone that Mr Munga is not from the Akamba tribe and they may be able to recognise that he is Giriama, but that is of no consequence. All Mr Samson needs to say, if he is asked, is that he is a guest in his house and a distant relative of a brother cousin. No one will pay any further attention.'

'What about me?' Joseph said.

'You, sir, will have to remain at the hotel with Karisa and I. A *mzungu* will cause too much notice and that would not be good for your friend.'

I could see that he was not happy about this and opened his mouth to speak again but I put my hand on his arm to calm him and he remained silent. He pulled me to one side of the room once Mr Munga and Samson had left. 'I need to have a word with you.'

We both made our excuses to leave and return to our room.

'You must not leave the hotel and must return once this is done,' Wambua said.

On closing the hotel room door behind us, Joseph said that we ought to inform Angela's family what was going on with their mother. I was very afraid to do that and told him so. I told him of my concerns with Mark and felt that he would blame me for what had happened to his mother. But he was sure that the family must be told and thankfully, he offered to do this.

'But first, we need to get our story straight. I don't want to alarm them unduly, but, heaven forbid, if something does happen to Angela and they aren't aware of this, then it would damn us in Hell for all eternity.' It was strange to hear Joseph talking about Hell. I had never known him to be a believer or attend any church and this news brought me comfort.

I closed my eyes to pray as he picked up his phone to dial Mark's number.

Chapter Forty-Eight
Angela

The conversation with Nzoka I'd had a few hours ago was running round my head. There was a side to him that was kept hidden. A side that had been hurt badly by something, and I was intrigued by it. But as night fell, I was confronted by the old Nzoka.

'Get into the room and do as you are told.'

I could hear his voice and, seconds later, Rose was forced into the room and took her usual place on the floor by the door. He followed immediately behind her. She seemed even more uncomfortable than usual and found it hard to settle down. Once or twice she asked if she could go for a walk outside, but this was forbidden.

'Why do you want to walk with the snakes at night? You are much safer in here where I can keep an eye on you.'

I recognised that feeling of everything being forbidden and felt pity for her. Nzoka liked to control, just like George, but all it bred was resentment and I could see that in her eyes and the way she clenched her jaw. There was hate but Nzoka was oblivious to it. He made himself comfortable on the sofa and faced me.

'So, *mzungu*, since our last conversation, I have had many thoughts about our situation, but I do not trust you as I know that you do not trust me. The only way forward for both of us is for the lawyer to come to us here and the papers can then be signed. You must phone him and ask the question.'

'I don't think that this will be possible,' I began.

'But how can you know if you have not contacted him to see if it can be done? I believe that Rose has the number.'

Nzoka handed me a phone to use but realised it needed charging and told the guard to go and get it charged at a local *duka*. He left the room to get the charger. 'Come, Rose, help me look,' he said, leaving me alone with the guard.

This was my chance and I knew I had to take the risk that the guard would help. 'Please could you try and get my phone charged also,' I said digging it out of my bra. 'I don't have the charger but maybe you could find one for me.'

He turned his head to look around to check that no one could see us and then swiftly put the phone in his pocket. 'I will do my best,' he whispered before Nzoka came back into view, carrying his phone charger.

'You must remain with the phone as it charges fully. I will stay in this room to guard this woman.'

It was beginning to annoy me that he never used my name. 'I have a name,' I said. 'I would be grateful if you would address me so.'

'Okay, Mrs Trippett.' He laughed. 'But of course there is the other Mrs Trippett, the first Mrs Trippett. You are only number two.' He knew he had angered me and that made him laugh even more. 'So, number two, what do you think of me? You can tell me the truth. I can see it in your eyes.'

I wanted to slap him hard but I was too far away from him and the distance was my safety for what I was about to say. 'Okay, if you want the truth… then I think you are a bully. A cruel man who likes to always be in control and doesn't have a heart.'

He broke into a smile as I spoke. 'If I do not have a heart, as you say, then how do I keep breathing?'

'Oh, you may physically have a heart that pumps your sordid blood around your body, but you don't have a heart that cares,' I said.

'How do you know?'

'What?'

'How can you be so sure that I do not have a heart that cares? You do not know me at all,' he said.

'I know enough of you to form a judgement. I've seen your cruelty to your own sister, the way you've beaten her, and I believe that if I wasn't a means of money to you then you would probably do the same to me. That's not a man who cares. That's a monster.'

The smile disappeared. Had I gone too far? I could not afford to make him angry, not while we were alone. 'You make your judgement very easily, but you do not know anything. Sometimes things can happen that change us forever. Sometimes things that we would have thought of as sinful once may not seem so bad when they are necessary...' He looked at me for a reaction. I refused to give him one. He continued.

'You *mzungu,* you have no idea what it is like to live my life. You have all the riches that you need, you have free education and you have free medical, what more can you need? But you talk of me not having a heart that cares and yet you hold your greed in your heart. My sister is entitled to the money from your husband's will for the suffering she endured from him, and yet you hold onto this money. You remain rich while those that have suffered remain poor.' He looked at me with disgust and went to leave the room, but realising that the guard wasn't there, was forced to remain outside by the door.

I stumbled to the door. 'What suffering?' He didn't speak. 'You mentioned suffering for your sister. What suffering was it?' I shouted.

'It was nothing,' he said. 'Forget I spoke of it.'

'Now that it's been said, I can't forget it. Nzoka, I'm learning things that I didn't know about my husband and if you know something and you know for certain that it's true, then you must tell me.'

'I do not have to tell you anything, *mzungu*! But if you want to hear about your wonderful husband and what he did to my family, maybe I *will* tell you.' He turned back into the room and sat down. 'My sister met your husband a long time ago, as you are aware. I warned her about him. I quickly understood that he was not a nice person, but she would not listen to me and she would go off to meet him whenever she could.'

'Where did she meet him?' I asked.

'My sister was an educated woman and she worked in an office in Nairobi,' he said. 'I am not sure, but I believe that she met him in this office. What does it matter?'

I noticed that he'd said his sister '*was*' an educated woman, but I didn't mention it to him. I didn't want to stop him talking. I already knew that the Rose with us couldn't read or write, she'd admitted the lie when we'd spoken.

'She saw him many nights a week. She shared a room with two other girls, and it was them that told me when I went to visit that there were nights when she did not come home. In Kenya, this is the sign of a bad woman, a woman who has fallen from God and has become sinful. I told her this many times, but she would not listen. I kept all this from my parents as I did not want to concern them. But I think they suspected that something was wrong when she stopped visiting them. She told them that

241

she was an important secretary and was too busy to come home. That was wrong; no one should be too busy to visit their parents. They had educated her. Many people had told them not to bother with educating a daughter and it would be a waste of time. That she should be taught how to wash clothes, cook meals, fetch water, and prepare for the day when a man would take her as his own. But they did not listen. Rose was bright, they used to say, brighter than me, and she should be educated. And so, they saved as much as they could and they sold what they had to sell. When I had finished my secondary education, I was sent to work on my uncle's *shamba* to help to pay for her education. She went to college. I had to stay on the farm and work my fingers to the bone to help to pay for that, and she said she was too busy to visit the parents that gave her everything. She was a very bad woman.'

Nzoka began to pace the room, his fists were clenched. I was frightened and watched nervously as he continued to walk back and forward, but I wanted him to carry on. 'Was it just your sister and you in the family?'

He stopped and looked out of the window, like he was searching for someone or something. 'There were other children born to my parents, but like most families in Kenya, they did not survive. The sickness of malaria got them and I remember my father many times carrying the body of one of my brothers or sisters outside and digging a hole to bury them. They were so small and the holes seemed so deep for their tiny bodies. In total, eight children were born. Two survived. I was the second son born but the only son left and therefore I was destined to be the head of the family. But I was not as smart as my sister and the education that should have been mine, went to her.'

'What happened to your sister when she got involved with

my husband?' He paced like he was caged.

'For a long time I did not know. Nobody knew. She could not be found. I used a lot of the money that I had loaned from people to travel into Nairobi to look for her. Her friends said that she had left the rooms they had shared, and they had not heard from her since that time. I even went to her office, but they also told me that she had left and gone away. I had no idea where to look next and so I stopped looking and went home to my parents. All the money spent on her education and she had abandoned her family. That was when hate started to grow in my heart. Up until that point, *mzungu,* I had been a good person.'

He was about to continue when the guard returned, holding up Nzoka's phone fully charged. Suddenly, his mood changed.

'But, as you can see, I did find her and I brought her back home with me. She is happy. Now, Mrs Trippett number two, it is time for you to do as you said you would and phone your lawyer. I have the number written down here.' He handed me a crumpled up bit of paper. 'It is time for us to get what we are due. I have good hearing, so I will hear everything that you say, do not worry about that.'

As Nzoka turned away the guard quickly handed me my phone. I hid it before anyone saw.

243

Chapter Forty-Nine
Angela

The phone was answered immediately.

'Why are you ringing me again?' a voice snapped.

'I am sorry; perhaps I have the wrong number. My name is Angela Trippett and I'm wishing to speak to Mr Daniels. I'm sorry to disturb you.'

'No, please do not hang up!' The voice changed to the simpering, whining voice that I recognised. 'It was me that mistook the number on my phone. I didn't realise that it was you,' he said. I wondered who he thought was ringing.

'Whoever you thought it was made you very angry,' I said.

'That is of no matter; we now know who each of us is talking to. So how may I help you, Mrs Trippett?'

With Nzoka standing outside, listening hard to what I was saying, I knew that I had to get to the point that he wanted to hear. 'I believe that I've located the woman that's mentioned in my husband's will.' The lie stuck in my throat. 'Therefore, I know that this is very irregular, but I was wondering if you'd be able to travel to us to complete any necessary documentation. It appears that she's unable to travel to your office.' I expected excuses but there were none.

'I don't see that being a problem at all. Of course, there would be extra charges incurred in doing this. But I'm sure that you're more than happy to pay these to get the matters finished with. Shall we say tomorrow at noon?'

'That will be fine,' I said, and before I could say anything else, he rang off. I hadn't given him any information about where we were going to meet. Nzoka was very happy when he re-entered the room.

'That is a good job. We can soon get this sorted.'

He didn't stay for long, and the minute he left, Rose came into the room. Nzoka was giving her much more freedom and she was able to almost come and go as she wished, or so I thought. But he was using her to clean the school as payment to his uncle for using his room for the past few days. She didn't seem to mind. 'I prefer it to sitting in this room all day waiting to see what mood that man is in.'

I told her that the lawyer was coming to us tomorrow, but didn't mention my concerns about his part in all this.

'I heard Nzoka speaking to him a minute ago,' she said innocently.

'Why would he be speaking to the lawyer?' I asked.

'Oh, I do not know, I thought perhaps you had told him to do so.' I asked her if she'd ever spoken to him and she said she'd never had a reason.

'I have to get a message to my friends,' I said. 'Can you tell me the name of the school?'

'I am not sure that I should. If Nzoka finds out, he will beat me severely.' I understood her reluctance and so I didn't push it. But I could tell that she was thinking about what I'd just asked. She got up to leave. 'St Anthony's,' she whispered and left.

Now I had the name of the school as well as the name of the nearby church, I had to take the risk of sending a message quickly to Karisa before anyone returned to the room, so I typed the details and pressed send. I immediately turned the sound off and hid the phone once again in my bra. I hoped that the

245

message had gone through, the signal was very weak but I didn't have any other choice. I'd just hidden the phone when Nzoka returned and I challenged him.

'I've contacted the lawyer as you told me to, but I have a real concern. He told me he would be here tomorrow, but he doesn't know where '*here*' is. He rang off before I could tell him.'

'I do not understand what you are saying,' he said.

'What I am saying, Mr Nzoka is that I didn't give him any details of where we were to meet and he never asked for them. Why do you think that is? It's like he knew where to come.'

I caught a snap of fear in his eyes but it quickly disappeared. 'The man must be an imbecile. You must call him back and give him the details immediately. He is a very stupid man.'

He handed me the phone once again and I called the number. This time he didn't answer. I pretended otherwise and spoke the details of the meeting. The phone remained unanswered. I handed the phone back and Nzoka shoved it in his shirt pocket without question.

'Now all we can do is wait until noon tomorrow. So make yourself comfortable. This could be your last day with us. I have arranged a feast for you. Today we will eat meat. Uncle has slaughtered a goat for us and we shall enjoy that later in your honour.'

I told him that the only thing he could do in my honour would be to let me go.

'Maybe tomorrow,' he laughed.

My ankle had been improving steadily and I wanted to walk to build up my strength, but my requests to go outside had always been denied. Today, however, Nzoka was in a much better mood and he allowed the guard to escort me to the school and said that I could do my exercise in the empty classrooms. It had been closed for the holidays and the uncle should've been preparing it for re-opening the following week. But now he had Rose to do his work for him, and I found him fast asleep on two plastic chairs. He woke up, though, as I drew near. He was still wary of the *mzungu*.

The ankle held up well on the short walk from the room to the school. I left the guard in the school hall and went to find Rose. The school was no different from other schools I'd seen in Kenya, a flat single storey, built of breeze blocks with a corrugated tin roof. The classrooms looked very small for the amount of desks that were piled up at one end of them and I could see where Rose had swept. There was very little breeze blowing through from the tiny windows and I imagined how hot and sticky it would be for the children trying to learn.

Looking around, I thought of Gabriel, laughing and joking, running about in his new school in the village. I missed him so much. I sat down at one of the teacher's desks to rest my ankle, and looked at the torn posters on the wall, showing the human body and the different parts of a plant. I remembered learning them myself at school a million years ago. I pictured my boys starting school, both of them so brave. Their father had told them not to cry, that only women did that and, bless them, they did as they were told. They were too afraid to do otherwise, we all were. I was still miles away when Rose came into the classroom.

'Are you okay, Angela?'

'Yes, I am. Don't worry. I was just thinking of my children back in England.'

'You have not spoken about your family. How many

children do you have?' she asked.

'Oh, Rose, they aren't children any more. They have grown up and left home. I have two boys, but they'll always be my babies, even if sometimes our relationships are difficult. Do you have children?'

'I am not blessed so, and for a Kenyan woman, that is a great tragedy. Without children to look after you as you age, you will die early. I am too old to have children now and so life will be very tough for me.'

'What about your brother?'

'Both you and I know, Angela, that man is not my brother. He does not care for me. He just uses me and I allow him to do so because I have no one else.'

I felt so sorry for this woman sat beside me. As we spoke, two women bound by the circumstances of my husband's death, it didn't seem to matter whether she was the other Mrs Trippett or not.

The guard appeared before we could talk anymore and told us that Nzoka wanted me to return immediately to the room where he wished to speak with me.

'Did you enjoy your exercise?' he said, as I walked through the door. 'Is your leg fully recovered now?'

I told him I'd enjoyed the walk but I played down how much improved my ankle was. I didn't want my movements curtailed any more that they were already. So I made much effort in sitting back down on the sofa. 'You said you wanted to talk with me?' I said.

'Yes, I wanted to make sure that you have arranged for the money to come with the lawyer tomorrow.' For obvious reasons, I hadn't mentioned this to the lawyer as I was still very suspicious of everyone involved and I didn't have the money to give but I told Nzoka that I'd done as he'd asked.

'Are you sure you have done so?'

'Yes, I am, why are you questioning me?'

'I am just checking, because if this was not the case and the money did not arrive, then it would be very bad news for Rose and yourself. Do not think for one moment that you can cheat me. For if you do, then I will have nothing to lose, will I?'

I knew then, that he'd been in contact with the lawyer while I'd been in the school. He knew I hadn't mentioned the money.

'If I was you, I would phone him to make sure he understands fully what his task is tomorrow.' And for the third time, he handed me his phone.

This time I did as I was told.

Chapter Fifty
Karisa

I thanked the Lord God Almighty that I had received a message from Angela! This message was the answer to all my prayers and I rushed to show it to Mr Munga and Wambua. I wanted to show Joseph first but he had driven to Nairobi to collect Angela's sons. It unsettled me to meet Mr Mark again. I did not know the other son.

Mr Munga was happy to read the message from Angela.

'This is good news, my friend. Now we know exactly where she is being kept. Let us hope that they do not move her before we are able to get to her.'

'So we must begin soon?' I said. 'I will phone Joseph and let him know. Her family will be very happy when they get here and see her back with us.'

'My friend, we are not going to bring her back today,' Mr Munga said. 'As I said before, the people that are holding her are not the people that we seek. They have not moved her for a reason and that must mean something is about to happen very soon.'

'But she is in great danger. We know where she is and we need to go and collect her and bring her back to safety.' My voice rose along with my anger. Why would they not let us go to find my Angela?

'Please try to understand, Mr Karisa,' Wambua took over. 'She is not in any danger at the moment that we can safely assume. As Mr Munga here says, she is being kept in the same place for a reason. Her last message said she was near the "Jesus loves me" church, and this does not seem to have changed. Please let us wait for another day and see what happens. In the meantime, Mr Samson and Mr Munga can go out and about in the area again to see if they can determine anything. The people round about that area now have seen that Mr Munga is a guest of Mr Samson and so will not be suspicious of them. If all of us go there now, even without the *mzungu*, then Nzoka is likely to get knowledge of it and they will move. Please be patient that is all we ask, and trust us. We know what we are doing.'

I was unable to trust them but I did not tell them. The most important thing was that Angela was returned to me quickly and without harm. But at least we would have some good news for Joseph and Angela's sons when they arrived at the hotel.

I was wrong. Her sons were very upset that Angela was not back with us and they were extremely angry that we knew where she was and we had done nothing to help her. Mr Mark particularly was not happy and he regarded me with hateful looks when he came into the reception. The other son introduced himself to everybody as Josh, and I remembered him being the son Angela had spoken of. Mr Mark demanded that everyone went to the room to talk rather than out in public. I was not included.

'I don't want that man anywhere near me or my mother. This is his fault, I know it is, and I'll see that he pays for this.'

Joseph placed his arm around my shoulder and led me away from the reception. 'Don't worry; he's just very angry and upset. He'll see reason I'm sure of it.' He left me alone while he joined the others.

I sat outside the hotel. I needed to feel the air on my face. There was heaviness in my heart, not just because I ached for Angela, but also because I was being blamed. I had done nothing wrong and yet I knew that Mr Mark believed that I had caused everything that had happened to her. He had always believed that I wanted to take her money away and this gave me great hurt. I loved Angela with all my heart. I did not want even one shilling that was hers, but that was difficult for people to understand. I could even see it in the faces of Wambua and Mr Munga. They had seen it many times before. The young African who clung to the older *mzungu* in order to gain a better life and more money in exchange for a little loving. But Angela and I were different. I would die for her!

Joseph came to check on me occasionally but the rest remained from me for many hours, finally, as the meeting ended, both he and Samson came to find me.

'Let's go and eat,' he said. 'Away from the hotel, and then we can tell you what was discussed.' The three of us walked out into town and found a place to talk freely.

'First off, Karisa, please don't worry about what Mark is saying. He's not in his right mind and he needs someone to blame for what's happened to his mother. It's easy to blame you because of the arguments that you've had before, and he has no one else to. He's not brave enough to blame me because he knows that I'd challenge him, but deep down he knows there's no evidence around you. As for the meeting, Samson here will tell you that there was nothing spoken about that we don't already know. Angela's sons had a lot of questions to ask and we had to give them answers that they were satisfied with. They don't understand the way of Africa and they, like you, were angry that she was now involved in something much greater than finding a woman mentioned in their father's will.'

'That man Mark is very angry,' said Samson. 'And his anger is blinding him to reason. His brother is much calmer and speaks with wisdom. Mr Joseph is right; you must not worry about the crazy one.'

I thanked them both for letting me know what had been said and told them that I felt much better knowing that they were now with me. We all ordered some *pilau*, but my appetite was gone and I ate very little. I offered what was left to Samson; he took it outside in a plastic bag and gave it to a beggar on the street. 'How can I be greedy and eat more than I need when there are people hungry outside the door?' he said.

When we arrived back at the hotel, I went to the room, while Joseph and Samson went to find the others. Within five minutes of lying on my bed, there was a knock at the door. I ignored it, I wanted to be alone, but the knock came again and so I opened the door a small amount to see who it was.

It was Mr Josh. 'Karisa, I'm sorry to disturb you, but I would like to talk with you.'

'Is your brother with you?'

'No, he's not. It's only me and all I want is to have a quiet conversation with you. I know a little of what's been going on with your journey up country with my mother, and I know that she's very fond of you. My brother is angry and I understand that because I was angry with my mother too. I know you and him have argued in the past. I know my brother, I have lived with him all of my life, and we don't always see eye to eye. So this is why I came to find you. I want to hear what you have to say about matters and then I can make my own judgement.'

I was not sure that I could tell this man everything that had happened, but he was Angela's son and so he deserved to be told about our journey. I was not ready to trust him yet with my feelings for his mother. He listened very quietly as I told him about Gabriel, about his mother being ill, and about being directed to Wambua, through Joseph's contact in Mombasa. The rest I left safely tucked deep in my heart.

'So you had no idea that my mother was going to be taken like this?'

'That is true. In fact, I tried to stop your mother from meeting up with Nzoka, but she met him on her own and she was going to do so again even after she had injured her ankle. I did not want to go but I would not let her go alone. I myself was held prisoner by Mr Samson for a short while. But deep down he is a good man, and I was able to talk him round, at great risk to himself. Both he and I thought that your mother would only be gone for a couple of hours in order to meet up with this woman Rose but she never returned. I know your brother believes that I only want your mother's money, but you must believe me that I do not. The person that directed us was a contact of Joseph's, not mine, and the same with Wambua. Surely if I had wanted your mother's money, I would have done this myself without these people. Your mother is a good woman who has suffered a terrible loss with her husband. She is my friend and I would lay down my life to know that she is safe.'

'Let's hope that none of us have to do that,' he said. 'I want you to know that I believe you. Both Wambua and Mr Munga confirmed your innocence in these matters, but my brother can sometimes be foolish and doesn't easily forgive. I ask you to try to understand his anger and don't let it get to you.' He shook my hand and walked towards the door.

'You are a very lucky man to have a woman such as Angela as your mother.'

'I know,' he said and was gone.

Laying back down on the bed to think about what Mr Josh had said, I was once again disturbed. This time by Joseph, asking me to come downstairs to meet with the others.

I could feel the anger from Mr Mark as I entered. He was not happy that I was there. Everyone was there and it was Mr Munga who took control.

'I am concerned that there are those of us among this group who may feel the need to take matters into their own hands,' he said. 'I have to tell you this now that it cannot be so. We are dealing with a police investigation and we are at a critical stage. I know that some of you have concerns about the way that this is being dealt with and are worried about the safety of the captive...'

'That "captive" you are talking about is my fucking mother,' shouted Mr Mark. 'And you are damn well right we are concerned. I swear to God if one hair on her head is...'

'Mark, for God's sake, will you shut up and bloody listen for once in your life?' Mr Josh shouted back.

He muttered something under his breath and sat back in his chair, his arms folded tight and a look of murder on his face.

'I am sorry, Mr Mark, I did not mean to offend you, but as we have said numerous times, we do not believe that your mother is in any danger at the moment. However, because she has not been moved, we believe that something may be about to happen and we cannot make them suspicious. That is why, as we planned earlier, myself and Mr Samson will be returning to the area of the "Jesus loves me" church to see if we can pick up anything. It is really, really important that the rest of you remain in the hotel and do not try to follow us or begin any enquiries of your own. Wambua will stay here to ensure that you do as we request and when we return, we will all meet up again and we will give you all a full report.'

So Mr Munga and Samson left the hotel. We all watched them go. When they he had been gone for a few minutes. I turned to Joseph. 'I have to go too. I cannot sit here waiting now that I know exactly where she is.'

'But Karisa, you don't know the area, so how can you know where to go? Plus, if you are going then I'm coming with you.'

'That cannot be, I am sorry to say. You would attract much attention with your white face. I have been to the area before – not to the school, but it cannot be far from the church, and my face will not make people look. You must stay here with Mr Mark and Mr Josh. They will not miss me and I must go to make sure that Angela is safe. I hope you understand this thing?' I left the hotel by the fire exit and quickly made my way to the "Jesus loves me" church with a blessing from Joseph.

The way came easily to me as I had done it twice before but I was very surprised when I heard someone calling my name from inside a *duka*. Samson rushed out to greet me.

'I thought you were with Mr Munga, what has happened? Why are you not looking for Angela? He knows where they are being kept now,' I said.

'Do not worry my friend, Mr Munga is very close by to the school but he sent me away. He fears for my safety if I am seen by Nzoka. He will believe that I have led you to them and he will take revenge, so he told me many other police would be with him very soon and I was to leave. I was just buying some water to drink.'

'So do you know exactly where this school is?'

'I do, and if you so wish, I will take you there.'

'But if your life is in danger…?'

'You are my friend and I will not let you down. Let me pay for my water and I will show you the way.' He disappeared inside.

In my heart, I was very relieved to meet with Samson. I had been concerned that I would not find the school in time. He soon came back outside and without another word; we walked off in the direction of the church.

It did not take us very long to reach it and, walking a little way past it, turned off and into what looked like a dead end. But before we reached the end of this small road, we turned off again and there stood the building painted blue and white, the colour of all schools in Kenya. Angela was close by, I could feel it.

Chapter Fifty-One
Angela

Rose was strangely quiet this morning, which concerned me, and the minute Nzoka left the room, I asked her why.

'Surely this is the day you get your freedom back?' I said.

'Do you really believe that? He is not a man to give anyone their freedom once he has control of them. I owe him money that I borrowed from him to pay my rent. He will take your money today but my debt will still stand.'

'Are you telling me that he has no intention of letting me go?'

'Oh, he will let you go. After all, once he has the money, he has no further use for you, and it will be dangerous for him to keep you. For me it will be very different. I have played the game he wanted me to, but he is not a man to keep his promise to wipe off my debt to him. For me nothing changes, except I have now met the woman whose husband I was supposed to have married, and I like her.'

'And I've met the woman who was supposed to be married to my husband and I like her too,' I said and we managed a quick hug before Nzoka entered.

He seemed in a very buoyant mood and was full of smiles. 'So, number two, this is the day that we say goodbye to each other. The day my sister here gets what she is owed.'

'I wouldn't be so sure. You haven't got your hands on the money yet.' I wanted to put doubt in his mind, even though I hadn't a clue what I was going to do when he found out there was no money.

He was unbothered by my words. 'But she is the woman mentioned in your dead husband's will, of that you have agreed, and once the documentation is dealt with by the lawyer, then it is perfectly legal. You will not get any joy from the police by reporting anything that has happened between us. Also, you must understand that if I believe that you have done so, then it will be Rose who will suffer, I will make sure of that,' he said.

I looked at her. She was terrified. I knew that she was innocent in all this and I couldn't be the one to give her more suffering in her sad life. I'd got myself into this situation. I should've stayed in England. I had no business being here. It would backfire, I was sure of it, and there was a real likelihood that Nzoka would win in the end. I just wanted to be away from this man and this room and even this bloody country, and back home in my house in Somerset, safe and sound. Except that it would never be my home again. I was about to lose it all.

Nzoka left us to go and meet the lawyer. He was still not aware that I hadn't given him the details of where we were to meet. The fact that he was confident that the lawyer would be at the designated place confirmed to me that that sleaze ball knew exactly what was going on, which must have included my captivity and the fact that Rose wasn't the person named in the will.

The more I thought about it, the more I realised this had all been set up. Karisa and I'd been directed here via Joseph's contact in Mombasa. Was Joseph part of all this? Wambua had been sent to us from the same contact and had taken us to Nzoka. Maybe he was part of it too? I'd spent three days with these people and there'd been no attempt to rescue me or even

259

to come and find me. The guard said that he knew Wambua, but he'd done nothing either, so what guarantee did I have that Nzoka would let me go as he promised? I doubted that man had ever kept a promise in his life. So while he was away, I texted the only person in all this that I felt I could trust.

'Karisa, there is a meeting at noon today, at the school, the lawyer, and Nzoka. I need your help please!'

Rose looked over at me as I was writing the text, but said nothing. Her mind, no doubt, on other things. Almost immediately I felt my phone vibrate on my chest. I'd forgotten to turn it off.

'Angela, trust me help is on the way!' the reply came quickly.

Help is coming, he'd said... I could only pray that it came in time. Within a couple of minutes, Nzoka entered the room followed by the lawyer.

'I believe that you two know each other?'

'I'm sure that I'm not the only one who knows Mr Daniels here.' I looked straight at Nzoka.

He laughed. 'Who is to say?'

Mr Daniels touched my hand to shake it but I yanked it away. He paid no attention to this snub and followed Nzoka out of the room and across to the school. Rose and I followed with the guard.

A classroom had been laid out for the meeting, I assumed by the uncle, who was on hand to serve *chai* and chapattis.

'It's good of you to give me some refreshment,' said Mr Daniels, 'I've had a long and expensive journey.'

'No doubt that will be going on the bill,' I sniped.

'Mrs Trippett, you don't sound very happy today. If you remember, it was you that got me here. I'm here at your bidding to try and conclude this important business. If there's an issue then you must tell me now.'

I could see that Rose was petrified and so once again I bit my tongue and mumbled for him to carry on. I prayed to God that this help that Karisa had promised would arrive soon.

'Do you have the money?' Nzoka said.

'It's being prepared, Mr Nzoka, don't worry. But as Madam is aware, we have some formalities to complete before I can hand it over. It's a great deal of money and I'm not going to wander around with it in my pocket. But trust me; I'm in a position to transfer the money once we're all done and legal. So first of all, Mrs Trippett, are you happy to go forward with the proceedings? I mean Mrs Angela Trippett, not Mrs Rose Trippett.' He gave a chuckle and I wanted to slap him hard.

Even though I suspected they knew each other, I could sense the animosity between them. I was watching two bull elephants sizing each other up before the fight. But I had a bigger concern. There was no money and so I knew that the lawyer was bluffing just as much as I was. There wouldn't be any money until the house was sold and I'd no intention of ever doing that. I'd wanted to find the truth but I'd got myself into a situation that was very dangerous. Once Nzoka knew there was no money God knows what he would do.

'I'm sure that you'll find that it's all in order,' Daniels said. 'You did tell me on the phone that you believed that this lady was the Rose that you sought and was the person mentioned in the will did you not?'

'I just have some concerns about this situation,' I said. 'There's something that bothers me in the back of my mind.'

'Well then, my good lady, you must let us know what your concerns are. I'm acting on your behalf and if you've any doubts about these people you must say it now,' he said. This man deserved an Oscar for playing the part of a concerned and trustworthy lawyer!

'That's the thing, Mr Daniels. I know all about these people and they're just as I suspect them to be. Nzoka is a bully and a cheat and Rose is a very frightened woman, but you... You, I thought I knew, but now I'm not so sure,' I said.

'I don't understand you, madam. I'm your lawyer.'

'But are you? I didn't appoint you. I don't know who did, but you seem to be in the middle of this. You told me in your office, that Rose had a good case, and yet you've done nothing to help me. You very quickly offered to come when I asked you to. I never told you where to come for the meeting, and yet here you are. How did you know where the meeting was? That is my question to you,' I said.

The room was so quiet; I could hear the cicadas outside until Nzoka spoke. 'Angela, you are mistaken. I heard you tell Mr Daniels all the details on the phone. I was in the room with you when you did so. You must have forgotten.'

'You heard me say the words, but are you certain that I was connected to him when I was saying them?'

'Yes, I am, I gave you my phone, you dialled the number and spoke. That is what you did and that is what I heard. So do not try and confuse matters now. He knew where the meeting was because you told him. That is it,' he said.

'May I suggest that you look at your phone log from yesterday? You'll see what you said is quite correct. I did dial the number and I did speak the words as you say. But he didn't pick up the call. I spoke as the phone was still ringing and you can check this on your phone. So this is my confusion and I'll ask the question again to Mr Daniels. How did you know where

262

the meeting was being held?'

I felt the tension in the room rise and I waited for something to happen.

'Madam, how I got to know about the meeting is of no consequence now. If you wish me to leave then I will do so. But please remember that I'm here at your request. You may not have told me where the meeting was, but it was you and you alone who asked me to come. Now the decision is yours: do I stay or do I go?'

Chapter Fifty-Two
Angela

'You stay!' yelled the voice from the doorway. 'You all stay. Nobody is to move.' And suddenly there was a rush of people in uniform storming into the room. I watched Nzoka jump through the window and the guard jump after him. So much for him being on my side, I thought, he must have told him everything that was said between Rose and me. A man headed towards me.

'Thank goodness you arrived, just in time,' I said. He was not in the mood for pleasantries and as I put my hand forward to shake his, he grabbed hold tight and snapped it into handcuffs.

'Hang on! I am the innocent party here, what the hell do you think you're doing? I have been held against my will for three days. Tell them, Rose,' I shouted, looking at her for support, but it was too late; she was being dragged out of the room by a couple of policemen and she wasn't talking.

However, both Mr Daniels and the uncle were, and Mr Daniels was professing his innocence strongly as he was being handcuffed also.

'Shut your big fat mouth,' I heard a man say. He came over to me. 'Just remain calm and do as you are told. Everything will be fine.'

Rose and I were helped into the back of one vehicle whilst Mr Daniels and the Uncle were pushed into the other. It was very cramped as we were hemmed in by four policemen, all looking about seventeen years old but fully armed with rifles and batons. Mercifully, the journey was not long and the heavily fortified gates of the police station were almost a relief. I knew Karisa would be there waiting for me.

But as our names were taken and we were quickly dispatched to separate cells down a dark pungent corridor, my relief turned to panic. He was not there. Hearing the door lock behind me heightened the panic and I gulped at the air from the small barred window in the metal door. I was just in time to see Mr Daniels and the uncle being pushed down the corridor to their cells. Mr Daniels was still protesting his innocence and threatening to throw the book at all and sundry. The uncle, however, was sobbing quietly to himself and for a fleeting moment, I felt sorry for him. Maybe he too owed money to Nzoka and that was the reason he'd put himself at risk in hiding us. My sympathy evaporated as my panic rose. I had my own worries.

I sat on a concrete block that must serve as a bed and tried to control my breathing. Excrement had been smeared down the walls by unseen hands. A rusting metal bucket sat lopsided in the corner. I stayed well away from it. The man had promised me everything was going to be okay, but how? Nobody knew that I was in a police cell. I couldn't help myself; I began to cry. Within minutes the door was yanked open and Wambua was standing there.

'Come with me and try not to make much noise, I do not want others to see what is happening.' I tried to get up from the block but my legs were shaking so much. He helped me to my feet. 'Take it easy, Mrs Trippett. We do not want you to hurt your leg again. Please accept my profound apologies for having to put you in that place. It was the easiest thing to do when dealing with everyone. I hope you were not too distressed. But do not worry you are safe now, your family are waiting for you when we have finished signing you out.'

His words confused me. He must've got this wrong. My

family were in England, safely unaware of all this. I dreaded to think what Mark would have to say about all this if he knew. He took me to a much larger room, sat me down and offered me a wonderfully cold bottle of water from the fridge in the corner. I used a grubby tissue to wipe my tear-stained face, while he went to get the papers.

'Just a formality,' he said.

He was true to his word, returning in a matter of minutes with them to sign, allowing me to be released. He'd said that my family were waiting but that was impossible. I was thinking about how I could get back to the hotel when the door opened once more and I was engulfed by two huge arms wrapping tight around me.

'Mum, are you okay?' a voice said into my neck and I realised immediately that it was Josh, my beautiful son Josh. 'We were so worried about you. Please say something, Mum.'

But I couldn't say one word as the tears returned and the anguished sobs racked through me, making it impossible to breathe.

'There is someone else here to see you.'

Karisa… I knew he would come; I so desperately wanted to see him. I tried not to let my disappointment show when I saw Mark stood in the doorway. I went to hug him and he tried not to pull away. But he did.

Wambua was keen to get us all out of his office. 'Mrs Trippett, You will need to return for further questioning over the next couple of days, but for the moment, enjoy your time with your family.'

'Why do I have to come back? You all know what was going on. I'm the innocent party here. It was you who told me to meet him one more time and look what happened!'

'I understand your concern, but the problem we have is that Mr Daniels says that you requested him to come to the meeting

266

with the money. You said that you believed that the woman was the person mentioned in your husband's will. Is this all true?'

'Well, yes, it is, but I was put under pressure by Nzoka to say those things, and if I hadn't, I don't know what he would've done. Plus I didn't have the money the solicitor in Bristol knew that. But Daniels said he had it.'

'There *was* money, Mum,' Josh looked towards Mark before he continued; 'Your phone call worried me so I sold my car and borrowed the rest. It was in my bank account and if the police hadn't arrived then the transaction would have taken place.'

'But this is my problem. Mr Nzoka is not here, and without any confessions from him, then the case is very weak if there is a case at all. Mr Daniels will be able to walk free, Rose is too scared to say anything and without Nzoka, there is not even a charge of kidnapping. So at the moment, I can get you released but I will need to question you at some time. I just thought that you may want to see your family and bathe. I will keep you updated with any developments and I will do my best to keep that lawyer of yours behind bars for as long as I can. Goodbye, Mrs Trippett, for now.'

The sun blinded me and I lowered my head from the glare. That's when I saw it; the pale band of skin around my finger. It had gone; the ring was no longer there. I climbed into the back of the taxi that my sons had kept waiting for me and breathed a sigh of relief. I was free.

Chapter Fifty-Three
Karisa

I heard shouting but I stayed hidden, then I caught sight of Mr Munga rushing into the school, followed by others. I did not move. I did not know where to move to. Should I go into the school or should I go back to the hotel knowing that the rescue was taking place? In the end, I did nothing. I just stood and watched; my fear had returned. I could see two men running towards me. I remained until a man I recognised rushed past me. Nzoka!

'Help me to catch that man!' a second person yelled as he also ran past, and without thinking I, too, ran. I would not let him escape.

I felt my years and more, as I gasped for breath trying to keep up with the others. Nzoka knew the area well and dashed in and out of small alleyways, trying to get away. But no matter how hard he ran or where he ran to, he could not find any refuge. The other man was very fast, and my anger at Nzoka brought energy to my body and speed to my limbs.

I saw him turning his head to look at the two of us and I sensed him begin to tire. I knew that we would catch him and I spurted ahead of the second man without fear. This man would be captured by me and it would be me who would bring him to justice. I owed Angela this.

Finally, he stopped and turned to face me for a fight. I was not prepared for this and I stopped my chase. My hesitation gave him chance to escape once again through a small café, and as the second man ran past me following him, I heard his words.

'Fool!'

I felt my anger rise, not at the man or even Nzoka but at myself. Yes, I was a fool, I should have faced him. Now was not the time to return to my cowardly ways. So once more I ran, quickly catching up with them and this time there was no stopping me, my eyes firmly set on Nzoka. He began to throw things in our pathway. Tomatoes, potatoes, crates of soda, a wooden cart full of vegetables, but I would not let this slow me down. My anger had given me the agility of a gazelle and I scrambled over the obstructions easily. Once again, he turned to fight, but this time I did not stop, I put my head down and charged straight at him like a buffalo. I felt the blows on my head and back as I held onto him tight, but I would not let him go. I then felt someone pulling him from me. I had done it, I had captured Nzoka!

A big crowd gathered around the three of us and I was concerned that some of his friends would come to cause trouble, but the crowd seemed full of joy that he had been caught and they laughed and jeered as we dragged him into a *tuk-tuk* to take us to the police station. It was only then that the other person introduced himself as the guard that had been with Angela all the time.

'No real harm would have come to her; I would have made sure of this.' He explained that in reality, he was a policeman working for Wambua. Nzoka was furious and increased his effort to escape from the *tuk-tuk* by spitting in the guard's face.

'You can spit at me all you wish, but it is you, not me who will be the one in prison. Then I can come and spit on you whenever I like. So carry on while you are still able. You, my friend,' the guard turned to face me, 'Are a very brave man. Not many people would have chased this man as you did. Not many people would have run him down like you did. I am sorry for what I called you. Forgive me.'

'You were speaking the truth; he could have got away if you had not run straight after him. I am not brave, my friend. This man held my very dear friend prisoner and has to pay.' I looked at Nzoka and no longer felt afraid.

After arriving at the gates of the police station, we were directed to a building where Wambua and Mr Munga were waiting. As we parked, I saw a taxi leaving the compound. Angela was in the back with one of her sons and I put my hand up to wave to them, but the look on Mr Mark's face in the front of the vehicle made me stop. He was laughing. They all were laughing. I was not noticed.

Seeing her with her family together brought many feelings to me. I was happy that she was okay, but deep down in my heart, there was also a sadness that I could not understand.

'My friend, can you please help me with this man?' the guard was shouting. Nzoka was fighting with him and so, putting away my thoughts; I grabbed hold of his hair and dragged him through the door. Other policemen had heard the shouting outside and come running to help us and so once we were through the door I was able to bid my farewell to the guard and be on my way. Nzoka was in the police station, Angela was with her family, I was no longer needed.

I went for a walk. After seeing the family all together, I was not in a hurry to return to the hotel. Angela was safe and happy; that was all that mattered to me. I was not familiar with the area of town that I was in, but it did not matter, I did not have any particular place to go.

I knew I should have been back at the hotel finding out what had happened and what was going to happen going forward. But I also knew that no one would miss me and I felt like an intruder, now that the family were with her. Mr Mark, I knew, would be very pleased for me to be out of the way. It would be *wazungu* together. There would be no place for me.

As I had been running after Nzoka, I had felt my phone vibrating in my pocket but had forgotten all about it until now. I checked my phone; I had a missed call from Kadzo and a message waiting to be heard.

'*Karisa, please pick up the call, I need you to phone me back. Something terrible has happened.*'

I thought only of her parents or, that something had happened to my mother or to the boy and so quickly dialled her number. She answered almost before it had rung.

'Thank goodness you rang back. Oh, Karisa, it is so bad.'

'Kadzo, tell me what the problem is. What has happened? Is it something at home?'

'I never imagined this would happen, it is too bad for words,' she was yelling down the phone at me and I was losing my patience.

'I can only help you, if you tell me what is wrong. Is it your parents?'

'What...? No, it is not my parents, how could you think that? It is Vincent. He has left me for someone else, for some rich, stupid, ugly, two-timing lady.' She began to cry.

I felt the anger burning my face as I listened to her. I wanted to shout at her foolishness, but listening to her tears was difficult to do, so I tried my best to calm her down. When she found out how close I was to Nairobi, she said she would come to meet with me where I was. I did not want that so I promised I

271

would go to her.

I had not planned to see her again after our last meeting, but maybe leaving this place would be a good idea. I knew that I had to go back to the hotel to pack my small bag, but when I got there my cowardice returned. I could not speak to Angela and so I crept back into my room unseen. It had been cleaned and the beds freshly made, and the temptation to lie on one of them was great, but I had made a promise to Kadzo, so I grabbed my bag, packed my things, and then wrote a note for Joseph. I had lost my courage to go and find him. I paid as much of the bill that I could afford and told reception that Joseph would pay the rest on his return. I would repay him from my wages in Mombasa.

Chapter Fifty-Four
Angela

It was strange to be back in the room, all freshly made up, with my clothes still hanging in the wardrobe and my cosmetics in the bathroom as if I had just popped out for something to eat. I'd spent what seemed like hours in the shower trying to scrub away the dirt and also the memories of the last few days. It hadn't worked.

I was very surprised to see the boys at the prison. I didn't think I'd ever been so happy to see anyone in my life and since coming back to the hotel we'd had a chance to talk for a short time. But I was meeting them in a few minutes for dinner and we would be able to continue our conversations then. Joseph came to greet me when I arrived back, but Karisa didn't. Joseph said he left the hotel, that morning, saying he was going to help in the search, but he never returned. Mark still believed that he had something to do with my captivity and was forceful on giving us his opinion.

'He's done a runner. He could see the plan wasn't working and he's pissed off before he was caught.'

Neither Joseph nor I believed this for one minute and we told him so.

'I'm telling you, he was part and parcel of it. I mean, Mother, if he's such a good friend to you, where is he now?'

As I did my hair for the first time in what seemed like forever and enjoyed the luxury of clean underwear, I thought of

Karisa. I couldn't understand why I hadn't seen him since I returned to the hotel. I truly thought that he'd be waiting for me and, if he did leave the hotel this morning to join the search, then what had happened to him? It worried me. Before I could ponder any more, there was a knock at the bedroom door and it opened slowly.

It was Joseph. 'Hope you are decent, sweetie? Thought you might like a gander at this before you meet the boys.'

He handed me a folded sheet of paper. I recognised the writing straight away.

'Mr Joseph, I have gone away for a few days to speak with a close friend who is having a hard time at the moment. I did not want to leave without letting you know. I have paid as much of the room bill that I could afford and I hope that you will pay the rest by lending me the money from my wages. I saw Angela leave the police station with her family, she looked very happy. Please try to speak to her alone if you can and tell her where I have gone. I am full of joy that she is now safe and I hope that everything will work out well for her. Please send her my best wishes and tell her that I will remember our friendship in happy memories. I am glad she is back in the heart of her family and that she is happy. I promise that I will be in touch once I am free and will get back to Mombasa as soon as I can. I leave the Land Rover for Angela and her family. I will travel by bus.

Rafiki Yangu

Karisa.'

I refolded the note and looked at Joseph. 'He has gone. He has left me.'

Before I had chance to reread the note, the boys arrived.

'I'm starving. Hey, Mum, you look great. Do you think she's now clean enough for you to hug your mother, Sir

Marcus?' said Josh.

Mark gave him a playful clout around the head and moved to give me a hug. I knew that he was trying his best, but I could still feel a slight pull away from me. I didn't remark on it. I was just grateful that they were both here. But I was heartbroken that Karisa had gone. We headed downstairs and into the dining room.

'Nice to see you again,' said the receptionist on the way. 'I hope your visit was successful?'

I had no idea what he was talking about so just smiled and nodded in his direction as I was guided away by Joseph.

'Just a little white lie we told him to explain your absence.'

After we'd ordered, talk turned to my ordeal, but I changed the subject, telling them that now it was all over I'd rather forget it and that it was my own silly fault for getting into the situation in the first place.

'Couldn't agree with you more,' said Mark. 'I told you it was stupid to come out here.'

'Oh, I'm sorry, Mark, my memory must be failing in my old age. I could've sworn that it was you who phoned me and told me to find "that woman immediately". I also could've sworn it was you that flew over here to "sort it all out" as you couldn't trust me to do the job.'

'Yes, Mother, and looked what happened to you the minute I left. You go and get yourself kidnapped.'

'Steady on there, old boy, I wouldn't say for one minute that your mother did it on purpose.'

I gently placed my hand in Joseph's and held it tight. I couldn't face a fight with Mark tonight. 'Look, boys, can we please just be nice to each other tonight? Whatever has happened has happened, but now it's over...'

'Apart from the fact that it isn't, is it?' said Mark. 'Regardless of how this situation arose, it's far from over. For a start, the guy who held you captive is still free, and the lawyer is likely to get off scot-free because the stupid police went in too quickly and so, in the eyes of the law, and I'm assuming he knows it better than we do, he's done nothing wrong. All he's done is attended a meeting that he was asked to attend by you. And as for that Rose, we know she's not the woman we are looking for, and as she can say she was being held captive too, there is no case against her either. So everyone walks away from this without a blemish on their record. Hardly a raging success, is it, Mother? Plus, somewhere out there is the real Rose, and when she's found we will still have to hand over fifty thousand pounds. Turned out fucking brilliant, wouldn't you say?'

All eyes turned to the arrival of two police officers, approaching our table in full dress uniform.

'May we join you?' the first police officer asked, and as he removed his cap, I could see that it was Wambua. I didn't recognise the other police officer.

'Well, this is a surprise,' said Joseph. 'Angela may I introduce you to Chief Inspector Munga here? He was my contact in Mombasa.'

'Yes and a bloody mess he made of it. He nearly got my mother killed, just to sort out one of his bloody cases.'

'I understand your anger, Mr Mark, but if you would permit me, I would like to give you some reasoning behind why, when Mr Joseph came to ask me for my help, it was an opportunity too good to miss. God smiled on our police force that day.'

Mark went to speak but Josh, put his hand over his mouth to shut him up. 'Go on...?'

'When Mr Joseph came to see me, I did some investigation concerning this sort of incident and a pattern began to emerge. It appears that there had been other cases similar to yours and although we did not have any proof, we believed that the lawyer Mr Daniels was involved in all of the cases. Initially, we did not believe that he was getting the money in the previous cases, but he was most certainly being paid very well for his services.'

'But this case was different,' broke in Wambua, 'This time we had a feeling that he himself may be profiting. We could not understand this until we began to look further into it and spoke to his secretary. They will tell you lots of things if you have something that they want. In this instance, her husband had been arrested because he had been fighting in a bar, the family had had to search a long way to find the money for his bail, but he was still due to go to court. We were able to lose the file and drop the charges for her help.'

'Ah, good old fashioned corruption!' said Mark.

'Are you saying to me,' snapped Wambua, 'That your whiter than white British police force do not strike deals with people in order to get to the criminals?'

'They definitely do,' said Josh. 'Please go on and ignore my ignorant brother.'

'As I was saying, this time, the case was different and we wanted to know why. Daniels knew Nzoka, who is greatly in his debt. He'd got him off some very serious drug charges and to this end; Nzoka will probably spend the rest of his life repaying that debt. Anyhow, he was not in any position to say no to Daniels, and so a plan was made to defraud you of a substantial amount money.

'Daniels knew your husband well and had been the one to do the original will. Apparently they had fallen out, but your

277

husband had never made a new will so, when he died, this one was valid. From what I can gather, you were just to hand over the money. They did not bank on such a determined lady as you and that is when things got out of hand. We do not believe that Nzoka ever intended to take you captive, he just panicked. We already had a man who was working undercover in the area finding information about the big drug problems and so it was quite easy to make sure that he was part of Nzoka's group of friends and able to monitor what was happening. It was luck, or maybe God smiling down on us, that he was chosen to go with Nzoka that day. And so, Mrs Trippett, as you were refusing to co-operate, things got out of control. Nzoka is well known for his temper but he is not a stupid man, he knew he could not take out his anger on you and so it was the woman Rose that suffered, the guard has testified to that. You were very smart to get those texts out to your friend Karisa and that made all the difference. It allowed us to know where you were and to make sure that no harm came to you. But as much as we wanted to rescue you and your friends wanted us to do the same, we needed to make sure that Daniels was there with you and that is why nothing happened until today. I apologise for that, Mrs Trippett, but I hope you understand our reasoning.'

Mark couldn't keep quiet any longer. 'But it doesn't make one bit of difference, does it? There's nothing you can charge this lawyer with because you let that man escape and without his testimony you have nothing. My mother went through hell for your so-called investigation and you blew it!'

I opened my mouth to snap back at Mark, but Joseph put his hand on my shoulder and I remained quiet.

'But Mr Mark, we have all the evidence we need,' said Mr Munga. 'The guard is able to testify to conversations that took place within the room. He tells of the great intelligence of your mother. You are a very lucky man to have such a smart lady as your mother and I hope that you respect that. We also have the testimony from Nzoka himself. You see, he did not escape. Yes, he may have got away from us at the school, but the guard chased after him. I think you would have seen that, Mrs Trippett. Am I correct?'

'Eh. Yes, I saw that but I thought he was making his escape too. So the guard managed to catch him then?'

'Actually, the answer to that question is no. If it had been the guard only, then he would have escaped. No, the person who caught him was your friend Karisa. He was very brave; he did not care for his own safety. He chased him for a long time and then he brought him down and made sure he could not get away until the guard caught up. I am here to shake that man's hand and to thank him very much.'

I didn't know whether it was me or Joseph who let out the biggest gasp at this news. Joseph explained to everyone that Karisa had gone to Nairobi to help a friend in need and may not be coming back, but returning straight to Mombasa.

'That is a great shame,' said Wambua. 'He was a very brave man and I would like to have told him so.'

Chapter Fifty-Five
Karisa

Not so long ago, seeing Kadzo would have brought great feelings of love, but now there was nothing. My heart did not have room for her anymore. It was full only of Angela, and though I knew she would be leaving me, there would still not be space for anyone else.

'I am so glad to see you.' She leaned in to kiss me as I got off the bus. I could smell the tang of stale tobacco and I pulled away from her. She did not notice. 'Karisa, I have been so sad. That horrible man, I cannot even say his name, has left me.' She could not wait to tell me of her troubles.

It was as I had feared back in the village. He had found someone else, someone more beautiful and younger or richer, and gone to her. I did not know what to say. She needed sympathy and I did not have any to give her. I could think of nothing other than Angela, my love, sat in the back of the taxi happy. It broke my heart – not because she was happy, I would always wish happiness for her – but I wanted her to be happy with me. I was jealous. I had never felt this before.

I paid little attention to her as she spoke until we stopped outside an open door. I could hear the sound of children crying and a woman shouting. The smell of rotting rubbish caught my throat. She pushed open a broken wooden door to the side revealing a dark space which we entered. The room was very poor, with rags at the small window to stop others seeing inside, a long thin piece of foam on the floor and a *jiko* in the corner. She must have seen my disgust.

'Do not look like that; this is only for the moment. I have many friends who will help me.'

I asked her why she was staying in Nairobi when she could return home to the village and they would look after her?

'You heard my father; he would not allow me back, even if I did want to return home. This is my home now, I am a city girl.'

I had heard her say this so many times, but this time I felt sadness for her. She might be educated but she would never fit in here in the city. She would always be used by men. 'I am sorry but I do not know what I can do to help you. Why did you ask me here?' I said.

We sat on the floor and she began to cry. I was feeling a great tiredness; it had been a very difficult day. Kadzo shouted at me and I realised that I had not been listening to her. My thoughts had been solely with Angela. 'I do not think that you have heard me at all?' I saw anger flare up on her face.

'I have had a very difficult day and I am a little tired,' I said. 'Please forgive me and I would be very happy if you would tell me again and I promise that I will listen.'

'I asked you if you were free and you nodded. I asked you if you missed me and you nodded. Is that true?' she said.

'Of course, we have known each other for a very long time, since we were small children, and I enjoy it when we are in each other's company. But things are different now; you have your life here in Nairobi. You say your life is not back in the village, but mine is. And as for being free, I do not understand what you are asking me. I still have my job which ties me.'

'I was not asking about that, I was asking whether you had

a woman in your life. Karisa, we all make mistakes in our lives and hopefully, God will forgive us. None of us is perfect, is that true?'

'That is very true,' I said, thinking of Angela. Had our love been a mistake?

'I made a big mistake going off with that man. I was very foolish but I loved him. Now I am alone and I remember our times together. We have always been good together. Have we not?'

'Yes we have, but...'

'That is what I thought. And that is why I ask again if you have a woman.'

I suddenly realised what it was that she was saying to me. Kadzo wanted to get back with me and, with her next breath, she said as much.

'I am sure we could work something out. I know at the moment you need to be in the village with your mother. But she is very old and when she is late, then you will be free to move to be with me here in Nairobi. We will find someone to take the boy; that will not be a problem. I am asking that we forget what has happened and go back to being as we were, promised to each other. I know it would make our parents very happy.' She jumped to her feet, smiling. 'What do you say?'

I knew then the reason that she had called me. She needed someone to pay her bills and to allow her to get back to the life she had enjoyed before she had met Vincent. She expected that person to be me. I could not face the conversation that I would have to have now, I needed to clear my thoughts and sleep, and it was very late.

Although I was exhausted sleep did not come as I lay on the bare floor while she slept soundly on the mat. She had offered to share this with me, but I could not. I must have slept for a little while because I dreamt of saying goodbye to Angela at the airport with Gabriel standing by me. She showed no sadness as she left; it was only Gabriel and I that were heartbroken. It was with the same heavy heart that I watched the dawn break through the grubby window.

As the light grew stronger, I quietly got dressed and went for a walk. I cared for Kadzo. I even considered that getting back together could be a good solution for me as well as for her. I could go back to the village and, for the moment, help my mother to take care of Gabriel. If I asked Joseph for more work or got a second job in the evenings, then I would be able to give support to her, and as she said our parents would be very happy that we were back together. But would I be? I could never give up the boy.

My phone rang.

'Have you left me for good?' I could not speak.

'Karisa, please talk to me.'

'I am here, listening to you, Angela,' I finally whispered.

'Joseph showed me your note. Answer me; have you left me for good? I need to know. I know what you did, I know it was you who arrested Nzoka, but what I don't understand is why you left without seeing me,' she said.

'I saw you leaving the police station. I saw you with your two sons and that you were very happy. I did not want to change that for you and so I left.' I struggled to hear her voice, the traffic was too loud. I hid in a doorway.

'Don't you think that there may have been other reasons too why I was so happy? First of all, I was free and heading back to have a shower and change my clothes. I was no longer in captivity. And yes, I was happy to see my sons. I didn't

283

expect them to be there. But the main reason that I was happy as was because I was going to see you again. Or at least I thought I was. I was happy that maybe, just maybe you'd hold me in your arms again. But you weren't there, and nobody knew where you were, so, for Christ's sake, Karisa, answer my bloody question. Have you really left me for good?' She was crying.

'Angela, I thought I was doing the right thing and I cannot help but think that that is the case still. I do want to hold you in my arms; I want that more than anything. Please trust me. My feelings for you are unchanged.'

My bundle ran out and the line cut off.

Kadzo was awake when I got back to the room and was not happy that I had gone out and left the door unlocked.

'This is Nairobi, Karisa, not some backward village. You are not safe in your own home.'

'Then, this will never be a place that I can live,' I said.

'Oh, you will get used to it, I did. It doesn't take very much and you will soon be a city boy.' She lit up a cigarette and blew smoke into the air.

'I have made my decision and I am sorry but I can never return to how we were. It is not right for either of us. I know that this is not the answer that you want from me, but I cannot change it.'

'How do you know what is right for me? You cannot know,' she shouted. 'Are you rejecting me too, or is this because I will not come back to the little village that you think is so marvellous? Why should I give up the life that I have worked so hard for? I studied night and day to be a success, why should I give it up?' She sat back on the floor and folded her arms tight. I remembered this from when the teacher had chastised her at school. She had not changed but still, I spoke.

'It was your parents and all the other people in the village who paid for your education. People gave up food and medicine so that you could have this great opportunity and you are so ungrateful. You think that God is making you suffer. What, because you had to read books and attend lectures? Is this suffering? You do not know what suffering is and at this moment I am ashamed of you. Real suffering happened in our village, as people gave up on their own dream in order that you could have yours.'

'How dare you? Get out; I never want to see you again. You are nothing but a stupid village boy. You have nothing worth having. You will never find a woman.'

I quickly grabbed my things. 'I wish you all the best and I hope that one day you will find humility, surely I do. You talk about me never finding another woman. I have to tell you that I already have,' I said.

'Oh what, your old *mzungu* woman? The village news travels far, Karisa. So do not judge me for leaving you for Vincent, when you are doing the same with a woman who is almost old enough to be your mother.'

I banged the door shut, just before the wooden chair hit it behind me.

Chapter Fifty-Six
Angela

I had to call Karisa, I couldn't let him go. I needed to hear it from him and so, after a few hours' sleep, I rang and, oh my God, I was so glad that I did. Just to hear his voice and listen to what he had to say. I knew then that he had strong feelings for me. But I still didn't have an answer. He said he'd try to come and see me before we left to return home. Why did he assume that I would return home? I suppose because it was the sensible thing to do. To go home and let the police here and the solicitor in England sort it all out. But for me, there were so many loose ends. I still didn't understand why the lawyer wanted to do this to me and then there was Rose... I knew I should walk away from her and forget it all, but I couldn't forget how she'd tried to help me in her own way. I also couldn't forget the beatings she took from that bully and the despair on her face as she left me to be locked in the police cell.

As it was still early after I'd spoken to Karisa, I decided to go for a walk, but as I was leaving the hotel, a police vehicle pulled up and Wambua got out.

'Ah, Mrs Trippett, I am pleased to see you so early. I thought you may still be in bed. We need you to come to the police station to answer some further questions and to corroborate some evidence, if that is okay with you. Also, Nzoka wishes to speak with you.' He must've seen my hesitation because he added, 'If you do not wish to speak to him, I understand, that is not something that you have to do. But I do need you to come down to the police station, when it is convenient. It will not take long.' I told him I'd go at some point, but I needed to let my family know first.

'I understand, Mrs Trippett.' He got back into the car and drove off.

'No way should you be speaking to that man!' Mark was fuming. 'No way at all, Mother. You could get yourself into all sorts of trouble. He's trying to weasel out of all this and knowing you, you'd make it easy for him. I forbid you to speak to him!' And there it was, that word 'forbid' again.

Joseph took hold of my hand. 'I think you *should* speak with him. I mean, sweetie, where's the harm? Wambua will be there all the time, so what could happen? I know, Mark, that you're angry and concerned about your mother...'

'I'm more bloody concerned that she'll make this into a bigger mess than it already is.'

'What I want to say' – Joseph's irritation was beginning to show – 'Is that of everybody here, including the police, Angela probably knows that man better than anyone. It is her decision alone. I know if it were me I'd want to get some answers in all this. I'd want to understand the full story, and maybe Nzoka is the man who can provide that.'

'All he will tell her is a pack of lies to save his own skin,' Mark said.

'And maybe you're right, but if she doesn't go to listen to him, then she'll never know. That's my opinion anyhow, darling.'

'Thank you, Joseph, for talking some sense. Mark, I do wish sometimes that you would credit me with just a tiny bit of intelligence. I may not be as smart as you, but somewhere in my ageing head is a brain that has served me for many years and I'd appreciate it if you occasionally acknowledged that it might exist.' Both Mark and Josh began to speak at the same time but I held my hand up to stop them. 'I've decided that I will go to the police station. I'll answer their questions and then I'll meet with Nzoka. Joseph made sense when he said I needed to know why.'

'Please don't tell me you need "closure." I've heard so much of the psychobabble from my therapist. For God's sake, Mother, don't you start.'

I stood up quickly, knocking my chair over backwards. 'I'm not talking bloody psycho… anything, I just want to have a stab at finding out the truth. Is that too much to ask? And I'd ask you to keep your nose out of my business, all of you!' I felt the tears of frustration stream down my face as I turned and left all three of them staring at me, speechless, for once.

As I travelled to the police station in the taxi, I pondered on the wisdom of my decision to come alone, and for what seemed like the millionth time in the last twenty-four hours, I thought of Karisa and how I wished he was with me. Wambua was there to greet me and led me into his office once more.

'Thank you for coming, Mrs Trippett. This should not take too much time.' All I had to do was confirm that I hadn't known either Nzoka or Rose before I came to Machakos, that he had held me against my will and that he'd beaten Rose. As things stood, however, there would be some difficulty in getting a conviction. Namely that I had gone with Nzoka freely, that I had asked Daniels to come to the meeting and I'd told him that I was happy that Rose was the person named in the will.

'This will not make things easy for us to make sure they all get the sentences they deserved,' Wambua said. 'This is my concern. If you knew that Rose was not his sister or the woman that you sought, why did you tell the lawyer otherwise?'

'She'd been beaten and was very frightened of him. I didn't want to get her into any more trouble by admitting that she'd told me the truth.'

'Okay, I understand that. This woman may be innocent but she was happy to deceive you about your marriage,' he said.

'She was desperate and I want all the charges dropped against her.' The words just came out. I hadn't even considered this but now that I'd said it, I knew without a doubt it was the right thing to do.

'What? Are you sure, Mrs Trippett? She lied to you about your husband and even produced a marriage certificate. Are you sure that you are going to let her walk free?'

'Yes, I am. She helped me when I needed it. She's suffered enough. I want her released.'

'Okay, it is your decision, but my next concern is Nzoka. He says you came with him of your own accord and that you asked him to take you to find Rose. I was not there and so I cannot say if this was true or not. He says that you were free to leave at any time, but you chose to stay and it was your idea to phone the lawyer to get it all sorted.'

'That's partly true. Yes, I did ask him to find her, and yes, I did go with him alone even though Karisa told me not to, but I'm telling you I was held captive for three days. You only need to ask Rose or the guard.'

'I am sure we will get the whole truth from her once she knows she is being freed. At the moment, she is saying very little. She does not want to incriminate herself any further. But you did phone the lawyer and ask him to the meeting?'

'Yes, I did because Nzoka made me. He threatened more trouble for Rose if I didn't do it. But I didn't tell Daniels where the meeting was, so that must surely prove that he and Nzoka were in cahoots.'

'Cahoots? Mrs Trippett, what is this cahoots?' Wambua looked confused.

'It means that they were working together...sorry,' I laughed.

'Ah, now I understand... Cahoots, I must write that down.' He quickly scribbled it down. 'Daniels is saying that he is innocent and that he was asked to come to a meeting by yourself to conclude the matter of this money from your late husband's will. The problem is all that we have at the moment is this and the fact that he was carrying a promissory note for fifty thousand pounds on him, which he says you, requested him to bring. Now as far as I can see, the only person who can help us to convict Daniels is Nzoka and at the moment, he is not talking very much. He knows that as it stands, he could face some time in prison, but as you went with him freely we cannot get him on abduction. We have a lot of suspicion that Daniels has been involved in many other cases like this one, but without some real evidence I have very little to convict him on.'

'So what happens now?'

'Nzoka is asking for you and says he will not talk with anyone else. He does not want a lawyer present. He says it was a lawyer that got him into this situation and he cannot trust another. I think he has something he wants to tell you. Once we have heard it, then we can make a decision as to what to do next.'

I closed my eyes to think and I heard Jeannie's voice, as clear as if she had been sat next to me. *'The truth, Angela, you need to know the truth!'* I nodded my consent to Wambua and he left the room.

As I waited for the arrival of Nzoka, the nerves returned, but the sight of him shuffling into the room, shackled hands and feet, dispelled them.

'Mr Nzoka, how lovely to see you. I'd shake your hand but

I can see that would be impossible.' I couldn't help the sarcasm. For once, I had the upper hand.

He lifted his head and looked at me. 'Thank you for seeing me,' he croaked. The bully and the arrogance had disappeared and as he was pushed into a chair in the corner of the room, I felt a glimmer of pity. I told myself to pull myself together, that the real Nzoka was still in there and this was just a part he was playing to save his skin.

'So you wanted to speak to me?' I said. 'Well then, go ahead, I am listening.'

He began very quietly. 'Well, madam, you may remember when we spoke together and I told you about my sister.'

'Yes, I remember. You said she was an educated woman, and yet the Rose you presented to me as your sister can't read or write. Did her education disappear?'

'No, it did not. You know that woman is not my sister. I realised after I had spoken to you and hoped that you would not remember. But you are not a stupid woman. I will admit that the woman you know is not related to me. I will admit that I asked her, no, I told her that she must play that part. She has a debt to me and so she could not refuse.

'But I spoke to you about my real sister. I told you about her relationship with your husband and how he took her away from her family, the family who had given everything so she could be employed, the family that she should have been supporting with the money she earned. She was our only hope out of poverty. I did not have her brains. But your husband, madam? He took that away with no concern for anyone but himself. His voice had risen to such a level that Wambua warned him to cool it down.'

'Mr Nzoka, if you remember, my husband wasn't my husband at the time, so you can hardly blame me for what was done,' I said.

'Forgive me,' he said, looking nervously at Wambua. 'This was my family that was suffering, and the responsibility to find and bring my sister home was mine alone. So for six days a week I worked on my uncle's *shamba*, and then on my rest day I would spend what little money I had left looking for the sister that had ruined my life. I told you, madam, that sometimes things happen to change us. This was when my anger began.

'I tried to speak with your husband, but he would not meet with me. I even turned up at his work and the place where my sister had worked, but I could not gain entrance. Eventually, I met up with someone who had worked with her. She told me that she'd heard a rumour that Rose had been with your husband until recently but had then left. She gave me a place to visit where she thought she was staying. I expected a nice place, but what I found was no more than a broken-down toilet. Yes, madam, your husband may have been "with" my sister long enough to make her pregnant, but once he found out, he did not want her. When I walked in, she ran to me like some crazy woman, screaming and shouting. I bought her medicine to calm her and she told me what had happened. She told me she had nothing left, no money, no clothes, no food. She did not blame your husband; she was still in love. She blamed God. She said it was his fault, that he had made her pregnant and that she wanted to be rid of it so that she could go back to the life that she had. I told her she was a fool and offered to take her back to the village with me. She would not go. She said she was a shamed woman and that she did not want them to know.'

Nzoka asked for a drink of water and this gave me a chance for a little break. I stepped outside.

Almost immediately, I was called back. He was anxious to get on with his story. I wasn't so sure that I wanted to hear it but I returned to the conversation. Wambua had removed the handcuffs and he had his hands together like he was praying. He began speaking again almost before I'd sat down.

'I did as my sister asked and kept it from my parents. I could not even give them the comfort of knowing that their daughter had been found. They would have wanted to see her and take her home but I had given my word to Rose that I would not let that happen. So every off day I carried the lie of searching for her, but often I went to visit her and bring what comfort I could. Madam, I spoke about my anger and at this time it was very high indeed. I tried to force my way in to see your husband at work. I found out where he lived from Rose and tried to speak to him there, but he would not talk to me. One time I was nearly arrested when your husband called the police to get rid of me. But I managed to get away before they caught me. Another time I was not so lucky. It cost me two thousand shillings that I had saved for my sister to bribe the police to set me free.

'As the time came near to the birth, she began to act crazier and crazier. I found a *mganga* to try and help her with some herbal medicine but it did not make any difference. I found out from a neighbour that my sister had been trying to get rid of the baby. She still believed that she could go back to her old life with your husband if she was not pregnant! The abortion attempts had failed and so, as the pains started to tell that the baby was coming, she began to drink. She drank the local brew which is very dangerous, so dangerous even I would not drink it. I was with her as the pains got worse and I was scared for her. The whole neighbourhood heard her agony and a mama from across the way, came in to help. She had helped a lot of babies into the world and that she knew what to do. She sent me outside. "A man should not be at a birth. It is bad luck," she said. I walked down the track but I could still hear the screams of my sister. I hear them now sometimes.

'The baby did not survive for long, of course. How could

293

it? My sister had done everything she could to get rid of it and finally, she had her wish. The baby died within the hour. It was a boy. It would have been the first grandchild for my mother and father. They would have been so happy, regardless of the circumstances that he had been born into the world, but they never got the chance to meet him. They never knew that he existed. The only person that held that boy, madam, was me, his uncle. His mother did not want him. The mama left the minute he was born. She knew he would die and so, as the baby lay wrapped up in a dirty cloth where he had been born and tried to summon up the breath to cry, I picked him up and held him close. I walked the room with him and sang him some of the songs from my village and I gave him all the love I had until he died in my arms.

'My sister did not once ask to see him and barely made a sound. She just lay there while her baby died and then, when I told her that he had breathed his last, she told me to take him away from her. So I put him in an old sack and took him back to the village with me. On my uncle's *shamba,* I found a shaded corner where crops would not grow and I laid him to rest. I could not even mark his grave. That day, madam, was the day my anger became my life.'

Chapter Fifty-Seven
Angela

I knew there was more to tell, but I needed a break of more than a few minutes and told Nzoka so, but promised that I'd return. I needed to get away from the room. I began walking around the grounds of the police station. I felt so restless. My head was bursting with everything he had said and, although there was a part of me that was still sceptical, his story broke my heart. Then I heard my name being called.

'Sorry, madam, Mr Wambua wants you back inside immediately. He says that Nzoka thinks you have left and will not be coming back. You must come quickly,' the man said.

He sat exactly as I had left him and I could see a slight smile on his lips as I sat back down. 'So you returned?' he said.

'I said I would, I'm someone who keeps their promises.' I could not resist more sarcasm.

He clasped his hands again in prayer, and took a deep breath. 'I did not see my sister again. She did not contact me and I did not contact her. The days I pretended to be searching for her got less and less, and I told my parents that I had run out of places to search and that if she wanted to be found, she would contact us one day. They did not believe me and they never lost hope that she would return. My mother died soon after, I think of a broken heart, if you believe in such things.'

I nodded. 'The days I told my parents I was going to the big city to search for her, I instead went to visit the grave of my nephew. I could not forget him. I know that may sound strange coming from the Nzoka that you know, but as I told you, I have known real love. It was not the love of a good woman. It was the love of my dead nephew.

'I tried to phone her to tell her of the death of our mother, but she did not pick up and I assumed that she was back where she wanted to be, with your husband. Months later I received a phone call from the woman who had helped me previously. She said the police had been to see your husband and she was concerned that something was wrong. We arranged to meet and she told me all that she knew. It seemed that my sister had tried to get her old job back and your husband had forbidden it. She had also tried to get him back but he had refused her. So she had made money in the only way that she could. Educated or not, she became a prostitute! I was glad that my mother was dead; at least she was spared the shame. The woman from the office did not know why the police were there but she heard my sister's name being mentioned. I went to find out. I expected that she had been arrested and that she had given your husband's name as someone who would pay the bribe money, but that was not the case. I was taken to the hospital nearby and it was there that I was shown the corpse of my sister. She was left in a corner, having been brought into the hospital by a police officer. She had been found by a passer-by on the side of the road. She had taken her own life. I did not know how she had done it; there were no visible signs and I did not have the money to find out. At that moment, I gave my soul totally to the devil. I lied to the police and the people at the mortuary and said that I did not know the woman, and then I walked away.

'It was only recently that the news of your husband's will came out. The lawyer contacted me as his investigations into the whereabouts of the Rose mentioned in the will had led him to me. I knew him already and was in debt to him. I told him I did not want anything to do with it and that it could not be claimed, as Rose was dead. I had still not told anybody about that day in the mortuary. My father had died still believing that one day his beautiful daughter would return home to him. None of it mattered now. But when Daniels offered to kill off my debt and pay me half of the money, I thought only of revenge on the man who had caused my sister's death. It was him that came up with the plan. All I had to do was to find someone to play the part of my sister. That was very easy to do. I had become a man to be feared in the years since my nephew's death and could easily find people to do anything I wished. I promised to wipe off the debt of the woman that you know in exchange for her playing the part. We could have put anything on the documents; it did not matter, she could not read them. But it was Daniels who decided to be greedy and to claim that Rose was your husband's wife before you married him and that they never divorced. Your husband had really left money to my sister. It was that man who made your husband into a bigamist, and I loved it. He arranged for the documents and together we put together a story.'

'Oh, and did that story include kidnapping?' I snapped.

'No, it did not. It was supposed to be easy. Daniels said you would just send the money through your solicitor. I expect you would have done if he had not been greedy. The will had been changed. The copy that was sent to your lawyer said fifty thousand, but the real amount was ten thousand. It was a good job; no one knew the difference. Your lawyer accepted it without question. It also mentioned that Rose was the wife. That was an addition too. But as far as I was concerned, I was doing nothing wrong. Your husband, for whatever reasons, had included my sister in his will. Maybe he believed his child had lived, I have no idea. But he had intended that money to go to Rose. She had to be living to collect the money. He did not know that she was dead, nobody did, and so what was wrong with the money going to the family that he destroyed when he took her away from us? There was nothing wrong, nothing at all. Surely you agree?' He raised his head and looked at me.

I couldn't speak... so there was no other wife?

'Nzoka, it is not for Mrs Trippett to give an opinion on your crime. Now carry on. Or are we to take you back to your cell?' Wambua said.

'She knows there is nothing wrong in what I did, I am sure of it. And it would have been very easy. We would have never met if that stupid lawyer had not wanted a lot of money for himself. The original deal was, he got five thousand and I got the other, it was *nusu-nusu,* as you say, fifty-fifty. But he wanted more. He did not like your husband. He told me they had quarrelled at some point. He believed he could get more money by claiming Rose was his wife and increasing the amount. He did not expect you to travel over to Kenya. He did not expect you to distrust him and he certainly did not expect you to search for the woman yourself, and that is why the Rose in the photos and the marriage certificate had to become the Rose in person. So in answer to your question, madam, no, the plan did not include kidnap; it did not even include meeting you in person. But you came.'

'Ah, so you admit to keeping Mrs Trippett against her will?' said Wambua.

'I did not have a choice. I deserved that money. I just had to get his crazy wife to give it to me.'

298

'Crazy wife! I tell you what crazy is, Mr Nzoka, it's giving up my valuable time to sit here listening to your bloody sob stories to save your neck.' I got up to leave.

He placed his head in his hands. 'I would not blame you if you left. Yes, I am a liar that is how I get by, that is how I get my daily bread, but I swear on my own life that I am telling you the truth. '

Wambua said that the conversation was at an end, and lifted Nzoka out of the chair. He struggled in chains to the door. 'I hope we may speak again,' he said, shuffling down the corridor.

I remained in the room for some time. Wambua hadn't returned and I was thankful for the chance to try and make some sense of it all. There was a part of me, a big part, that believed Nzoka, but it was difficult to hear his story about the man I thought I knew. This Rose must have meant something to him, regardless of what happened later; for God's sake, he left her ten thousand pounds. So what the hell was I supposed to do now, just walk away from it and leave them all to get their just deserts? After all, now that Nzoka had spoken, there was enough evidence to convict Daniels, especially as I was sure Rose would corroborate her part in it. So I was free to leave. I'd listened to him, I didn't want to hear anything that Daniels had to say and I certainly wasn't responsible for Rose. I'd dropped the charges and given her freedom, that was enough.

'Thank you for coming.' My thoughts were broken as Wambua walked back into his office. 'I thought you might need a few minutes to yourself.'

'Thank you, that's very thoughtful of you. I was just thinking of what I should do,' I said.

'Mrs Trippett, there is nothing for you to do. You have done a great deal already. The woman has been told of your decision and will be set free very soon. We are just recording her statement and I believe that she is telling the truth. Nzoka has now admitted to his part in your captivity and so, regardless of anything else, that man will go to prison. And now, thanks to you, we have enough evidence to convict the lawyer. So, there is nothing more for you to do. You may return to your life back in England with your family. I will show you out now and I thank you for all your help. I do not expect that we shall meet again, but I wish you a happy life,' he said and led me through to the reception desk to sign me out. 'Goodbye, Mrs Trippett. *Safiri Salama,* travel safely.'

Chapter Fifty-Eight
Karisa

I had just enough money to get credit for my phone and a bus ticket. I had promised Angela that I would try and see her before she left for England. I phoned Joseph as I got on the bus and he was there waiting for me when I arrived. I was very grateful to see him.

'Now then, young man, I think it's time to get a few things sorted, don't you? And I know just the place to start. I've found this beautiful cafe with a delightful garden where we can sit away from everybody and have a cup of tea. What do you think?'

I laughed and shook his hand and we walked the short distance to the cafe. It was the perfect place to talk. I would never have been able to afford to drink my *chai* in such a place and so I was thankful for his generosity. But I was anxious to see Angela.

'Now then, Karisa, you know I think an awful lot of you. You've worked for me for a long time and I can see that you're unhappy. I think I know why, but I need you to tell me and then we'll see what we can do?'

I did not expect to have this conversation but I knew that I could trust him with my feelings. 'Angela has become very dear to me. She is more than a friend to me. I have great love for her and I believe that she has feelings for me too. But we come from different places and there are too many obstacles to overcome. I wish there was something that you could do to help, but I am sure that there is not. She will return to her home, which is the right thing for her to do. She needs to be with her family. It is where she belongs. We can never have a life together and so, yes, I am very sad at having to say goodbye to the woman that I love. But that is my task to do.

'That is why I have returned from Nairobi. She phoned me and I promised to try to see her before she left. She asked me to come to her, and here I am. I would do whatever and go wherever she would ask me to if only there was a chance.'

'And who says that there's not a chance, Karisa?'

'It cannot be. That is life.'

'But who says?'

'God says, that is who! God has made us different, he has given me black skin and her white, he has given me poverty and her riches and he has given me Africa and her England. It is He who says that this cannot be.' I rose from the table, my heart was full. I did not want to show my feelings in front of him so I made my excuses and rushed to the toilet.

When I came out, I found Joseph was waiting outside and with him was the woman I loved. I could not move. I was stuck to the ground and my heart was racing. I was confused. She saw me and immediately walked to me.

'So you came,' she said.

'I came,' I whispered, and in the next minute, she had her arms around me and her lips on mine. I felt the heat in my groin as I kissed her deeply.

We knew that time was running out and that these hours together would be our last. Joseph left us and so we walked. We did not speak much; our words remained in our hearts. I told her why I had gone to Nairobi. She was very quiet. I was not brave enough to ask her about her journey home. I did not want to know. I could not bear that she would be leaving me.

She stopped walking and turned to face me. 'Do you still love her?'

I looked into her eyes and saw the pain. 'Angela, I am not going to be untruthful. I have a great fondness for Kadzo, we grew up together and she was to be my wife. But that has now changed and, no matter what happens in my future days, I know that the love I feel for you will never be over. I feel for you so deeply and will never forget you.'

'I love you too, Karisa.' We held each other tightly; my heart to her heart joined in our love, and cried.

Chapter Fifty-Nine
Angela

Wambua said there was nothing more for me to do concerning Nzoka and Rose but gnawing at the back of my head was still the money. Now that it could be proved that the will had been tampered with and the woman mentioned in it was no longer alive, there was nothing to pay. My home was safe and I could go back to things as they were. But life could never go back to as it'd been. I was scared to go back. Everything felt tainted, my home, my family, the money. I'd come here to save my home and now that I had it, I couldn't wait to get rid of it. Also what about the money? George had left ten thousand pounds to Rose, money he didn't have. That woman in the will was dead, but her brother wasn't and I'd met another Rose who needed my help. But I knew what the boys would say should I talk to them about it. Mark would tell me to stop being stupid and to keep the money. Josh, bless him, as always, would tell me it was my decision.

Karisa and I were back at the hotel. We arrived separately so that the boys wouldn't see and now he was back in his old room with Joseph. The plan was that they would return to Mombasa tomorrow. Mr Munga had left and as Joseph travelled up with him, he would accompany Karisa on his journey home.

Mark and Josh had already booked flights home for all three of us tomorrow morning and a meeting with the solicitor in Bristol the day after. It was all set. Tomorrow we went our separate ways and I couldn't bear the thought. I retreated to my room and told everyone that I had a headache and didn't want to be disturbed for a couple of hours.

My head had barely hit the pillow when I got the compulsion to return to the police station. I couldn't leave the country without talking to Rose again. Unfortunately, when I got there she had already been released, but Wambua was happy to send a police officer with me to her home.

'We have everything we need from her, Mrs Trippett; she has nothing more to tell us. But it is up to you if you want to see her,' he said.

It seemed a lifetime ago when I was last in her home, but it was only a matter of days. She was alarmed when the policeman entered, followed by me.

'I have told everything I know, madam. You must believe me.'

I told her that I did and she relaxed as the policeman waited outside for me. 'I've just come to say goodbye to you, and to thank you for the help you gave me when I was sick, and to say sorry for the beatings you received because of me,' I said.

I hugged her. I felt nothing but bones. There was no flesh to cushion them. What life did this woman have to look forward to now? She wept freely as we said goodbye.

As we started to make our way back, we walked past the 'Jesus loves me' church. I stood by the door looking in, and was hit by a cacophony of voices singing and swaying to the music, arms raised to heaven. There was such a joy to this place. In the midst of all the poverty and hardship, there was this immense happiness and I found myself getting caught up in it.

'We all have to hope,' said the policeman, who was engrossed in the singing as well. 'Without that, there is very little else. Whether you believe or you don't, without hope in your life, you have nothing.'

His words hit home hard and I phoned Joseph.

'I need you to meet me at the police station. I'm on my way there now, I'll explain everything. Just please try and not let the boys know where you're going. I need to talk to you. I need some sensible advice.'

Wambua was surprised to see me back at the station.

'I thought you would have gone back to your hotel. Is there anything wrong?'

'No, don't worry, I'm meeting a friend here in a minute, but then I may want to talk to Nzoka again. Is he still here?'

'He is here and he is not talking to anyone at the moment, but he may talk to you,' he said.

I walked back out into the sunshine to wait for Joseph, who came rushing up, having been dropped at the gate by a *tuk-tuk*. 'My dear, what on earth is the matter? Your phone call scared me a little. I don't understand why you are here. I thought it was all finished with.'

'I need to talk to you about something that I'm thinking of doing, and I want you to give me some honest advice,' I said.

He nodded his agreement and we found a fallen tree trunk to sit down on as I began to tell him my idea.

'I've just been to church, the "Jesus loves me" church.' Joseph raised his eyebrows, but said nothing. I continued, 'I saw Rose to say goodbye to her and it breaks my heart to leave her like this. She's so poor, and I've just taken away her hope. She still has her debt to pay to Nzoka and there's no chance for her.'

'But my dear, Angela, there are thousands, hundreds of

thousands of people living this way in Kenya, in the whole of Africa. None of them have hope. That's their life.'

'But the difference is that I know this woman. I've spent time with her in captivity; she's taken beatings because of me. She's not one of the faceless thousands. She's my friend.'

'Okay, so what are you going to do about it? You need to be very careful. You have only known her for a few days. She has lied to you. You must understand she may not be the friend that you think she is.'

'This is where I need your advice. I am not about to rush into anything and, although you are right, it was only a few days, I feel I do know her and I want to help her financially. Not just by giving her money but by making sure that she can make a better life for herself. Her age is against her and she has no children to depend on. I suppose I want to give her hope.'

'Well, this needs some thinking about, as what's the best way to go. The easiest way would be to move her away from the slum that she lives in, but sometimes that's not the right thing to do. She has neighbours there and friends that she can depend on, whereas if she moved elsewhere, then she wouldn't have anyone. She's too old to be starting afresh somewhere else. That's not to say that you couldn't do her place up a bit, make sure the walls and the roof are in good repair, get her a bed to sleep on and food to eat. That would be very simple to arrange.'

'But this is my problem, Joseph. I leave Kenya tomorrow and you live in Mombasa and I don't know anyone that I can trust to help her and to make sure that the money is spent wisely. I was hoping that maybe you could manage to do this for me but I realise I'm asking too much of you. You must return to Binty and your home. I think I'll just have to give her some money and let her get on with it,' I said.

'Well, yes, you could do that Angela, and that would salve your conscience, but if people get to know that she has money then it could put her life in danger. There are many desperate people here, and if they believe that she has money then they'll force her to give it to them, and she will be beaten or worse if she doesn't. But if you give me an hour or so, I have someone who may be able to help us. He's a friend of Karisa's. You've yet to meet him, but he helped us greatly in getting you released. His name is Samson.'

'That sounds great,' I said. 'But there's one more thing that I need your advice on and this one is much more difficult.'

'Go on, I can see by your expression that you are struggling to tell me. So spit it out, old girl.'

'I want to drop the charges against Nzoka. I want to set him free. And I want to help him too.'

Joseph's smile disappeared and he stood up quickly. He went to walk away but suddenly turned and sat down again. 'I'm not sure this is a good idea. Have you spoken to Wambua or the family about this? I mean, this is a huge decision. Nzoka is a nasty man. He kept you prisoner and he beat Rose. This is not just someone with a hard life, this is the person that makes other people live in fear. What good do you think letting him go will do for the people in Rose's community? It'll make her life more difficult, that's for certain. And what does it say for law and order? '

As he spoke I realised how foolish I'd been to even consider getting Nzoka released. I couldn't just play the white saviour in this country. It wasn't my place. Who was I to dictate who was punished or not? That was the place of the Kenyan judicial system not some middle aged woman from Somerset playing judge and jury.

'You're right, Joseph. Forget I ever mentioned it. I wasn't thinking straight. The only thing is that I genuinely believe that Nzoka is a victim of his circumstances and, while he must still serve his sentence whatever that will be, I still want to help him. He lost his sister because she was involved with George. He wanted her to have the money. I would've handed over the money had it just been the ten thousand, even if it was to the wrong woman. At least the real Rose's family would have got some money. Now nobody's getting anything.'

'Look, let me get Karisa to arrange a meeting with Samson, I'm sure that he can help us. But Angela, we can't do it all in the few hours you have left. So let's do what we can,' he made the call.

I told Joseph that while we were waiting for Karisa to arrange the meeting, I wanted to go and say goodbye to Nzoka. I could see the concern on his face. He offered to come in with me, but this was something I wanted to do alone. 'Just be careful that your heart does not rule your head.'

'You sound just like Mark.' I laughed and walked inside.

Wambua was waiting in his office when I returned and quickly went to get him. Nzoka seemed pleased to see me, and we even managed a little smile to each other. But the sight of him still bound wrist and ankle brought back the pity in my heart. I told myself to remain calm and be sensible and to not promise anything that I couldn't fulfil.

'I've come to say goodbye to you. I'm leaving Kenya tomorrow.'

He looked up and I swore I could see regret in his eyes, or maybe I was just imagining it. He was a broken man and this was all because of George and his bloody selfishness. So many people caught up in him and his sordid little life. I felt the guilt finally lift and I knew I had done the right thing. George was dying anyhow. I hadn't killed him, I just hadn't helped him, and if I had that choice again, I would do exactly the same.

His voice brought me back. 'I know I am going to prison, but when I get out, I am going to put a cross on my nephew's grave and I am going to add another cross for my sister. I do not know where she is buried. She would have just been thrown in a hole somewhere, but I am going to reunite her with her son, even if it is just in my heart. I am sorry for everything that I did to you. I can see that you are a good woman.'

He began to cry, huge sobs that made his whole body double over. Was this what remorse looked like? I nodded to Wambua, and turned around and walked out of the room and back into the sunshine. My tears came then.

Chapter Sixty
Angela

Samson looked concerned as he walked up to me with Karisa and was introduced. I recognised him as the man from the bar, and was surprised and very pleased to hear the part he'd played in helping to get me released. Joseph explained what I wanted to do for Rose and asked if he could help. Karisa thought it was a wonderful thing to do to get him involved. They'd become very close over the past few days and he had great belief that this man was very honest and wanting to make amends for being involved with Nzoka.

'Mr Joseph, madam,' he said. 'Please, I will do everything within my power to help this woman. I do not know her well, but from how she helped Madam, I believe deep down she is good. She deserves your help and I thank God for it on her behalf.'

I told him that I didn't have time to visit Rose again, but I would hope to do one day should I ever return. I saw Karisa flinch. I asked that he explain everything to her and I promised him that I'd look after him for doing this. We said our goodbyes and Joseph, Karisa and I made our way back to the hotel to spend our last few hours together and to explain to the boys what my decision was about the money.

'You are doing what?' Mark shouted. 'After all that's happened you're still handing over the money? Fucking amazing!'

Even Josh was a little bewildered at my decision. 'Mum, have you really thought this through? I mean this woman could just keep asking for money.'

'First of all, boys, I'm not totally stupid. I've spoken with Joseph at length about this and we will make some contingency plans. Ten thousand will be held in a fund and will be administered by Joseph, myself, and his lawyer in Mombasa, a reputable one before you ask, and it will be this money only that will be spent. So don't worry yourselves, no one is going to touch your inheritance. This is what your father wanted.'

'Oh Mum, we weren't thinking about that at all,' Josh said. 'We're just concerned about you and being taken for a ride. Ten thousand pounds is an awful lot of money to spend on this one woman, don't you think? She isn't even the woman in the will.'

I drew a big breath and prepared myself. 'The money is not just for her; it's to help Nzoka when he's released from prison.'

I heard the gasp from every one of them.

'Angela, my dear, I thought we'd agreed...' Joseph began, only to be interrupted at full bellow by Mark.

'Are you fucking mad? The guy kidnaps you and you fucking reward him for it?' I tried to get him to lower his voice but he was ranting like a madman. 'I can't believe you, Mother, I just cannot fucking believe what I've just heard you say.'

He stood up and walked towards me, but Karisa was there in a shot.

'And you can just piss off.' He pushed him away. 'What's your problem anyhow? No money left for you? Didn't work out as you planned, eh? Well, don't worry, go and see your friend Nzoka. He'll have plenty of money spare in a few years, courtesy of my bloody mother.'

I felt Karisa's fury, he clenched his fists and faced Mark;

thankfully Joseph intervened and led him outside.

'Well that went well, Mum, what are you doing as an encore?' Josh said, trying to lighten the situation.

I sat there completely shell shocked. I hadn't expected it to be easy and I knew that Mark would've plenty to say, but I thought that eventually, they'd see reason. But who was I kidding? Here was I newly rescued from captivity, and Mark was right, it did look like I was rewarding Nzoka. But they hadn't been there; they hadn't listened to his story. All I was doing was giving out the money to Rose's family and helping a desperate woman who'd helped me when I needed it most. I needed some air.

Joseph and Karisa were sat on a wall outside the hotel when I went outside. Joseph started to walk towards me to say something but I stopped him in his tracks.

'I've made my decision and as you said, it was my decision to make. Please can we leave it? I don't want our short time left together to be spent arguing. You and Binty have been so wonderful to me since I arrived in Mombasa. I know you didn't expect to be involved in all this, but I can't thank you enough for being there for me. I left some luggage with Binty when I left; nothing much just bits and bobs. Please give it to whoever you wish.'

Joseph, as perceptive as ever, realised that this was me saying goodbye. He kissed me on both cheeks and told me to take care of myself and then gave me a big hug for good measure. That just left Karisa. This was the goodbye I dreaded the most.

It was late afternoon, but I'd already decided that I'd be having dinner in my room. The thought of being with the boys and having to listen to Mark go on and on again filled me with dread. I wanted to be with Karisa spending my last few hours in Kenya with him alone. I'd thought of nothing else since my release. I'd struggled with the decision to go home or not, but the boys had made that decision for me and it was probably the right one. I'd gone over it so many times in my head, wondering how we could have a future together but I couldn't see any way. Also, there was Gabriel. I so much wanted to see him again, but I knew that it would upset him so much when I had to leave again. No, the best way was to just go, like ripping off a sticking plaster. It would hurt a lot but hopefully in time the pain would lessen.

I asked Karisa to follow me. He stood up without a word and we went back into the hotel. Luckily the boys were nowhere to be seen, but if I was honest, I didn't care if they'd seen us. These were my last hours with this man and I wanted to cherish every moment. I held his hand tightly in the lift. I felt brave. We both knew what was going to happen when we got into my room but said nothing. I was no longer worried that Mark and Josh's room was just across the corridor from mine, but I could sense that Karisa was.

'I do not want to cause problems for you,' he whispered as I closed the door behind him.

'There won't be any problems, believe me,' I said and without another word I slowly began to undo his shirt, taking my time over each and every button, not taking my eyes off his body as, button by button, it was revealed to me. I noticed a pale cream scar underneath the right-hand side of his collarbone. I gently ran my fingers over it. 'How did you get this?'

'I fell out of a palm tree when I was a young boy. I was trying to climb it to get at the coconuts.' He laughed, taking me in his arms and holding me tight.

'And there was I thinking it was a warrior wound or some tribal mark.'

'Sorry to disappoint you, just a young boy hungry for coconuts.'

He lifted me into his arms and carried me to the bed. Karisa looked at me, all of me with so much longing and so much love, my heart was breaking. This was our goodbye. I didn't want to let him go and we spent the next three hours making love, gently, fiercely, passionately. Eventually, happier than I had ever been before, I fell asleep entwined in his arms. When I awoke, even though it was still dark, he was gone. I knew he would be.

I never saw him again before the taxi came to take the three of us to the airport, but I knew he would be watching from his room. I could sense his eyes on me as we loaded our luggage into the taxi and I felt his pain as we drove away. I didn't look back. I just mouthed 'I love you' and silently blew him a kiss without anyone noticing. We never said our goodbye... and now we never would.

Chapter Sixty-One
Karisa

I had to watch her leave. I had given her my heart and she was taking it back to England with her. There was nothing else that I could do other than return to Mombasa. There was a little boy who needed me and I had to take care of him. I would not tell Gabriel the story of what had happened, but I would tell him of the love I had for Angela and the reasons why she was unable to stay. I would not give him false hope that she may return, that was something I did not expect. We had spoken long in between making love and we both knew that it would be very difficult for her to return. As we always knew, she had her life in England and mine was in Kenya. There was no other choice.

Joseph had insisted on driving for most of the way back to the coast. He promised he would let me know when he was tired and then I would take over. I was grateful for this. My mind was full and I would not have been able to concentrate on the road ahead. He had known this also and had taken control. He had stirred when I had got back to the room last night but had said nothing. I tried to close my eyes but every time I did I could picture Angela in my arms, I could feel the great feelings I got as I made love to her and the joy I felt when I satisfied her. Now she was gone.

The journey back was many hours and as we came to places I had visited with her, I dropped my head to look at the floor until we passed through. I would never visit those places again; I would make sure of that. The memories would be too painful. Joseph tried his best to cheer me, talking about my home village and the boy, but it did not help. Then he said he was suddenly very tired and needed me to take over the driving. I knew he was not telling the truth, he had been fine a minute ago; he was doing this so that I would have to take over the driving and my mind would be on the busy road ahead. We were not far from Voi and I caught sight of the gate into the safari park, where we had entered. I missed her so much. But as we travelled, the road becoming busier, I had to shake her out of my mind to get us both home safely.

Binty came out to greet us as I sounded the horn. I had no idea how much Joseph had told his wife about the last few days, but I saw a look of great concern on her face.

'Come on in,' she said. 'Leave the bags, you can get them later. You must be exhausted travelling all that way. Have you eaten?'

He hugged his wife and told her that we were famished and they walked into the house arm in arm. I stayed at the Land Rover for a while. The tears were falling and I did not want anyone to see them and so I sat in driver's seat waiting for them to stop.

'Excuse me,' a voice shouted from behind the vehicle, 'Do you need any help with the bags?'

I quickly wiped my eyes and muttered that I was okay and jumped out of the driver's seat – straight into Angela's arms! I could not believe it.

'What are you doing here?' I pulled her tight.

'Well, that's a great welcome,' she said. 'I couldn't leave you.' She pulled me into the house. I was greatly confused but filled with happiness, God had answered my prayers.

'Well, young man, who would've thought it? I always said you cannot trust these women.' He laughed. 'Think I need a drink, don't know about anyone else.'

'You will not touch a drop until you've eaten. If you start drinking on an empty stomach, you'll end up squiffy.' Binty took the glass from his hand.

'See what I mean, Karisa, they rule your life and boss you around. And the bloody awful thing is they think that they're always right…and you know what… they always are. Come on then, old bean, let's get some food inside me then I can hit the G&T,' he said, grabbing Binty by the hand and leading her to the kitchen. 'Let's leave these young things alone. I expect they have a lot to talk about.'

'Joseph, I love you,' Angela shouted after him. 'You can call me a young thing as many times as you want.'

I was filled with joy that she was with me, but I still did not understand the reason. I took her outside to the garden so she could explain.

'I had every intention of getting on the flight to England, but when I got to the check-in, I couldn't do it. It all became clear to me in an instant that I couldn't leave without saying good-bye. I know it sounds stupid, but I knew I had to see you one more time.' My joy disappeared as I realised she had only delayed her journey. She was still leaving. 'The boys were very angry, but Karisa, I'd never been so certain of anything in my whole life. I knew I had to see you. It was easy enough to change the ticket back to the UK and get a flight to Mombasa, I just had to change terminal, and within two hours, I was getting a taxi from the airport to here. Binty was so surprised to see me, but understood exactly why I'd done this, and promised not to phone Joseph to tell him but to help me to surprise you.'

'But Angela, what is the point? You will be leaving again soon. Nothing is different.'

'The thing is Karisa, I want to seriously talk with you about the future, our future, and if we do indeed have the chance of one. So that's why I've done this to give us some time to try and

318

work this out. I've rebooked my flight for three days' time.' I held her tight in my arms.

It felt like such a long time since I had visited my home village. My mother was pleased to see me but I could see she was still worried that I would leave, especially when she saw Angela get out of the vehicle.

'Why does she come?' she said. 'There is nothing for her here.'

'She comes to see the boy,' I said, 'And we both come to speak with you. This is the woman I love, and we are looking to find a way to have some sort of future together if we can.'

'There is no way,' she snapped, and walked back into her home.

'Then you must say goodbye to me now and I will take the boy. If you cannot show hospitality to this lady, then I cannot show respect to you.'

She came back outside and I introduced Angela to my mother once again, with all the respect both of these women in my life deserved. Only time would tell whether bridges would mend but, for the moment, they were at least sitting together sharing a cup of *chai*. I went to look for the boy.

I did not have to go far, news travels quickly in a small village such as ours, and Gabriel came running towards me at full speed.

'Baba, is it true,' he yelled, 'Is Mama here with you?' I saw the immense joy on his face. He did not wait for an answer and ran straight past me into Angela's arms.

'Mama, Mama, you came,' he said, before bursting into tears.